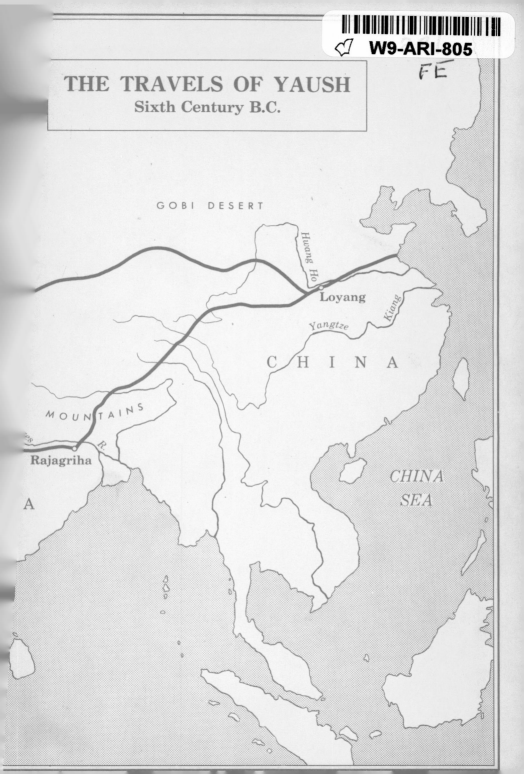

FÉ

THE TRAVELS OF YAUSH
Sixth Century B.C.

GOBI DESERT

Huang Ho

Loyang

Kiang

Yangtze

C H I N A

M O U N T A I N S

R.

Rajagriha

A

CHINA SEA

Wanderer

Upon

Earth

Then the prophet Ezekiel held up his hand with a commanding gesture. "Stay," he said, gazing upward as before. "It was written that you, Yaush, should escape and journey to Babylon to bring us the message that the city was smitten. You were spared for a purpose, my son. You alone are free to travel to far countries and hear the teachings of strange peoples that you may know at last what is false and what is true. Such knowledge will be needed when Jerusalem is reborn, but see that you are not deceived by false divinations. Go in peace, wanderer upon earth."

In silence I turned to obey his words.

[Page 65]

Wanderer
Upon
Earth

by Jack Finegan

Harper & Brothers Publishers New York

Contents

Wanderer
Upon
Earth

Prologue

DUST SWIRLED IN CLOUDS ACROSS the excavation site. The sirocco was blowing from the deserts of Transjordan, laden with sand and burning with heat. Working conditions would soon be intolerable in the subtropical depression of the Jordan. I was glad we had decided to bring the season's dig to a close that day.

As I stood there I reflected upon the satisfaction and the frustration of archeology. This site was almost certainly what we believed it to be—the town where King Zedekiah had taken refuge on his flight from Jerusalem. It lay at the point where the Wadi Musa opened into the Jordan valley. This would have been the logical way for King Zedekiah to have come because Wadi Qelt, leading directly to Jericho, was too well known, and Wadi Kedron, winding through the hills farther south, was too devious.

Since the flight of Zedekiah was made in July the bed of the Wadi Musa would have been dry, and because the ravine plunged steeply and directly to the floor of the Jordan valley it was little used; therefore it offered the best route for the attempted escape. Leaving Jerusalem by night, the king and his men of war could have been at the exit of the wadi by dawn. Then they would have required a place to hide themselves during the day, hoping to proceed when night came again, down the shore of the Dead Sea to the Arabah and so eventually to Egypt and safety.

We had selected this site at the mouth of the Wadi Musa as the logical location for a village—and that is precisely what we had discovered. A process of pure reasoning and dead reckoning had led us to the place, and we took some pride in having discovered an ancient site previously unrecognized by any scholar. Occupying a slight elevation above the debouchment of the gorge were the ruins of a small town.

Now at the close of a season's excavation in the ruins, we felt that the results accorded with our expectations. The pottery we had unearthed showed that a settlement had been made here in the tenth century B.C. and had continued to exist until the sixth. Then at a time which we judged was in the first quarter of the sixth century the village—for it had never grown to be larger than that—had been completely destroyed. The houses of the period had been forcibly demolished, and a heavy layer of ashes still remained from the conflagration which evidently had accompanied the end.

Why had a minor town been so terribly punished? We knew, of course, that the Chaldean armies destroyed many cities in their invasion of Judea but, as the conspicuous example of Lachish showed, these cities were usually strategic and fortified strongholds. The only hypothesis which seemed to us to explain the virtual obliteration of this village was that it was indeed the place which had given sanctuary to Zedekiah and his warriors. The swiftly pursuing Chaldeans must have found the men hiding there and flushed them out like a startled covey of quail, seizing Zedekiah on the nearby plains of Jericho, slaying or scattering his fighting men, then returning to wreak vengeance on the village. Woe to any who in any wise acted against the king of Chaldea!

To be sure, our hypothetical reconstruction of the situation fell somewhat short of positive proof, but a degree of uncertainty attends almost every conclusion in archeology, and the facts appeared to us to add up to a satisfactory conclusion. If only we could have found an inscription, some written document—but such were rare from the Palestine of that time. Of course, there had been some potsherd letters uncovered in the ashes of Lachish, a fortress also destroyed by the Chaldeans within a year or two of the time with which we were concerned, but their finding was an unusual circumstance not likely soon to be paralleled.

On the whole, I reflected, we had every reason for satisfaction. Our expedition had succeeded in its primary objective: to find and excavate the town where Zedekiah must have taken temporary refuge. We had discovered and dug a hitherto unknown town of pre-exilic Judea; we had made a convincing case for its identification. When our results were published they would fill another small niche on the shelves of that slowly accumulating knowledge through which modern man seeks to gain historical perspective on the problems of his own life.

Early the next day I returned alone to the site, a gesture of respect I was accustomed to make to a place where I had devoted a long period of work. Our tents were struck, sand was already beginning to pile up around the ruins, and what we had labored so hard to bring to the light of day would soon again enjoy the oblivion to which the desert so relentlessly consigns the works of man. Already our selection of objects to be taken back to the museum at home— chiefly pottery—had been approved by the archeological authorities and had been securely packed into cases and even now were en route with our gear somewhere between Jerusalem and Tel Aviv.

We had scheduled our departure to make exact connections with a steamer sailing that night. This was a good time to be leaving for there had already been much skirmishing between rival political parties in Palestine, and there was talk of outright war. As a matter of fact, driving out to the site this very morning it had seemed to me that I glimpsed far more armed patrols than ever before. I was glad that our artifacts were safely out of the country. Yet I wondered if they would be safe even in the United States of America, since a world war seemed again in prospect. Perhaps it would have been better if we had left the precious potsherds buried in the sand, to be excavated only in some future century when men had learned better how to live together! At any rate we would soon be safely at sea, and what we were bringing back would be welcomed by the world of science.

The hill above our excavation site was rocky and steep, and I had always wished to climb to the top of it to survey the larger scene spread out below. There was just time to do so now, I thought, and thus to take my farewell view of the whole region. Clambering up its slopes with difficulty, just below the top I slipped and fell. A large boulder arrested my fall sufficiently to allow me to regain my footing, but the jolt dislodged the boulder—doubtless already in precarious balance due to erosion beneath it—and sent it hurtling down to the floor of the valley.

To my mild surprise the dislodgment of the boulder opened the mouth of a small cave. In curiosity I squeezed through the narrow entrance and turned the small light I always carried upon the walls of a rocky cavern of some size. Then I started with amazement. In the center of the cave was a man-made cairn of rocks which provided a support and an enclosing protection for a tall pottery jar. In our digging we had recovered only broken fragments of pottery; here was a completely intact specimen. Moreover, it was different from anything we had found below. Drawing upon such knowledge as I had, I guessed that it was Neo-Babylonian in origin and late sixth century in date. Then I saw that the top was securely sealed with linen cloth and bitumen. Later, when a portion of the cloth was tested by the radiocarbon method, the date indicated was approximately 538 B.C.; thus my initial surmise as to date was verified from the side of nuclear physics.

I could not refrain from gently breaking the ancient sealing and looking within. Then I reached in and withdrew an object which appeared to be a long, tightly wound roll of thin leather. To unroll it would be a matter for the laboratory, but one corner was already bent back and there I saw strokes of writing. The script appeared to be similar to that of the Lachish letters, to which I had devoted special study the preceding year; I judged it might be half a century later in date. Here, too, my initial impression was later substantiated when the entire text was made available for study. Thus the evidences of paleography, radiocarbon analysis, and comparative ceramics converged on the conclusion that the jar and the scroll it contained were to be dated in approximately 538 B.C.

When I emerged from the cave with this entirely unexpected treasure in my hands, my thought was of course to drive back to Jerusalem immediately, register the discovery with the archeological officer, and await his instructions as to its disposition. However, my ears were greeted by the rattle of distant gunfire and, looking from my elevated vantage point, I saw puffs of smoke rising along a battle line which stretched from horizon to horizon. Evidently the more numerous patrols of the morning had been advance detachments of large-scale army movements, and the long-dreaded major hostilities had at last broken out in earnest. I was hopelessly cut off from Jerusalem. There was no way out save by the course which Zedekiah had long before taken to Egypt. So I followed his route. The hardships of my journey, first by car, later by camel, need not here be recounted. Suffice it to say that I arrived at last in Alexandria, communicated by radio with the rest of my party, then at sea, and secured passage home by air. All the way my valued jar with its scroll inside accompanied me, wrapped as if a part of my exceedingly meager personal effects.

Hostilities continued in Palestine for years. The scroll remained unavoidably in my private possession, and I devoted myself unceasingly to its study. Only now have I received authorization to publish the find, which I do herewith. The translation is my own, and I have supplemented the remarkably concise text of the author with such additional material as seems necessary to make it intelligible to the Western reader. In particular I have rendered the dates of the original into terms of our own calendar, as has only recently become possible through the publication of astronomically based Babylonian chronological tables.

As the story unfolds, if it should seem remarkable that one man should have traveled so widely and met the outstanding prophets of pre-Christian history, this is not more remarkable than that Zoroaster, Mahavira, Gautama Buddha, Lao Tzu, Confucius (K'ung Tzu), and several of the Hebrew prophets should all have lived in the same period of world history. As I explain in "A Note on Chronology" at the end of the manuscript, there was already good reason to believe that these teachers were contemporaries, and the present manuscript seems strikingly to confirm that deduction.

Book One

ESCAPE

1

The Water Tunnel at Jerusalem

THE WATER TUNNEL AT JERUSA-
lem held a weird fascination for me. As a young boy I felt its lure
even as its dank darkness filled me with a peculiar foreboding.
Legends about the tunnel and the spring which supplied its water
were part of the heritage of my youth in Jerusalem. Indeed, I cannot remember when I heard the first of them nor from whom—
stories of mysterious passageways in the rock, the unpredictability
of the flow of the water so that sometimes in the dry season a great
boiling of the spring would fill the tunnel with surging water, stories
about "the old days" and even about the days before the "old
days."

The lower end of the water tunnel was familiar to every resident
of Jerusalem. Here spring water from some distant source emptied
into a large pool safely inside the great city wall. I often went there
with my foster mother, for it was there that the women of Jerusalem
came daily to wash their clothes, perform their own ablutions or fill
their earthenware vessels with water. When bored with the gossip
of the women, I gazed in fascination at the latticework of iron bars
that had been laid across the tunnel entrance to discourage exploration. One day when my foster mother was ready to turn her steps
homeward she saw me perched on the latticework peering intently
into the cavernous darkness.

"Come away from there, Yaush," she said sternly. "I will punish
you severely if you ever play there again." Then she went on to say

that in the past before the latticework was ever put there, brave souls had gone forth to discover the secret of the water tunnel but none had returned. "It is not for us to know," she warned, "and you are not to try to find out. At times great floods of water sweep through the tunnel and no one knows when they will start or stop."

I moved ahead of the women as they took up their burdens to return home, but I could not help overhearing my foster mother's remark, "He is so different from the other children—more like an old man at times." I kicked the pebbles in the path and stirred up a cloud of dust. I could be a boy, and a thoughtless one, if that was what they wanted. Almost immediately I was ashamed of this childish anger—after all I was ten years old. I waited for my foster mother to overtake me and then I relieved her of one jar of water.

"You are very thoughtful, Yaush," said Ruth, the younger woman walking with us.

"It is nothing," I replied, but I was happy to see my foster mother straighten a little and walk with an easier step. Although I knew, of course, that she was not my real mother, I loved her as if she were, for it was on her shoulder that I had sobbed for heartbreaking hours after my parents were taken from me. It was at her knees that I had heard the tales of our people told as not even the men in the temple could recite them. I loved her and someday I would repay her for all the care and love she had given me, an orphan.

She was right about one thing—I had no interest in the silly games the other boys played—tossing stones into marked-out squares, or hunting small animals in the nearby hills. I wanted to explore, to find the answers to my questions, and many of the questions were about the water tunnel. I listened intently whenever I heard it mentioned, but I held my peace and never gave up my plan. I would sit by the hour and listen to the tales of a much-traveled mendicant who begged for alms in the market place. It was he who helped me piece together the legends into a marvelous story.

The story began back in the time of David when Jerusalem was a small but important town called Jebus, and inhabited by a tribe called the Jebusites. The town was safely built on a limestone hill, impregnable to any enemy. At the foot of this hill, on the east side, was a spring of fresh water which the city fathers recognized would be an even greater asset to the people, especially in time of war, if its waters could be brought within the city walls.

To accomplish this end they dug into the hillside and diverted the waters through a crude tunnel into a deep-lying pool within the city. But precipitous rock walls surrounded and overhung the pool, so in order to make the water accessible to the people, the Jebusites built a sloping passageway to a point where they could cut a vertical shaft through the rock down to the pool. Now the women could fill their water jars without ever leaving the protection of the city walls. They lowered their jars by ropes over the edge of the shaft and drew them up filled to the brim with the cold, clear spring water.

The day came when David and his men of war camped in the valley and threatened to lay siege to the city, but the Jebusites mocked them. "Were this city of Jebus defended only by the halt and the blind, you would not be able to take it," they boasted, for they were proud of the strength of their walls.

They gave no thought to the tunnel and water shaft that led into the city. But David did. "Whoever first smites the Jebusites will become my captain," he said, offering a prize which made the eyes of all the strong young men gleam. "And whoever will go, let him give heed to the water shaft," David added, providing a clue which only Joab caught.

In the dead of night Joab slipped into the spring and swam back into the inner pool, holding his small lamp up out of the water to keep it dry. Supporting himself against the side of the pool, he lit his lamp and shone its beam up at the shaft which opened above his head. Yes, it could be done, he decided.

Insinuating his toes into small cracks in the rock and seizing every available protuberance with his hands, he worked his way upward. As he neared the top, the opening was so narrow that he could brace his knees against one side and his back against the other and inch his way up. With a mighty effort he pulled himself over the lip of the shaft, worn smooth by the ropes with which the Jebusite women lowered their water containers. He lay there for a while, breathing heavily. Then he rose and made his stealthy way along the sloping passageway which led up into the town.

As he came out into the midst of the sleeping city he slipped like a wraith along the streets to the main gate. An hour before dawn he slew the drowsy and unsuspecting guards and flung open the gates to David and his men, who swarmed in and took the city.

With the passage of three hundred years the city boundaries were enlarged, new walls built, and the shaft and passageway fell into disuse; even their exact location had been lost in antiquity. It was not until the reign of good King Hezekiah that interest in the spring as a strategic asset was revived and the present water tunnel was constructed. When the king of Assyria threatened to lay siege to Jerusalem, King Hezekiah, who was no weakling to submit meekly to the attack, set about to increase the city's defenses and provide for his people in case of a prolonged siege.

As he pondered the problem he thought about the spring in the valley outside the wall. Except for private cisterns filled by rain, this was the only source of water for the inhabitants of Jerusalem. If the enemy were encamped in the valley, the good water would be theirs and nothing would remain for the people of the city but the diminishing supplies in their own tanks. Why not build a conduit through the rock beneath Jerusalem's wall to lead the spring water to a pool within the city? Then let the valley entrance to the spring be covered over, disguised and hidden completely. If the Assyrian king came up against Jerusalem his troops would thirst in a dry valley and the people within the walls would drink fresh water. Hezekiah called his engineers and gave the order to proceed.

One day as I followed the old man's story intently I asked, "Where is the upper end of the water tunnel?" The old man did not answer so I went on excitedly, "And where would *you* guess the ancient shaft was? You know many things hid from the eyes of other people."

The bearded face turned toward me abruptly and sunken, penetrating eyes peered at me. "The upper end of the water tunnel has been hidden since the days of Hezekiah," he replied with meaning. "I doubt that the oldest inhabitant of the city would know where to look for it, and as for the ancient passageway and the shaft of the Jebusites, some say it still exists, but I know of none who could locate it. It is possible that it is guarded by an evil spirit." Then he added, "And no good will come of trying to uncover the secret."

This veiled warning did not keep me from turning over in my mind the various possibilities, and even as I did my daily work for my foster mother my imagination led me into the rocks and hidden recesses. But the explorations during my free time brought no profit except greater determination to solve the riddle.

It was during my twelfth year, and entirely by accident, that I discovered the long-lost entrance to the waterways. I was wandering down an old alley with its crumbling brick walls where men were wont to stop for natural reasons, when suddenly I detected a whiff of dank air which even in this malodorous atmosphere had a distinct odor of the underground. Working along the wall, I traced the peculiar odor to a tangle of thorns around an outcrop of rock. Regardless of thorns, I tore aside the mass of tangled bushes and discovered a narrow opening in the rock formation. I tried to see into the passageway but darkness as of midnight concealed anything that might be in its cavernous depths.

Attracting as little attention as possible, I pulled the thorn bushes back in place and nursed my wounds as any scratched-up boy might do. Then, since I would have to explain my appearance to my foster parents when I reached home, I joined some of the other boys playing at war on the hillside, which would afford reason enough to account for my battle-scarred appearance.

Naturally I told no one of my discovery but the first day I could slip away again I returned to it, this time carrying a little lamp in the folds of my garment. Squeezing into the opening I lighted the lamp and walked cautiously along a narrow descending corridor. Only at its entrance was it stone-choked; beyond it was relatively clear of debris, so hard was the rock out of which it had been hewn. At last I came to the opening of a vertical shaft which led straight down. Cautiously I leaned over the edge but I could see nothing. My tiny lamp illuminated only the top of the black hole; I would have to come back another day.

The next time I went back to the secret passageway I took with me some cord so that I could lower my lamp slowly to the bottom of the shaft and examine the nature of the cutting of the rock sides.

There could be no doubt about it now—I had stumbled onto the long lost Jebusite passageway and shaft! I was breathing so hard that I fairly gasped for air, more from sheer excitement than anything else. I had no fear, only a sense of wonder that I, Yaush, a common boy of Jerusalem, should be a link between the days of great King David and—. I did not complete the idea because my mind was seeing fantastic visions of secret meetings, underground consultations, and stealthy forages in which I, of course, was the hero on whom every success depended.

When this elation passed I again faced the fact that I was alone and had better find out a little more about my surroundings. I found that the Jebusites had left a shoulder of rock jutting out, perhaps to pass their ropes over when hauling up heavy loads of water. This ledge would serve me well as a place to attach one end of a rope and make it fast so that I could lower myself down the center of the shaft. To procure a sufficient length of rope cost me no little trouble, but the next time I came back I was equipped for the attempt. To give myself courage I recalled the exploit of Joab; copying the pressure technique employed by this hero, I found I could let myself down to the pool and pull myself up again.

After I had practiced this descent until I could negotiate it easily and without fear, the day came when I was ready to venture on into Hezekiah's tunnel. This offered still greater hazards for no one had ever been able to predict the ebb and flow of the water, and it was well known that at its peak it became a torrent that would sweep away a full-grown man as if he were a fallen leaf.

The first few times I ventured inside the tunnel the water was at low ebb so I could explore at will. I found that the tunnel was uneven in both width and height. In the first section the average man could extend his arms and just touch the walls on either side; other places were narrower, and still others were fairly wide. The variation in height was even greater. In the first section I had to stoop to make my way through the tunnel while in other places the ceiling was at least ten feet above my head. Thus a maximum flow of water would fill the tunnel completely in the first section but would not reach the top further along. I also discovered in this latter part some rock ledges beneath the roof where it was possible to pull myself up and rest. I was both petrified and fascinated as I imagined myself crouching on one of these ledges just out of reach of the roaring torrent below.

As I repeated my trips of exploration into the tunnel it became evident even to an untrained boy like myself that the engineering work by which the tunnel had been cut through the rock was crude. Obviously there had been two crews of workers boring toward each other, one from each end. Legend held this to be true, also. In the dark bowels of the earth it was not easy to maintain the course and effect the junction, so that the result was a tortuous passageway with many turns and angles. The manner in which the work was done was confirmed in an inscription which I found cut in rough characters in the tunnel wall near the point of junction:

WHILE THEY YET PLIED THEIR DRILLS, EACH TOWARD HIS FEL-
LOW, AND WHILE THERE WERE YET FIVE FEET TO BE BORED
THROUGH, THE VOICE OF ONE WAS HEARD CALLING UNTO ANOTHER,
FOR THERE WAS A CREVICE IN THE ROCK ON THE RIGHT HAND. ON
THE DAY OF THE BORING THROUGH, THE STONE-CUTTERS STRUCK,
EACH TO MEET HIS FELLOW, DRILL UPON DRILL. THEN THE WATER
FLOWED FROM THE SOURCE TO THE POOL FOR TWO THOUSAND FEET.
ONE HUNDRED AND FIFTY FEET WAS THE HEIGHT OF THE SOLID
ROCK ABOVE THE HEADS OF THE STONE-CUTTERS.

It took me a long time to decipher these words in the light of my flickering little lamp. So engrossed was I in this task that I lost track of time and also failed to notice the sound of rushing water which was even then surging at my feet. The slimy walls offered me no immediate hold and I was swept off my feet only to be flung against the side wall of the tunnel and cruelly bruised. The next wave washed me into a section where I had wits enough to remember one of the rock ledges was to be found. Desperately I seized it and clung to it with all my strength. As time passed I could feel that strength waning, when just as mysteriously as it had gushed forth, the water receded. I dropped onto the wet floor of the tunnel, spent and exhausted. At least I had verified the stories about the uneven flow of the water.

My light had been torn from my hand by the flood waters, so I was forced to feel my way out. I crept cautiously testing every inch and trying to reconstruct the contour of the passageway from memory. Suddenly my fingers discovered a formation that did not feel familiar. Where had I lost the main tunnel? I entered a very narrow passageway of which I had heard nothing in the tales of the spring. It led at length to an opening high on a side wall, apparently a fissure of natural origin. I followed its devious twistings and turnings through the mountainside until I came at last to an opening that led to the valley outside the city walls.

Thus it was that I discovered a deep secret—the water tunnel could be entered from outside Jerusalem as well as from within the city.

2

A City Built on Unrighteousness

TO MAKE THIS CHRONICLE COM-
plete it will be well for me to tell my story from the beginning. I,
Yaush, was born on the first day of the tenth month, the month
Tebeth, in the sixth year of King Jehoiakim of Judah, which was
the twelfth day of January in the year 602 before the Christian era.

King Jehoiakim began his reign as vassal to Pharaoh Nekau of
Egypt. Jehoiakim's father, King Josiah of Judah, had fought with
Nekau on the battlefield of Megiddo and been carried home dead.
His son, Jehoahaz, born of the king's favorite wife, Hamutal, and
always popular with the people, took the throne. But having learned
no lesson from the fate of his father, he was still trying to reassemble
the scattered fragments of the army which had been defeated at
Megiddo when, three months later, the Pharaoh came back and
dragged him off in the bonds in which he later died in Egypt.

Jehoiakim was only twenty-five years of age but, having witnessed
so much, was become wise. His mother, Zebidah, also possessed a
kind of wisdom won the hard way through her years in second place
in the king's harem. So together they planned the obsequious acts
by which Jehoiakim persuaded Pharaoh Nekau of his loyalty and
received from him the throne. Jehoiakim's very name was given him
by the Pharaoh; at birth he had been called Eliakim. With co-opera-
tive planning, Jehoiakim and his mother swung the machinery of
government into the business of collecting the taxes which were necessary to pay the tribute which the Egyptian master imposed.

But the day came when it was to Jehoiakim's advantage to change his loyalty. Since his loyalties were always loyalties of convenience, they were not hard to shift. This move was necessitated by events that took place two years before I was born. At that time Nebuchadnezzar, heir to the throne of Babylon, met Pharaoah Nekau in battle on the Euphrates River and defeated him soundly. Soon after, upon the death of his father, Nebuchadnezzar became king. It was evident that the Babylonian monarch, rather than the Egyptian Pharaoh, was to be master of the world. Although his mother was no longer alive to counsel him, Jehoiakim was able to see the direction in which affairs were moving. There was a brief lull while Nebuchadnezzar returned to Babylon for his enthronement ceremonies, at which time he consolidated his position. When Nebuchadnezzar came again into the West, Jehoiakim was ready with acts of ingratiating servility and payments of large sums of money. Thus it was that King Jehoiakim of Judah served King Nebuchadnezzar of Babylon, and such was the state of affairs in the sixth year of Jehoiakim when I was born.

My father took no part in political affairs, but like every one of his fellows he felt the burden of them. Although he worked longer hours than ever in the dark hole that was his metal shop, he seemed never able to meet the demands of the tax collectors of Jehoiakim. Every month they came, every month they demanded more, and every month they stated their demands more inexorably.

Every month, also, the officers of King Nebuchadnezzar waited upon King Jehoiakim, carefully counted the tribute which the royal treasurer paid over to them, and rode off across the desert with it to Babylon. However, not all of the ever-increasing revenues which Jehoiakim extracted from his people were employed to purchase from the Babylonian master the right of Judah to continue as a state. Jehoiakim spent an increasing proportion of the taxes to gratify his own love of luxury, a fact which did not long escape the knowledge of the people. Although they were always told that the exactions they suffered were the price Nebuchadnezzar demanded for their national existence, they could not fail to see the new wings added to the royal palace, and to notice the large quantities of expensive cedarwood imported from Lebanon for new ceilings throughout the vast structure, or to hear about the vermilion paint with which all of its rooms were redecorated. Nor were they unaware of the many women, both wives and concubines, who were added to the king's harem, and they judged that these could not be supported cheaply. For King Jehoiakim's first wife, Nehushta, and for his eldest son, Jehoiachin, there was still popular affection. Jehoiakim had married Nehushta while he was still crown prince and only seventeen years of age; Jehoiachin, born the next year, was himself now seventeen and seemed as yet shy and unspoiled by his father's extravagances. But there was growing hatred for King Jehoiakim and the women and the courtiers and the tax collectors with whom he had in the later years chosen to surround himself.

As resentment accumulated, resistance increased among the people. My father noticed that more and more persons whom he had always thought to be quiet and law-abiding came to him for the small daggers which he executed with great skill. Also from time to time he learned that some tax collector had been found dead in a dark alley with one of these daggers in his back. When the police questioned him, however, he was never able to identify the person to whom he had sold that dagger because he made them all exactly alike and had a large number of customers. But he could take no pleasure in this increase of business. It was not well for so many citizens of Jerusalem to be needing daggers. The city was filled with unrest and a feeling of foreboding. So was my father's heart.

At the same time that King Jehoiakim found it increasingly difficult to gather all the revenues he felt he needed, he also experienced a growing frustration every time he saw the Babylonian couriers departing with their camels laden with his gold. He began to listen with favor to the position which had long been espoused by a pro-Egyptian party in his court. Was the Babylonian bear, after all, more powerful than the crocodile of Egypt? Was not the Pharaoh even then regathering strength for Asian conquest? Would he not soon march again where his predecessors had marched? Would it not be well to return to an alliance with Egypt before the Pharaoh came? The tribute formerly paid to Egypt was not as much as that now required by Babylon; and since the Pharaoh was eager to build a coalition, the price of the new alliance might be almost negligible. The crafty mind of Jehoiakim realized that such an alliance would let him make a gesture of tax reduction to his people, and at the same time leave more for himself in his treasury. Why should he not make the move?

He received the Egyptian envoy at court, but under humiliating circumstance. Nebuchadnezzar's couriers were also there, and as they rode off with their tribute the Egyptian envoy strode into Jehoiakim's audience hall with a scarce concealed sneer on his face. His body gleamed with precious ointments and was adorned with jewels. Even the slaves of his retinue were more handsomely attired than the free citizens of Jerusalem.

"From my Lord Horus, Mighty Bull, Appearing in Saïs, Crocodile of the Marshes, Enduring of Kingship, Falcon of the Sky, Splendid of Diadems, the King of Upper and Lower Egypt, Enduring in Might, Nekau"—thus the envoy began, and as he recited the titles of his master no one would have thought that only seven years before that same Nekau had been fleeing in terror of his life, ignominiously running from Babylon's Nebuchadnezzar. "Greetings to his brother, Lion and King of Judah, Jehoiakim—" In this wise the envoy continued, but it was evident from the look of distaste on his face that he considered Jehoiakim scarcely a king and no lion at all, else why would he serve a lord of such doubtful strength as Nebuchadnezzar? The gist of the communication which followed in sonorous eloquence was that the Egyptian Pharaoh would deign to receive Jehoiakim as an ally and would only expect from him those minimum periodic tokens that one friend would naturally be disposed to send to another. The advantages which would accrue to Jehoiakim from this relationship were so numerous that they could not be detailed (and they never were specified anywhere in the entire impressive speech). He went on to add that the mighty Pharaoh would be pleased to receive the reply, and the first token of friend-

ship, which the envoy with his large caravan was prepared to carry
back to the land of the Nile.

Because of his fear of Babylonian spies Jehoiakim maintained an
apparent indifference and turned the envoy away without an answer
and without the hoped-for first installment of tribute. But as soon as
it could be done with the necessary secrecy, he sent his messengers
to Egypt to accept the alliance and to seal the agreement with tribute. The amount of the payment was so much less than would have
been exacted by Babylon that Jehoiakim decided to use the difference to celebrate the beginning of the eleventh year of his reign.
This date was the first day of the seventh month, the month Tishri,
corresponding to the nineteenth of October, in the year 598.

The celebration was highlighted by a vague announcement of a
general tax reduction, but magnanimous and benevolent as the declaration sounded, it failed to impress the citizens. "How much less?"
some asked, going straight to the heart of the matter. "How much
goes to Egypt?" others inquired, proving that the reorientation of
national policy, carried out in such supposed secrecy, was already
common knowledge. "How much does the king get?" still others
asked boldly, showing that respect for the royal authority had
greatly waned.

The failure of Jehoiakim's new policy to evoke popular enthusiasm was matched by its failure to solve the problem of Judah's international relationships, for Babylon was now to be feared. In the
king's court, members of the pro-Egyptian party encouraged the
king by reporting that Pharaoh was assembling a great army on the
border of Egypt—that he was about to march north—that he had
plans for the re-establishment of an Egyptian empire in Asia which
would be as extensive as that once created by Thutmose. They con-
gratulated the king on having acted with the wisdom of a great
statesman in foreseeing the advantages of a strong alliance with
Egypt. But the reports remained nothing but reports. The true state
of Egyptian affairs was set forth in a chronicle written by a historian
working in an inner office at the court. If his writings had come to
the knowledge of Jehoiakim, undoubtedly they would have cost the

scribe his life. "And the king of Egypt," wrote the historian, "did not come again out of his land, for the king of Babylon had taken all that belonged to the king of Egypt from the brook of Egypt to the river Euphrates."

On the other hand, the leaders of the pro-Babylonian party sought almost in vain to gain audience with the king. When they did obtain opportunity to speak, their words were vibrant with fear and it was evident that they were desperate men. The reports they brought were to the effect that the king of Babylon was incensed when his couriers returned empty-handed, that far from having lapsed into insignificance—as Pharaoh's envoy had said—he was rapidly making himself the mightiest monarch who had ever reigned in the East, and that he was about to launch a new western campaign. According to the pro-Babylonians, Nebuchadnezzar might be expected at the gates of Jerusalem by spring. But when King Jehoiakim deigned to listen, it was obvious that he was bored with the tedious mouthings of a discredited group whose members he considered old, tired and timid men attempting to save face.

The truth of the matter was that the pro-Babylonians were right. Jerusalem was in grave danger and the time was short. Moreover, these men knew well enough that when Nebuchadnezzar and his forces thundered at the gates of Jerusalem they would be in as much danger as anyone else. While it was true that they had steadfastly urged maintaining the alliance between Judah and Babylon, it was undeniable that their efforts had failed. It was not likely that when Nebuchadnezzar came to punish a recalcitrant state, he would spare a small group of his supporters merely because their intentions had been good. Fear for their own lives, combined with terror for the fate of Judah, prompted them to desperate action. They would bring themselves to the attention of Nebuchadnezzar in such a fashion that he would have indisputable proof of their loyalty and might condescend to be merciful.

It was now mid-winter. Jehoiakim's eleventh regnal year, which he had thought would be so glorious, had run through only three troubled, contentious months when word came that Nebuchadnezzar was on the march, having started earlier in the year than ever before. Now the pro-Egyptians trembled, for there was no sign of any movement on the part of their great Pharaoh. They began to wonder what they could do to reverse their position and put themselves in a better light when Nebuchadnezzar arrived.

It was at this point that the prophet Jeremiah spoke—and not for the first time. He was constantly making himself unpopular at court, and sometimes with the common people, because of the punishment and doom he pronounced against the land of Judah. But his own integrity was so unquestionable, and his aloofness from all schemes of the politicians so well known, that there was never any question of his playing for favor. In the middle of the third month of Jehoiakim's eleventh year, the prophet strode unannounced and strangely unchallenged by the guards into the courtyard of the royal palace. He took his stand by a tall column and began to speak:

"Woe to him who builds his house by unrighteousness, and his upper rooms by injustice; who says, 'I will build myself a great house with spacious upper rooms,' and cuts out windows for it, paneling it with cedar, and painting it with vermilion."

Those who were listening looked around at the new wings and stories which Jehoiakim had added to the palace.

"Do you think you are a king because you compete in cedar?" The prophet was now speaking in direct address to an absent and unnamed person, but there was no doubt as to whom he meant.

"Did not your father eat and drink and do justice and righteousness?" he asked, and the hearers remembered the constructive reign of Josiah. "He judged the cause of the poor and needy; then it was well. But you have eyes and heart only for your dishonest gain, for shedding innocent blood, and for practicing oppression and violence."

He flashed a burning glance at those assembled before he raised his deep eyes heavenward and with upraised arm proclaimed: "Therefore thus saith the Lord concerning Jehoiakim, the son of Josiah, king of Judah: 'They shall not lament for him, saying, "Ah my brother! or Ah lord! or Ah his majesty!" With the burial of an

ass he shall be buried, dragged and cast forth beyond the gates o
Jerusalem. His dead body shall be cast out to the heat by day and
the frost by night.' "

Two weeks later his prophecy was fulfilled. Exactly what the
prophet had predicted was unfolded before the horrified eyes of the
people of Jerusalem. But not according to the well-laid schemes of
the pro-Babylonian plotters who had planned to assassinate the king
and then send his ring to Nebuchadnezzar as proof of his death and
of their fealty to the court of Babylon. The would-be regicides were
spared their trouble by an act of a petty official in the financial office
of the palace. Ordinarily a quiet, self-effacing person, this minor
official reached the point of blind rage when Jehoiakim's vaunted
tax reduction proved to be another injustice added to a thousand
which already filled his heart with resentment. The dam of his self-
restraint broke and he took his revenge. One evening as he came
out of his office he saw the king walking down the corridor of the
palace unattended. The assassin shrank back into the shadow of a
doorway until the king came abreast of his hiding place, then madly
flung himself upon the king and sank his dagger into the royal heart.
Palace guards seized the fanatic and killed him.

There was strangely little uproar over the king's death. It was as
if everyone in Jerusalem felt the deed was necessary. The pro-Babylonian plotters gathered around the corpse like vultures. Since the
major drama had been taken out of their hands there was little they
could do now to convince Nebuchadnezzar of their Babylonian sym-
pathies except to desecrate the corpse, which they proceeded to do.

No one objected when they tied the king's feet together and with
a long rope dragged his body from the palace. No one protested—
in fact, some of the bystanders cried out epithets against the king—
as they proceeded through the streets of Jerusalem, pulling the
corpse of the king behind them. The body rolled down steps, struck
roughly against sharp corners. The royal robes, already clotted with
blood and stained with the dirt and dung of the street, caught upon
rough places so that they were torn and shredded, and by the time

the city gate was reached the body of the king was stark naked. Thus they dragged him forth and let him lie outside the wall.

This was the burial of an ass, for when a lowly beast of burden expired within the city its hind legs were tied together and it was pulled forth just as the king had been. So the corpse of the ruler lay unattended and unmourned, exposed to the sun by day and the icy chill of the winter by night. It bore no ornament in its nakedness except the dagger which was still in the back. The dagger had been made by my father.

The day of the assassination was the last day of the ninth month of the calendar year, the month Kislev, or January 15, 597. Of his eleventh regnal year, Jehoiakim had lived out only three months. The next day, the first of Tebeth, was my fifth birthday and became the coronation day of Jehoiachin. This youth, then eighteen years of age, was not only the natural heir to the throne, but seemed also favored by all parties in Jerusalem. Because he was mild-mannered, each group thought to control him readily; because he was affable of person, the populace liked him. Perhaps he could lead the country to safety! Only Jeremiah took no interest in Jehoiachin and evidently had no hope for what he might accomplish. Actually the prophet had already condemned him when he had said of his father: "He shall have none to sit upon the throne of David."

However, these words appeared belied by the turn of events which put Jehoiachin on the throne. And as far as continuing seed were concerned, Jehoiachin seemed to be doing his best to insure a strong line of descendants. When at the age of sixteen he took his first wife, his mother, Nehushta, remembered that she had married Jehoiakim when they were only seventeen, and she smiled upon her son's marriage. At the age of eighteen Jehoiachin had four wives and five children, three boys and two girls. Nevertheless, the pessimistic prophet was correct. The entire reign of Jehoiachin was three months and ten days in length; no one of his children ever occupied the throne.

Nebuchadnezzar came on inexorably. The murder of Jehoiakim and the substitution of the son for the father upon the throne did not alter his opinion of the rebel state. Nor did the machinations of the plotters against the king lead him to think they were deserving of any special consideration. Jerusalem was to be punished for its defection, and when this was decided it was also done. Punishment might not, however, mean obliteration, unless that became necessary.

In the third month of Jehoiachin's reign, the Babylonian armies invested the city. On the first day of Nisan, Nebuchadnezzar arrived, the city capitulated and the king surrendered. The officers of Nebuchadnezzar went systematically through the temple and the palace collecting treasure. A vast quantity of gold and silver vessels was brought together, including many objects which had been placed in the temple by Solomon. Some of the golden vessels of Solomon were too huge to transport, and these were cut in pieces to make it possible to carry them away. At the same time the people of Jerusalem were subjected to careful scrutiny and the best were selected for deportation. This group included the members of the king's court, the chief men of war, and a large number of craftsmen and smiths. Among them was my father. They were given but twenty-four hours to make arrangements for their departure. The thing my father had so greatly feared had come upon him. With bowed shoulders and lagging steps he made his way home to consult with his wife.

She looked at him, her dark eyes stricken. Then she lowered her head in submission. "My place is with you, my husband," she said, "but the child must not go with us into exile."

Among the poor of the land who were to be spared deportation were some childless relatives of ours and under cover of darkness my parents sped to their home, made arrangements for me to be brought up as a member of their household. They hoped that I would forget the tragedy that had transpired before my childish eyes. Only when I was sixteen years old was I to be told the whole story of what had happened and where my own father and mother had been taken.

On the following day when all was in readiness, the signal was given for departure. Jehoiachin went forth first, followed by his mother, his wives and children, and the people of his court. Then came the warriors, stripped of their arms and burdened like slaves with the treasures to be carried to Babylon. After them marched the smiths and craftsmen, heavy laden with the implements of their trades which they would henceforth ply for the benefit of the king of Babylon. I remember my father as he passed; he cast a heart-broken glance at a small son staring in solemn-eyed bewilderment at this strange procession and clinging to the skirts of his foster mother.

Last of all came wives and other family members who were permitted to accompany their men. As my mother came abreast of where I stood she tried to smile and wave but it was a sorry attempt. I saw that she was silently weeping and I made a desperate effort to break from the grasp of my foster mother, but she picked me up in her arms where I broke into inconsolable sobs.

In all, three thousand and twenty-three persons made up the melancholy caravan which moved off into exile. It was the tenth day of Nisan, April 22, in the year 597.

3

Flight in the Night

ONLY THE POOR IN THE LAND OF
Judah did Nebuchadnezzar leave behind, with King Zedekiah to
reign over them. The new king was another son of Josiah and a
half brother to Jehoiakim. Originally named Mattaniah, he had
been given the name Zedekiah by Nebuchadnezzar, the conqueror.
Following the example of other members of his ill-fated family,
Zedekiah pursued a vacillating course and ended by making the
wrong guess and the wrong move. His fatal act was performed in
the ninth year of his reign and was in no wise new or original. It
was a deed of rebellion against the king of Babylon and consisted in
withholding the usual tribute, an action based upon the same mis-
placed hope of Egyptian help which had deluded his predecessors.

Nebuchadnezzar made reprisal immediately, as anyone who understood him might have expected. He sent his troops, and on the
tenth day of the tenth month, January 15, 588, Jerusalem was besieged. For a brief time it looked as if assistance might be forthcoming from Egypt for the Pharaoh put an army in the field, and the
Babylonians withdrew from Jerusalem to meet them. However, it
was only a face-saving feint on the part of Egypt and Pharaoh was
soon back safely behind his border, while the forces of Nebuchadnezzar were around Jerusalem, fighting Zedekiah and the remnant
that were in the city.

Thus it was that when I celebrated my sixteenth birthday on
the first of Tebeth, January 14, in the year 586, Jerusalem had been

nearly two years under siege. Food supplies were very low in the beleaguered city, so the birthday repast was of the simplest, but nothing could dim the importance of the day for me. Vague memories of my parents had always haunted me, but whenever I asked about them or the fate that had befallen them I was put off by my foster mother with the words, "On your sixteenth birthday I shall tell you all I know."

This evening as soon as the supper things were cleared away I waited eagerly for her to begin the story I was to hear. "Now tell me," I whispered.

My foster mother gravely took my hand and told me what she knew. When she finished I asked the question that was often in my mind. "Has any word ever come of how they fare?"

"No," answered my foster mother sadly, "but we believe they still live because we usually hear somehow of those who have died."

"Could I see them if I journeyed to Babylon?" I asked outright.

My foster mother shuddered. "Alas, we may soon be joining them in exile," she said. "Our homeland seems doomed. Over and over we have kings who care for nothing but pleasure."

"I know," I answered, standing at my full height. "I hear on the streets that we are ill-defended." Then I added more boldly, "But now that I am sixteen, I can join our army and help to defend our city, and avenge my parents too."

My foster mother reached up and laid a hand on my shoulder. "You are a man now, my son," she said kindly, "and a man decides these things for himself. Whatever you do, my blessing goes with you."

"And my thanks to you for all your kindness these many years," I replied, my voice hardly under control.

The very next day I bade my foster parents good-by and set out to find a man whom I had long admired, a member of the king's special guard of fifty picked men. He welcomed me with a warm smile and after the briefest of preliminaries I burst out, "I want to join the army. I am sixteen now, and strong. Is there any chance that you could use me?"

I waited expectantly while this man's eyes took a full measure of me. I knew that I was slim, but my shoulders were broad, and my legs and thighs were muscular. I had trained my body to do hard tasks and I could only hope that this discipline showed.

"You are a stalwart lad," answered the warrior, "made of good material, and well developed for your age. How would you like to be my personal armor-bearer until you learn the arts of war?"

For all my joy I tried to be restrained as I answered, "It would be an honor. I had no such hope." And so it was arranged.

It was with the youthful spirit of a boy wanting to right the wrongs of the world that I signed up for military service, but later as I looked out from the battlements of the city I began to see with the eyes of a man. This defense of Jerusalem was no mere adventure. The Babylonians surrounded the city on all sides, while the entire force defending the city numbered not more than five hundred men. All that the generals could hope was that by clever deployment and frequent changes in strategic spots along the city walls, the enemy could be deceived into thinking the numbers far greater than they were.

As it became increasingly evident that there would be no swift capitulation of the city, the attackers settled down for as long a siege as necessary, knowing that hunger, disease, and perhaps inward dissension within the beleaguered walls would soon be working on their side. From the forts which they had erected at intervals all around the city, Babylonians kept a sharp watch. Under cover of these forts they could freely bring up reinforcements and supplies, and prepare their siege machinery. The sorties they had thus far made against the city wall had been repulsed by the violent fire of the defenders, but the Babylonians were quite content to withdraw again to the security of their forts and wait for time to do its work.

Although Jerusalem maintained a brave appearance with pennants still flying and armored men visible upon the walls, on the inside the city was a pitiful sight. During almost two years of siege, no transportation could leave or enter the gates. There were no domestic animals or beasts of burden any more, for all had long since been slain for food. Only large rats scuttled across the garbage heaps, themselves pursued by men who haunted the dumps searching for some overlooked morsel. Most of the people were reduced to rags and their gaunt, undernourished frames were plainly evident. The skeletons of animals and men bleached in the corners of the walls, excrement accumulated in the streets and the stench that hung in the air would have been overpowering except that the inhabitants had gradually become accustomed to it. My foster parents succumbed to disease and starvation. Grief that I could not have helped them gnawed at my vitals sharper than hunger.

As spring passed and summer came, famine became more acute. Only the water supply remained adequate, coursing through Hezekiah's tunnel, but as the season proved unusually dry the flow of the spring at times dwindled alarmingly. Every day more people died of starvation and of the diseases which follow in its train. Driven to desperation, some persons occasionally slipped out of the city to seek for food. The Babylonians, who kept a sharp watch, caught them and used them as an object lesson to others who might think to do the same. Some they impaled upon stakes, others they decapitated, putting the heads upon poles which they set up in the valley in plain sight of the walls. Other desperate inhabitants of the city stopped at nothing in their madness for food. They chewed leather and ate scraps of papyrus. An ancient abomination in Israel was repeated when a family killed, cooked and devoured one of its own children, but even the report of this enormity scarcely stirred the populace, so apathetic had hunger made them. The men of war were now almost without food, and only in the king's house were meals still prepared, and even there the end was only days away.

When they found that their exploratory sorties were repulsed with less and less vigor, the Babylonians closed in for the kill. Helmeted and protected with large shields, the slingers and archers and lancers moved forward on all sides of the city, and the insufficient number of defending men was clearly revealed as they sought in vain to occupy all the necessary posts on the wall. At the north side of the city, where the terrain was most favorable, the Babylonians brought forward their heavy siege machinery. Catapults hurled huge stones through the air and under the protection of this bombardment battering rams were brought into place. Enormous tree trunks, bound with metal bands and terminating in metal ends of the greatest weight, were slung in cradles so that they could be hauled back and up, and then released, delivering blows so shattering that not even the heaviest stone walls could long stand.

All day the thunder of these machines struck terror into the hearts of the people. Defenders on the walls, who exposed themselves in an effort to repulse the operators of these mighty weapons, were picked off at long range by the expert bowsmen of the Babylonians, until Zedekiah's fighting forces were decimated.

It was on the ninth day of the fourth month in the eleventh year of the reign of Zedekiah, July 19, 586, while a merciless sun beat down from overhead, that the walls were finally breached. Not even the king ate bread that day.

The place where the city's once proud middle gate had stood was demolished. The towers on either side were reduced to rubble and the strong doors to splinters, while the walls were shattered far back. At the end of the day the chief princes of Nebuchadnezzar strode insolently through this great breach in the northern fortification. They sat down on the fallen stones and held their evening council of war in full view of the city.

Nergal-sharezer presided, the tall plume on his helmet rising imperiously. Samgar-nebo outlined the plans for the next day, drawing lines upon the ground with his lance to show the way the various detachments would move. Sarsechim and the Rab-saris and the Rab-mag and the others made their suggestions or expressed their agreement, and nowhere in the council was there any thought of pity for the city over which their gaze swept so coldly.

As night settled over Jerusalem, the death watch began. The Babylonian beast of prey crouching outside was content to wait till morning; the victim had no choice but to wait and could neither speed nor slow the hours. But for Zedekiah the night offered a promise of escape. While he was driven to make this attempt solely by the desire to save himself, and in so doing was basely abandoning the city which looked to him as its leader, he was able to present the scheme to a picked handful of counselors as a plan for preserving the kingdom in which he would take the hazardous and heroic lead. The proposal was, in brief, that the king with his sons, his counselors, and the remnant of the men of war, now only a few hundred in all, should leave the city by an old and unwatched exit under cover of darkness and proceed to Egypt. There they would re-establish the state, at least in miniature. Being there present in person they would soon organize with the Pharaoh a joint expedition of rescue which would march to deliver Jerusalem from bonds and rout the Babylonians forever.

It was clear that they should go as soon as possible, in order to make the most of the hours of darkness and also to be out of the city before any word of their plan became known, because if the desertion of the city by its king and defenders was rumored amongst the populace there was no doubt that in their fear-crazed state they would slaughter the traitors as quickly as would the Babylonians. On the other hand, to extricate several hundred men from Jerusalem without attracting the attention of either the inhabitants or the Babylonians would not be easy.

The men of war were summoned to come quickly but in small groups to the royal palace. This caused no comment on the part of those who saw them gathering, for the selection of the palace precincts as the place for a last stand on the morrow was logical enough. From within the palace the men proceeded silently through the king's garden to the gate at the far end. This exit from the king's garden had an unusual feature. It opened onto a stretch of wall that paralleled the main wall of the city. At one time it had been planned to double the city's fortifications, but the idea was found impractical and subsequently abandoned. Only this short stretch of the second wall existed but it was sufficient to conceal the escape of the king and his entourage.

As the long line of men slipped silently along in the shelter of the outer wall, I kept close to the warrior to whom I was attached. I

felt a vague sense of unease when I looked up at the main city wall
and thought of the sleeping people within, but we had been summoned too abruptly and the departure had taken place too quickly
for me to have much time to think. As we emerged from behind the
end of the wall we could see the dull gleam of Babylonian campfires
across the valley. Our best hope was that the day's success had lulled
the enemy into a watchfulness less sharp than usual.

The members of the special guard who were in the forefront of
the march flung themselves to the ground and began to descend the
ravine. Cautiously they crawled from boulder to boulder and shrub
to shrub, keeping one hand on their weapons wherever possible lest
they strike against a stone and the sound ring out in the silence of
the night. Behind his guard crawled the king, keeping well within
the shadow of the man ahead of him, and scuttling across exposed
areas with terrified alacrity.

South of the city the ravine led straight through the Babylonian
siege line, with a Babylonian fort on either side. Once a shield
clanged sharply against a rock. We froze in our tracks, but there
was no challenge so we crept on. The ravine now ran down into a
large gorge. The king expected to follow this route through the canyon all the way to the valley of the Sea of Salt, for this was the most
direct, but least used, way to descend from the high plateau on
which Jerusalem was situated. The torrents of winter had scoured
and seamed the rocky walls on either side, but now no drop of water
relieved the aridity of summer.

Although the night offered some relief, the heat increased op-
pressively as we groped our way toward the subsea-level depths of
the valley below. A partial moon whose light had been a menace as
we left Jerusalem was now a help, but it did not prevent frequent
falls, tearing of clothing and bruising of limbs as we stumbled on
down the gorge. Where the canyon emerged from the mountains,
the small town of Taloth lay upon the plain. As we staggered wearily
into view, dawn was lightening the sky and the village was stirring
sleepily to life. I followed my master as he walked up to the first
inhabitant he saw and asked to be directed to the headman of the

village. The man was plainly startled to be accosted at dawn by a warrior in full battle array, but reassured by the familiar Judean dialect he supplied the directions at once.

We located the town father with ease and my master addressed him as I stood by in respectful silence.

"My master, the King of Judah, has come with his men of war and would have food and rest here this day."

"And why does the great King of Judah come to this small village?" asked the headman. "And why do his mighty warriors," he continued, looking dubiously at our stained uniforms, "come to me?"

"Because," was the answer, "the city of the king is in great danger and his majesty goes with his forces to Egypt to obtain help in order to return and deliver the land from the hand of the oppressor. See, here is the signet of the king!"

So it was that the king and his men were taken that day into the homes of the poor inhabitants of Taloth, and given to eat and drink of that which was the scanty fare of the poor.

At Jerusalem the night passed without alarm, so silently was our escape completed, but with the earliest light of morning it could no longer be hidden from either the residents or the besiegers that there were no longer any defenders upon the walls. When it became known that the king was gone and his warriors with him, there arose an audible lamentation from the streets of the city thus left leaderless and defenseless to its fate. Actually, however, the stroke of doom was now delayed for when the Babylonians learned that their chief prey had fled, they left only a small force to watch over Jerusalem and to dole out limited provisions to keep its civilian population alive, while the rest went swiftly, in two mounted groups, to pursue the fleeing king. Correctly concluding that the king's ultimate destination would be Egypt, and his immediate route down to the Arabah, the first group of Babylonians moved at high speed along the main road to Jericho, the second descended the Kedron valley to the shore of the Salt Sea. Finding no sign that the king had yet passed that way toward Egypt, the latter group went northward along the seashore. In that desolate waste they met only one person,

but he was a hapless peasant from Taloth. Under torture he confessed that strange persons had that morning been received in his
village and, as far as he knew, were still there.

It was not long after noon when I was shaken abruptly out of
my sleep to find my master standing over me. "Get up the hill, yonder, and hide," he commanded, thrusting a sword into my hand,
"the Babylonians are coming."

I raced into the street. The other members of the king's party
came scurrying out of the houses like frightened rats and rushed toward the plain. Following orders I climbed the precipitous hill above
the village where I could see a cloud of dust moving up the valley.
Doubtless it was this raising of dust that had given warning that the
Babylonians were coming. Also from my vantage point I could see
something that was hidden from the men still in the valley—another
cloud of dust moving with all speed down the valley from the direction of Jericho.

Before I could give an alarm our men met the first contingent of
Babylonians. The fighting was fierce, the desperate men lashing out
in fury to fend off their pursuers. For an instant it looked as if our
little force from Jerusalem were to be victorious, but suddenly they
were set upon from the rear by the second band of Babylonians.
Now they were hopelessly outnumbered and mercilessly cut down.
At the end of the sudden attack, as nearly as I could make out,
there was no fighting man left alive—only the king and his three
sons who were taken prisoner and led away. The two merged groups
of Babylonian fighters moved into the town of Taloth. It seemed
dangerous to venture forth at this moment, so I crept back up the
hill and wedged myself behind a convenient boulder for protection,
only to find that a narrow crevice in the rock led into a cave, as was
common in this country. There I waited out the hideous sounds of
massacre that rose from the village below.

As darkness fell, I stole out of this hiding place and made my
way back down the hill to the village which was now reduced to
smoldering ruins. No living thing moved anywhere. As I silently sur-
veyed the devastation, I was struck by a pang of grief for my recent

master. He had been both a kindly superior and a good friend—in fact my only friend since my foster parents died. A great heaviness descended upon me as I reflected that it seemed ever my fate to be left behind. Should I return and surrender, or should I go on? Ahead of me all was unknown; behind lay a horror which I knew only too well, but the people were my people. Instinctively I turned in their direction.

I retraced the route we had taken the night before, only this time it was up the tortuous gorge, and this time I had no human companionship. Only by turning my thoughts to the problem of re-entering Jerusalem could I keep from dwelling upon the dangers of the night. If the Babylonian forts could be passed as they had been the night before, I would find myself under the south wall of the city. But if I followed the ravine to the west there was no likelihood that the gate into the king's garden would be open. Then I remembered the water tunnel! That was how I could re-enter Jerusalem without detection. I could safely make my residence in its friendly depths, finding food where and when I could. It offered the shelter I needed most. And thus I returned to the devastated city, the rubble of my home, and the grief of the populace.

As events transpired, Jerusalem had yet one month of life, by the pleasure and under the dole of the Babylonians. In the middle of the month came word of the fate of Zedekiah and his sons. They had been taken to the field headquarters of Nebuchadnezzar, far north at Riblah in the land of Hamath. There, so the story went, the monarch of the world was seated upon his portable golden throne and King Zedekiah and his three sons were brought into the royal presence and flung to the ground before him. In cruel sport Nebuchadnezzar ordered Zedekiah to a royal seat beside him. Here he was forced to watch the slaying of his sons. Then he was pinned motionless in his chair as a slave approached at a leisurely pace with glowing, red-hot irons and plunged them straight into his eyes. Sightless, tortured in body and spirit, he groped his way through such days as remained to him.

4

Jeremiah

fifth month, the month Ab, in the nineteenth year of Nebuchadnezzar, August 15, 586, Nebuzaradan rode into Jerusalem on a spirited
Arabian horse which snorted and reared and pawed the air each
time he pulled it to a stop. He looked as the special representative
of the king of the world should look. The sun glinted on his golden
helmet, fashioned like an exquisite wig with each hair standing out
in bold relief. His breastplate was adorned with silver inlays of the
symbols of the god Nabu, whose name was honored in his own
name. At his side he wore a short sword and proudly assumed the
need of no other weapon.

Nebuzaradan bore the title of Captain of the Guard and was
Nebuchadnezzar's supreme field commander. Even Nergal-sharezer,
Samgar-nebo, and Sarsechim, arrogant generals of the successful
siege against Jerusalem, recognized his exalted position. He had come
directly from Riblah to superintend the final disposition of matters
in the conquered city, and none would dare dispute his authority.

For one thing, the city had to be stripped of its remaining
treasures, and toward that end preparations had been in progress
throughout the month. Years earlier the large vessels of gold and
silver from both palace and temple had been carried away at the
deportation of Jehoiachin; what now remained were the objects of
brass and miscellaneous minor vessels of gold and silver. For centuries the brass work had been the pride of the temple, made at the

command of Solomon by a skilled artificer imported from Tyre, one
Hiram in whose family the art of casting and burnishing brass had
been passed down from father to son. The artisan had made forms
in the clay ground between Succoth and Zarethan in the plain of
Jordan, done the casting there, then had the objects transported to
Jerusalem and put in place in the temple.

Most famous were two hollow pillars of brass, six feet in diameter,
twenty-five feet in height. Adorning each capital was a delicate network of brass, hung with a hundred pomegranates executed in the
same material. Strength and Security were the names of the two
pillars, names which seemed strangely inappropriate now as Babylonian saws cut them into more manageable pieces for the long journey on which they were about to be sent.

Notable also was a brazen sea, as it was called. This was really an
enormous outdoor water basin, in which the priests performed ablutions. Around its upturned brim this bowl was thirty-five feet in
circumference, and it stood upon twelve bulls cunningly fashioned
of brass. Three of these animals faced outward in each cardinal direction, and from their distended nostrils to their male organs they
were so realistically made that one sensed their virility and almost
felt their hot breath as he looked upon them.

For the washing of offerings there were ten rectangular recep-
tacles of brass, six feet square and five feet high. To be movable,
these were mounted upon chariot wheels, and their paneled sides
were sculptured with bulls, lions, and winged cherubim. There were
also pots, shovels, snuffers, spoons, firepans, basins, and other vessels, most of brass, some of gold or silver. All of these and any other
objects of value throughout the city had been carefully collected and
catalogued; thus they awaited only the nod of Nebuzaradan to be
prepared for transport.

It was also part of his work to determine the disposition of the
remaining population of Jerusalem and for this end preliminary reports had been prepared. A good many people had attempted to
escape from the city, but no fugitive had succeeded and each had
been executed in some horrible way. Thus the conquerors made sure

that no one would carry news to Egypt or Babylon of what was happening at Jerusalem! If the Pharaoh wanted information let him risk sending his spies; and in Babylon none save the great king would announce his victories.

A second group was conveniently assembled in the hands of the Babylonian commander. These were the persons who, during the siege, had fallen away to the enemy. Managing to get outside the city walls and signaling their surrender, they had been impounded by the Babylonians and, as their numbers grew, had been placed in a special stockade.

A third group was still at large within the city. These were the leaders of the people who had not fled with Zedekiah and were still classified as dangerous on various grounds. Among them were Seraiah the chief priest, Zephaniah the second priest, and three other officials of the temple; a eunuch who was in the war office; a scribe who superintended public records; and sixty other men who were known either to have had influence with Jehoiakim and Zedekiah, to have been friends of Egypt, or to have made unwise utterances about the king of Babylon. All of these were now put in a special company and, when the long march northward began, were allowed to lead the way. If they were pleased with this distinction, it was not for long. When the caravan reached Riblah, they were executed in the presence of Nebuchadnezzar.

Finally, the fourth group was composed of the common people of Jerusalem. It was, therefore, the members of the second and fourth groups—those who had previously given themselves up to the enemy and the common people still in the city—who were to be deported to Babylonia. When the list of their names was completed it totaled eight hundred and thirty-two. Thus the entire population of Jerusalem was accounted for. A few peasants, the poorest of the poor, were left upon the land of Judah to be vinedressers and husbandmen.

Because I was making my home in the water tunnel I escaped being counted and forced to join those destined for exile. Each time I had ventured out to stand near some stall where the Babylonians were doling out food I risked my freedom, and on one occasion I was almost caught. I was just stepping behind the crumbling wall where the entrance to the water tunnel was hidden when an enemy soldier rounded the corner and shouted to me. Moving quickly into the tunnel, I waited, sensing that the soldier was groping around in the vicinity of the wall. Then he apparently blundered past the thorn bush and into the passageway. I fled swiftly down the familiar way, the soldier following awkwardly but persistently in the darkness. As my hands found the rope in the vertical shaft I thought I had left the pursuer behind, but a slight creak of the rope betrayed my whereabouts and unhesitatingly the soldier followed me. Plainly I was trapped. The soldier was armed whereas I had left my sword behind when I had gone out into the city for food. To flee to either end of the water passage, the one covered over and the other barred, would mean certain capture.

The only other possibility was to proceed through the Hezekiah tunnel as far as the side fissure and take that exit to the valley; but to emerge there in broad daylight and with a pursuer close behind would lead inevitably to capture by the Babylonians. Nevertheless it appeared the only way, and I made for the tunnel, taking long, powerful strokes through the pool, the soldier still in pursuit.

As I reached the narrow portion of the tunnel, I heard the fierce sound of rushing water. With my last remaining strength I raced into the forward section and climbed to the safety of the rock shelf. The Babylonian, trapped in the narrowest part of the conduit, was helpless in the path of the foaming torrent. Spewed forth by the monster which had destroyed him, his drowned body was swept past on a wave so close to where I was crouching that I could have reached out and touched him.

The last task of Nebuzaradan was to raze Jerusalem. Having carried out the treasures to be borne off by his caravan, and having marshaled the people in the valley in the groups in which they were to march to Riblah and Babylon, he began a systematic plan of destruction. Babylonian battering rams loosened the great stones in the mortar of the city's defenseless walls, and sent them crashing down into the valley. Only rubble remained to mark the course of the wall which had been the pride and strength of the capital of Judah.

On the ninth day of the month, Nebuzaradan inaugurated the final act. In the morning he rode through the city for a last inspection, his war horse snorting at every turn. Corpses lay in the streets, vultures flapped heavily into the air from gruesome repasts, rats ran from beneath his horse's hoofs. The sacred temple and the royal palace still stood, stripped of their gold and ivory but still splendid in stonework and cedar. So too stood the great houses of the rich and the miserable hovels of the poor, looted of everything of value, but habitable still. Save for his own cortege, no human being appeared anywhere within the compass of the former walls. It was a dead city and belonged only to the dead, but it was not yet razed to the ground.

In the afternoon Nebuzaradan rode into the court of the temple and, sitting easily in the saddle while his horse reared and pawed the air, let one hand fall in gesture of command. The poised battering rams thundered against one tall tower which was still standing, although thoroughly undermined, and it collapsed with a grinding roar. The valley beneath the wall was very deep at that point, and the huge stone blocks plunged down in a frightening avalanche. Contrary to any expectation, the capstone of the tower was projected backward rather than forward, and fell directly upon the officer in charge of the battering rams, crushing out his life in an instant. Thus the carefully planned ceremony was marred by an untoward event, and when some among the wretched prisoners learned of it, it seemed to them as if the very stones of the city were calling out for a higher justice.

Toward the end of the day Nebuzaradan gave the signal for which his men had been eagerly waiting—the signal to set fire to all that remained. The temple and the royal palace were the first buildings to which the torch was applied. While the foundation and walls of the temple were of carefully fitted stone, the entire building was covered both within and without with wood. This was indeed its chief pride. In league with Hiram, king of Tyre, Solomon had sent ten thousand men each month to work in the mountains of Lebanon to cut the great cedars which flourished there. The timbers were then floated down the seacoast in rafts, and taken thence to Jerusalem. Cut into beams and planks and beautiful panels, the cedarwood was used for the walls and ceilings and exterior of the temple, while the floors were of cypress and the doors of olivewood. All the walls round about were carved with figures of cherubim and palm trees and open flowers. The palace, too, was built of cedarwood in its beams, pillars, doors, posts, and porches, and was known as the House of the Forest of Lebanon. It was more elaborate than the temple, for Solomon had spent thirteen years in its construction as compared with seven years for the temple. Since that time other kings, especially Jehoiakim, had added to it, and so the palace was a very large structure. Aged for three hundred and fifty years, this wood was like tinder to the flame. The Babylonians flung their torches into piles of incendiary material that had been placed at the corners of the buildings and the great conflagration was under way. Then they rushed on throughout the city, firing the houses of the nobles, the lesser houses of the common people, the shops, sheds, and stables. Soon all of Jerusalem was ablaze, and the fire makers withdrew across the eastern valley to points of vantage from which to view the spectacle. The light of sunset faded from the sky, but the flames of the burning city leaped high and a garish light reddened the whole heaven.

The cool depths of the water tunnel were my refuge while Jerusalem burned. All the next day the city continued to burn, and the smoke of it rose aloft like a great column. As, long before, their ancestors had moved toward the promised land with a pillar of fire to guide them by night and a pillar of cloud by day, so now the people of Jerusalem marched away with a fiery light and a smoky pillar above them. Nebuzaradan let them miss none of the sight. He marshaled the entire caravan in the valley, while the victorious troops looked upon their work and the wretched prisoners gazed for the last time on their home. Jerusalem was become only a memory and a hope.

Strangely enough it was the gloomy prophet Jeremiah who uttered the hope. He was not to be taken into exile. Because he had always declared that Jerusalem would fall, Nebuzaradan treated him leniently and let him move freely among the people. At a place not far from the mouth of the fissure from which I watched, Jeremiah leaped to a rock by the side of the way and as the long files of trudging captives moved down the valley, he spoke to them: "Thus saith the Lord: 'A voice is heard in Ramah, lamentation and bitter weeping. Rachel is weeping for her children; she refuses to be comforted for her children, because they are not.' Thus saith the Lord: 'Keep your voice from weeping, and your eyes from tears; for your work shall be rewarded, and they shall come back from the land of the enemy. There is hope for your future, and your children shall come back to their own country.

" 'It shall come to pass that as I have watched over them to pluck up and break down, to overthrow, destroy, and bring evil, so I will watch over them to build and to plant. I will bring them from the north country, and gather them from the farthest parts of the earth, among them the blind and the lame, the woman with child and her who is in travail, together; a great company, they shall return here. Then shall the maidens rejoice in the dance, and the young men and the old shall be merry. I will turn their mourning into joy, I will comfort them, and give them gladness for sorrow.

" 'The days are coming when I will make a new covenant with the house of Israel and the house of Judah, not like the covenant which I made with their fathers, which they broke. I will put my law within them, and I will write it upon their hearts; and they shall all know me, from the least of them to the greatest.' "

I could not comprehend the full meaning of this poetic and even ecstatic declaration but I sensed that Jeremiah was telling his people that within themselves there was something precious and imperishable and that they should be true to it and they would live.

A feeling of exhilaration surged over me. I had a mission! I, Yaush, was the only inhabitant of Jerusalem who was still free. I would find my way across the desert to Babylon. Traveling alone

I could reach there long before the slow line of captives reached the city. I would tell the people of the first exile to make ready for the new captives. I would look for my own mother and father. And I would speak forth the prophet's words and cry out his hope for the future.

Book Two

COMMISSION

1

Ezekiel

THE FIERCE FIRES HAD BURNED
down and a pall had settled over Jerusalem when, at the end of the
tenth day of the month of Ab, August 18, 586, I emerged from the
water tunnel that had preserved my life and freedom. Once again
during the hours of darkness I descended the steep gorge to the
Jordan valley and with the early morning light took refuge in the
cave above the ruined village of Taloth. Before departing from
the cave in the evening I found a fragment of an old clay vessel and
with a bit of charcoal I wrote on this potsherd these words: "I will
go to Babylon, and someday I will come back again to Jerusalem."
I signed this statement with my initial, Y.

Since Nebuzaradan was marching north somewhere on the west
side of the Jordan, I thought it best to cross the river to the eastern
side. From Taloth I went across the sloping plain where my com-
rades and my king had been trapped by the Babylonians. I thought
of the warrior who had been my friend, and I felt within the small
package of my scanty belongings the shape of the sword he had
given me. I was glad that he had taught me to use it well.

At the edge of the Salt Sea I walked along on the sand, listening
to it crunch beneath my feet. Weird shapes of eroded saline formations rose around me, casting strange shadows in the moonlight. I
thought about the story I had often heard of Lot's wife who, fleeing
from a doomed city of the plain, looked back with regret toward its

49

sinful streets and was turned into a pillar of salt. I resolved not to look back until I had carried out the mission on which I was starting.

The waters of the Sea of Salt shimmered invitingly in the soft light, and stripping off my clothes, I walked in and swam a distance from the shore. When I came out the thick salt clung to me so I walked on to the Jordan intending to wash it off in fresh water. I was still some distance below the usual ford opposite Jericho, but I thought it best to cross the river here if possible. So I made a small, neat bundle of my clothes, placed it on my head and waded out cautiously. The force of the river was strong against me, and the boulders on the bottom were slippery and uneven so my progress was slow and I breathed a sigh of relief when I reached the other side and pulled myself up the bank with the help of overhanging tree branches.

After I had rested awhile I dressed and went on my way across the valley. Above me I saw the massive shoulder of Mount Pisgah, and at the foot I found a refreshing stream. From here I turned northward and went on up the valley on a course parallel to the eastern mountain range. When day came I found a hiding place from which I could look out over the valley. Although there was no sign of the Babylonians anywhere, I thought it best to continue to travel only by night. Thus, living on wild berries and wild honey and drinking from springs, I made my way cautiously northward.

As I proceeded I doubled my caution, making my way through deep gorges and up treacherous cliffs until after several nights of toilsome going, I arrived at the eastern side of the range. Here the trail descended and made junction with the King's Highway. This was the main north-south route on the east side of the Jordan, and was ancient in the days of Moses. Along its way caravans from Egypt and Arabia met those from Syria and Asia.

It was a caravan from Arabia to which I now joined myself. The long file of ungainly, arrogant camels came by with bells tinkling and loads swaying and then turned off the road into a clearing for the night's encampment. As I approached the camp, the drivers were laboring with their beasts, stripping off the heavy loads and preparing them for the night. Suddenly one of the camels swung sharply, striking a blow which knocked his driver to the earth. The other drivers whose animals were tethered for the night rushed to his assistance, but the frightened camel broke into a run, its half-loosened load cascading from its back and scattering in all directions.

Once I had had employment in a caravansary in Jerusalem, so camels were not strange animals to me. I sprang forward, seized the trailing rope, was jerked from my feet and dragged around the camp, but I hung on until I was finally able to bring the terrified beast to a stop. As I handed the rope over to one of the drivers I could see respectful half-smiles on the dark countenances of those gathered around. One stepped forward with a friendly gesture and indicated that he wished to conduct me to the caravan leader.

"You did well," said the sheikh. Then he looked at me sharply and added, "But you are not one of us."

"No," I replied truthfully; then untruthfully continued, "I am returning to my home in Damascus and would gladly join with this caravan if you would be pleased to accept me."

"What is your name?"

"Yaush."

I could hardly hope to disguise the accent with which I spoke, but since there were people of my country residing in Damascus I hoped the explanation would be sufficient. Evidently it was, for the sheikh took me into the company, assigning me to help the driver of the runaway camel. The other men accepted me without question, and it was pleasant to join them around the campfire and share their food—the first hot food I had eaten in weeks. It seemed to fill me with new courage.

As the caravan moved daily northward, Mount Hermon rose more and more majestically on the left hand, patches of snow still being visible on its upper slopes even though it was summer. Coming down from the eastern slopes of the mountain, the strong stream of the Pharpar River flowed across the plain. Farther north, the camel train turned into the valley of the Abanah and followed this river through its eroded rock canyon into Damascus.

The oasis of Damascus was a welcome sight to our weary eyes, the green of its orchards and palms contrasting pleasantly with the arid reaches previously traversed, and its rippling waters promising refreshment for men and animals. The caravan would stay here for some time before proceeding northward to Riblah and Carchemish, while the masters would sell some of their goods to the merchants in the bazaars, and the camel drivers would seek out the houses in the side streets where there were drinks and women.

I now separated myself from the caravan in order to live out the fiction I had invented that Damascus was my home, but also because I dared go no farther northward along the main caravan route. Ahead was Riblah and the field headquarters of Nebuchadnezzar, toward which the forces of Nebuzaradan were moving. I must find some way to go eastward across the desert.

While I was still haunting the caravansaries, seeking to find a party that was going to Babylon and picking up bits of information about the desert route, the first of Nebuzaradan's soldiers entered Damascus. These were scouts who were preceding the main body of troops and the captives. From necessity and long training, their eyes were alert to everything. In a narrow street I suddenly found myself face to face with one of these soldiers. The Babylonian, so recently come from Jerusalem, recognized something familiar in my features and he challenged me.

"Who are you? Where are you from?"

I found it difficult to formulate a reply, and began to stammer out something about my home's being in Damascus.

"You lie!" cried the Babylonian. "You are from Jerusalem, I can hear it in your voice. Those accursed people of Jerusalem, how long we fought against them! No one from Jerusalem is to go free."

With these words he lunged forward. I was quicker with my feet than I had been with my words, and dodged to one side into a doorway. The passage into which it opened looked like a way of escape, and I fled swiftly through it, but once inside I found myself in an arcade, lined on each side with wooden pillars, leading onto a central court, deserted at the time. I could see no exit and the Babylonian was pursuing me, brandishing his sword.

This was a game of life or death. Quickly I dropped my belongings to the ground, drew out my sword and wheeled to meet my assailant. Steel clashed against steel, but no telling blows were struck. Then the sword of the enemy flashed wildly. I danced lightly aside. Using one of the pillars as a shield, I made my next thrust. The enraged enemy lunged forward to return it, only to sink his weapon deep into the wood. As he tried to wrench it free I leaped from behind the pillar and ran him through.

The Babylonian slumped to the ground, the blood seeping slowly through his tunic. This was the first time I had ever killed a man, and for a moment I was filled with horror. Then I remembered my warrior friend lying dead on the Jericho plain, and felt that justice had been done. Carefully I wiped my sword on the tunic of the fallen enemy, picked up my belongings and made my way stealthily out of the court.

Knowing that the Babylonian would soon be missed and sought for, I quickly left the city. Having neither sufficient provisions nor adequate knowledge of the route, I was not prepared for the journey ahead. However, as I hurried from Damascus I secured such food supplies as I could, and a skinful of water. From the caravan people I had already acquired scraps of information about the way, so I started out.

At the outset the path was plain and the journeying not unpleasant. I followed a valley which led through the hills northeast of Damascus, then emerged upon a point from which I could look eastward across the Syrian desert. There were vast stretches of hard soil covered with gravel and stones, and many ridges of dark volcanic rock which rose up at crazy angles and formed grotesque patterns. As I trudged forward into this arid wilderness I came upon traces of a caravan route, which I followed. At last there came a night when I slept within sight of a small settlement, and the next day I was able to obtain more food and water.

Ahead now were almost unrelieved sandy wastes in the midst of which, according to my information, the oasis of Sabuya was the next goal of any traveler. It was now many weeks since I had left Jerusalem and I hoped that with the coming of the fall the caravans would be moving again on the route I had chosen to travel. Each day the sun rose blazing over the rim of the desert. Throughout the morning it gathered intensity until by midafternoon the heat was an oppressive force surrounding and bearing down upon every living thing, stifling breath and almost throttling life. But when the sun sank, the sands swiftly surrendered their heat to the dry air, and sharp and bitter cold descended.

I was still making my way alone, and the days were long and lonely. So far I had had no difficulty in following the trail, but I well knew that in the space of an instant a sandstorm could obliterate it, leaving me no trace. I did not allow myself to look far ahead for I knew, as did any desert traveler, what illusions could be conjured up by sun and sand. It was best to concentrate doggedly on one step at a time. It was thus that I had no advance warning when the trail suddenly ran out in a dune of sand created by the wind after the last caravan had passed. The sand was recently deposited. There was even a gentle ripple on its surface, undisturbed by the footprint of man or beast, but the trail was gone.

With sinking heart I took my bearings from the sun that day and from the stars that night. I had no idea how far it might yet be to the Sabuya oasis, so I hoarded my meager supply of food, and allowed only a trickle of water at a time to moisten my throat. The lack of anything to drink was soon a greater torture than the absence of food. My mouth was like wool, and my throat constricted so that I could not swallow. I came to a small shrub and dug frantically at its roots, but there was no discernible moisture. Then I saw the oasis! —a shimmer of water and a reflection of green, as if palm trees were mirrored in a cool lake. As I stumbled toward it, it seemed to move with me; then, as the light changed, it disappeared and there was nothing there except a dancing spiral of dust, drawn upward by an updraft of wind.

The mockery of the mirages lured me in one direction and another, until I became hopelessly lost. My strength failed rapidly, and my mind began to wander. I was a boy again, walking up the road to Jerusalem. I heard the voices of my father and mother calling to me. Then I saw one of the towers of the city wall, and began to run toward it. The Babylonians were pursuing me so I ran faster and faster, then stumbled and fell, stretching out my hands to clutch the corner of the tower. The whole army trampled upon me, and I sank into oblivion.

I opened my eyes to see a Bedouin bending over me, carefully holding a canteen of water to my lips. As the cool drink slipped down my parched throat I felt returning life. In accordance with the immemorial law of the desert where every wayfarer brings help to his brother in distress, the Bedouin not only offered water but kept pointing to his camel and urging me to rise. At first I was too weak to make the effort, but the Bedouin's arms were strong and finally, half carried, I managed to reach the spot where the beast was standing, its imperturbable gaze undisturbed. Slowly we made our way to this nomad's tent where I was cared for tenderly.

After some days I recovered my strength and had about formulated plans to continue my journey when the wind began to blow. It started in the morning, whipping up puffs of dust and causing little rivulets of sand to flow across the surface of the desert. By afternoon the sand was being lifted from the ground and driven forward in sheets with stinging force. The next morning the sky was so darkened by the sandstorm that it was hardly possible to tell that the sun had risen. No person ventured out of the tent, and within it the sand penetrated every aperture and filled every crevice, so that the atmosphere was almost as suffocating inside as out. In order to breathe at all, we wrapped rags about our heads and, almost stifled, drew in such air as we could get through the cloth. It was nearly a week before the storm blew itself out. When we emerged from the almost buried tent, every contour of the surrounding country was changed. There were depressions where there had been sand dunes, and where valleys had been were now hills of sand.

I was impatient to be on my way but I knew I could not continue alone. At length the first caravan came in sight on the horizon of the desert and I hoped that it would be one which I could safely join. While the nomad went out to meet them, I remained behind, prepared in case they were Babylonians to hide myself under the rugs in the corner of the tent. When the nomad came back the leader of the caravan was with him. He was a Syrian and the group he headed was made up of Syrian merchants carrying their goods to Babylon. In the sandstorm they had been driven off their course. Three of their men had gone out in the storm to try to find the way and had not come back. Later they found the bodies nearly buried in the freshly blown sand. The leader would be glad to have an able-bodied man join the party.

Day after day I rode upon the swaying back of a camel while the undulating sea of the desert flowed slowly beneath. White sand gave way to black, volcanic soil, and then the sand came again. A sharp ridge of rock rose like a reef, and the sand was driven against it like a wave. Great masses of volcanic deposit appeared to bar the way, but the path twisted and climbed through them until it came out at a high elevation beside a dry lake. Then the trail descended again and wound down through a series of wadis until once more the country opened out in its illimitable vastness. The oases which were the steppingstones across this waste were few and far between, and for that reason were welcomed the more gladly when they came into view. Our caravan missed one and we were forced to endure parched mouths until the next was reached. At such a time a pool of brackish water and a small cluster of palms was all we asked this side of paradise. We camped at each oasis until men and beasts were refreshed and ready for the next lap of the seemingly endless journey.

I could never entirely free my mind from the terrible experiences during the fall of Jerusalem. The sights, the sounds, the stench, the heat of the final fires, the captives as they turned their backs upon their homeland. Although I was free, I often shared the hopelessness of the captives. Then again I would be buoyed up by the knowledge that I was on my way to bring a message of hope to those already in exile. Jeremiah, the prophet—what was the faculty that he possessed? There were those in Jerusalem who had at first said that he had knowledge secretly obtained from the politically informed which he merely bleated aloud to the populace. But this theory was readily discredited by the nature of his prophecies, which often pleased no clique. Could it be that certain men possessed an ability to stand at an observation point on the edge of time and observe a greater distance than the common man can see? Judah had had other men "of vision"—were they poised on the border line between the finite and the infinite? Could there be prophets in other lands than Judah? I pondered these questions as I rode over the waste stretches.

At other times I tried to picture my future life. Would I find my parents in Babylon? What had been their fate, and what would be mine? If I did not stay with them, whither would I go? To the East? From these far lands many rumors and vague reports had come even to Jerusalem. Stories of fabulous wealth, of treachery, of customs so different from ours that we could scarce believe they could be true. With these thoughts I tried to make the journey less tedious.

Days were added into weeks and weeks into months. One day the caravan topped a slight eminence and I gasped at the sight which was spread out before me. As far as eye could see there was a perfectly flat expanse unbroken by as much as a hillock. This was the valley of the Euphrates and the Tigris Rivers, and this the stoneless alluvial soil which those mighty rivers had deposited over countless numbers of years. If the desert we had traversed was an ocean of varying moods and swelling waves, this was a sea of such absolute placidity that not a ripple marred its surface. There was no landmark anywhere, nor scarcely any way to tell where the horizon ended and the sky began. All was blended into a glaring infinitude of whiteness, across which the camels moved like spectral shapes, doomed to go forever forward and never to come to any destination.

I could only trust the leader to pursue the right course, and at length came a day when I again drew in my breath with sudden astonishment. Ahead was a definite line of green, stretching from horizon to horizon—the palm trees of the irrigated valley, precisely demarking the desert from the sown land. When we reached the palm line I dismounted and stood with one foot in a profitless waste and the other in a bountiful garden. The explanation was not difficult: thus far, and thus far only, came the life-giving waters. A canal ran here, and on a stone erected beside it was an inscription. Using knowledge of the Babylonian language I had acquired during the long trip, I made out:

NEBUCHADNEZZAR, KING OF THE UNIVERSE, IS A FATHER TO HIS PEOPLE. HE DUG THIS CANAL OF THE PLAIN, THIS CANAL OF ABUNDANCE, TO PROVIDE WATERS OF EVERLASTINGNESS, WATERS OF UNCEASING PROSPERITY, FOR THE LAND.

From here on the caravan route led beside the abundant waters. The small canal led to a larger canal, which in turn connected with an even larger channel. Thus a veritable network of waterways was spread out over the land. Water flowed through the main channels during the entire year, and when the season of irrigation was at hand the water was conducted across the thirsty fields. The prosperity of the valley was very great. At last the caravan route came to the Euphrates River, source of the canal water, a broad, turgid stream, flowing sluggishly but with irresistible power between low banks. Upon its waters men traveled in round skin boats, and from its banks they pulled heavy barges. As our caravan moved down along the winding river we drew ever nearer to the great city to which it led—Babylon, our goal across so many miles.

At last we entered the suburbs of Babylon which extended far beyond its walls. Small houses of the countryside gave way to finer buildings of the large estates and then, nearer the city wall, clustered the hovels of the poor. Next, massive double ramparts enclosed the enormous city, above which loomed a great staged tower. The main gateway, which bore the name of the goddess Ishtar, was adorned with bulls and dragons made of bright-colored, enameled brick.

It was here at the Ishtar Gate that our Syrian caravan drew to a halt. I had reached Babylon! Wearing the Syrian clothes I had acquired, I followed close behind the caravan leader as the latter went in through the gate to find the official to whom our arrival must be reported.

"We are forty camels and thirty-eight men from Syria, with wares for the market," the leader said, and the official perfunctorily noted down the statistics and greedily gathered in the gifts with which the Syrian purchased his good will.

The registration of incoming caravans was but one of the many official transactions conducted at the Ishtar Gate. Merchants and emissaries from many lands entered the city here, and citizens of Babylon from the highest to the lowest mingled on the great square. I searched the faces of the motley throng to see if I could recognize the features of any of my fellow countrymen. Then, idly, I watched the scribes of the House of Records, sitting cross-legged, as they wrote on their moist clay tablets and put them out in the sun to dry. With my very slight knowledge of the Babylonian language I could make out only enough to know that they contained notations concerning rations issued to persons resident at Babylon as captives and therefore dependent upon the government for their subsistence. So much barley, so much oil, was given to such and such a person, to such and such a family. Many of the personal names were strange and suggested faraway lands. Pleased with my ability to make out any writing on the tablets, I continued to glance over them. As I spelled out the names, I read, "Y-a-u-k-i-n, king of the land of Y-a-h-u-d."

With a start of amazement which I tried to conceal from anyone who might be watching, I peered more closely and spelled over the name again. There was no doubt about it. This was the Babylonian spelling for "Jehoiachin, king of the land of Judah"! This was the king who had been carried into exile with my own father and mother, and he was still living here in Babylon. Even as a prisoner, his royalty was recognized and he was fed from the king's storehouse. The tablet also showed that Jehoiachin had continued to beget progeny, for while it did not mention all the members of his family it did list his five sons, the royal princes. There had been three when he departed from Jerusalem.

With the discovery of the name of my king my heart was pounding and I continued to search through the tablets hoping against hope to find the names of my father and mother. A few names I recognized, Tobshillem, Shelemiah, Semachiah—but nowhere did I find the names of my parents. I could not risk asking where the captives from Jerusalem were settled, but day after day I haunted the courts of the Ishtar Gate and wandered through the market places of Babylon seeking some clue which might lead me to them.

One day as I was passing through a narrow street I was startled to hear a quiet voice say, "I am from Jerusalem." A mild-looking man fell in step with me and continued softly, "From your appearance I believe that you also came from Jerusalem. If so, walk on beside me to yonder square."

In spite of my Syrian dress I had been recognized as a man of Judah by one of her former inhabitants. I asked no questions until we reached the square and my companion indicated that we were safe to talk. Then I inquired eagerly about my parents.

"I do not know them," he said, "but if you will meet me here tomorrow morning I will take you to the community of captives from Jerusalem. There you can inquire for yourself."

The hours before the rendezvous seemed endless and I was at the meeting place long before the appointed time. When my fellow countryman came into sight he was heavily laden.

"May I not share your burden?" I asked, springing forward.

"That would be well," said my new friend. So we quickly divided the goods while he explained that he was one of the porters who was allowed to leave the community of exiles to obtain supplies, and if I were carrying also there would be less likelihood of any questioning.

We journeyed through the city and out a gate on the other side, then followed the paths along the canals. At the point where an erect stone marked the Canal Chebar we turned aside and I discovered that we were on the edge of an extended settlement, whose houses and garden plots were small but not untidy. The people were dressed in our native garb. With hungry glance I peered into many little shops where craftsmen plied their professions, but I found no sign of a metalcraft shop with my father's name over the door.

My friend broke the silence that had settled between us. "You can see that we are not too meanly located, but we cannot leave our appointed dwellings, and we must ply our trades for the profit of the King of Babylon. Our greatest misery is that we are absent from our homeland and have been so long without news of the fate of its inhabitants."

"I have come with news and—" I began, but was interrupted by my guide.

"Twice welcome then, son. But news must be told first to Ezekiel. We hold him to be the head of our community in exile."

"Ezekiel?" I repeated. "I do not remember him, but of course I was only a small child when the first captives were taken."

Instantly my companion picked up the clue. "Then there are others to follow? But tell me no more now."

"Who is this Ezekiel?" I asked.

"He is a strange man and he will not be surprised to hear that other captives are coming to Babylon. Your news will only affirm the message he has already given to us. It pertains to a siege of Jerusalem."

"But how would he know? Has he not been with you in Babylon for years?" I asked.

"Ezekiel has peculiar seizures," continued the man, shifting his burden a little, and I felt a note of respect in his voice as he spoke the name of the head man. "Ezekiel most certainly sees wonders not vouchsafed to others, but instead of proclaiming them aloud as did the prophet Jeremiah, he performs enigmatical acts whose meanings are not revealed until some time afterward."

"He told you about Jerusalem with no message from the outside?" I asked incredulously.

"In detail. And he communicated the news in a most unusual way. First, he took tile and clay and pieces of iron and made a likeness of Jerusalem; then he erected miniature forts and battering rams against it. Never will any of us forget the sight that greeted us when we were summoned to the prophet's house. As we filed in we saw the model and there beside it the prophet Ezekiel, his face as stern as if carved in stone and his arm upraised in a gesture of condemnation. He said no word but we all knew that Jerusalem had fallen under divine condemnation."

I responded in awe, "A seer who can sit in exile in Babylon and see what transpires in Jerusalem is one to be revered."

"And that is not all," agreed the Judean. "Next, Ezekiel fell prostrate upon his left side and lay there paralyzed for three hundred and ninety days. During this time he communicated with no one, not even the servant who fed and ministered to him."

"What was the meaning of the three hundred and ninety days?" I asked.

"They represented the period of three hundred and ninety years of Jerusalem's accumulated sins—from the evil-doing of David in his latter years to the rebellion of King Zedekiah."

"There have been weak and wicked rulers over the land of Judah," I agreed. "Perhaps it is no wonder it has come to this sad end. Did Ezekiel prophesy anything else?"

"As soon as he emerged from that trance he went into another rigid paralysis that lasted forty days. This signified forty years of desolation which were to follow."

"Do you mean forty years of exile?" I asked sadly.

"That is what we fear," came the simple answer.

"But does this Ezekiel never give word of hope?"

"Strange that you should ask that," replied the Judean. "For many weeks he was dumb. No word had passed his lips and he was forced to make his wants known to his servants by means of signs. But only last night the scourge was lifted and he spoke. We could hardly credit our ears when he gave a message of hope."

I said nothing. My mind flew back to the day I had stood concealed in the water tunnel at Jerusalem and heard Jeremiah speak words of encouragement to the captives filing out of their city. I had made this long and treacherous journey to bring this hope to the exiled people only to find another prophet who was speaking hope for Judah. In my mind I was very confused. This state of bewilderment continued as I was ushered into the presence of the great man. Then suddenly I was overcome with the thought that I did not have to hold my silence any longer—I was among my own people. Unceremoniously I burst out, "The city has fallen!"

"And now that the blow has fallen," said the prophet, as if he were not at all surprised by what he heard, "and the worst has already happened, we may look forward to the best which is yet to be. It was necessary that Jerusalem suffer for her sins, and it could not be other than that the chastisement fall upon the innocent and the guilty alike. But now the exiles will come here and we will help them make homes in this strange land. They will slowly learn the lesson we have already learned, that peace must be found within, and that when it is thus found, neither distance nor disaster can destroy it. Then someday, when the lesson is learned, the way will open. Jerusalem will be rebuilt, and will stand foursquare, and its name will be Yahweh-shammah, *the Lord is there*. But every person who is accounted worthy to live there will know that the Lord dwells first of all within the temple of the heart."

Ezekiel had spoken with unaccustomed plainness it appeared; but for his closing words he lapsed into the more poetic speech which often characterized his utterance. "Thus saith the Lord: 'Though I removed them far off among the nations, and though I scattered them among the countries, yet I have been a sanctuary to them for a while in the countries where they have gone. And I will gather you from the peoples, and assemble you out of the countries where you have been scattered, and I will give you the land of Israel. And when they come there, they will remove from it all its detestable things and all its abominations. And I will give them one heart, and put a new spirit within them; I will take the stony heart out of their flesh and give them a heart of flesh. And they shall be my people, and I will be their God.'"

During all this time the prophet's intense gaze had been fixed on some spot in the air above the heads of his hearers. It was as if he were reading a message written there. I stood in amazement. Here in the midst of exiles was a prophet who promised that one day Jerusalem would be restored. I looked around at the faces of those assembled and I could see that they had drunk in his every word and were comforted.

When the spell was broken the people flocked around me asking question upon question and I told them the story of the siege and fall of Jerusalem and assured them that even now a second band of captives was plodding across the desert under the Babylonian Nebuzaradan. I told them of Jeremiah's words. Then for a long time I answered questions to the best of my knowledge about the fate of relatives and friends. Almost immediately this community in exile began to make plans to receive the new captives.

Now I was free to turn to the matter of my own deep personal concern. A fear that I had not known during the treacherous months of my pilgrimage settled on me as I asked the prophet about my parents.

The luminous eyes of Ezekiel came to rest on me with a kindly glance.

"They are here and well," said the prophet. "Your father works every day at his craft. They have never given up believing that they would someday see their son again."

"I will go to them," I cried, as long-suppressed loneliness and longing broke over me. "I will make my home with my parents," I declared impetuously. "I will learn my father's trade, and be their support when old age comes upon them. Sir, will you direct me to them?"

"You may go to them, and there will be great joy at their table this day. But," the prophet went on somberly, "you may not stay with them. To do so would cost them their lives, and you yours. Perhaps it would endanger us all. The mighty king, Nebuchadnezzar, would be filled with wrath if any made known his triumphs until he comes himself and declares them to the people. Also, if it were discovered that you had eluded the Babylonian soldiers at Jerusalem, and had reached here ahead of his own triumphal return, you would be hunted to the death, and all who had received you would forfeit their lives. Even in the disguise of a Syrian, you are liable to recognition at any moment and if you came to our community here upon the Chebar, it would be no better. Every week our people are counted to be sure no workman is missing. Provisions are measured out strictly for an exact number and there is food for no more. To-morrow is the day of the counting. You may see your parents this day. Then for their sake and for your own, you must leave Babylon this night."

I recognized the truth of the prophet's words but for a moment I could not bring myself to accept this fate. Leave the parents whom I had buffeted storm and sand, treacherous waters and enemies to find! Leave them on the very night of our reunion day! As I stood there dazed Ezekiel took out of his pocket a private book of memoirs and repeated before me as he wrote: "In the twelfth year of our exile, in the tenth month, on the fifth day of the month, a young man who had escaped from Jerusalem came to me and said, 'The city has fallen!'" Even in records intended only for the prophet and his disciples, I must remain anonymous. Crestfallen, I turned to leave.

Then the prophet Ezekiel held up his hand with a commanding gesture. "Stay," he said, gazing upward as before. "It was written that you, Yaush, should escape and journey to Babylon to bring us the message that the city was smitten. You were spared for a purpose, my son. You alone are free to travel to far countries and hear the teachings of strange peoples that you may know at last what is false and what is true. Such knowledge will be needed when Jerusalem is reborn, but see that you are not deceived by false divinations. Go in peace, wanderer upon earth."

In silence I turned to obey his words.

2

Love in Death

I FOUND THE MODEST DWELLING of my parents and my heart pounded as loud in my ears as did my knuckles on the door. My father answered and in an instant he recognized his son. "My boy!" was all he said as he placed his hands on my shoulders. After a moment he continued in an unsteady voice, "Come in. Come in, my son." Then he turned and called to his wife, "Rachel, come."

A gray-haired woman came from the back room of the little house, wiping her hands and frowning slightly at the interruption. Then she caught sight of me and a great light broke over her face. A smile came to her lips, but tears to her eyes. She reached up and touched my cheek experimentally, almost as a blind person would do. "This time it is real," she said as if trying to convince herself. "I have dreamed of your coming so long!" She took a step back and looked at me intently. "The same brown eyes with the deep light in them; the same curly hair," she continued. "And you are tall, Yaush, tall like your father when he was young. You were only five then and now you are a man. Just four days ago you were seventeen. Oh, those years—" Quickly she collected herself before she completely broke down. "But you must be hungry. Sit here with your father for a few minutes while I finish preparing the meal."

So I began to tell my father of the events which had finally led to this reunion. When my mother set the evening meal upon the table I knew she had probably sacrificed her food allowance for the entire

66

week, but I could not disturb her shining happiness by making any comment. We sat long over that meal and my mother scarcely took her eyes off me. I was sure she was etching on her mind the picture of her son, for I knew she realized I could not stay with her even before we put the fact into words.

"The great prophet says I must not stay here," I forced myself to say. "It would endanger lives."

My mother sighed deeply. "Alas, that is true," she admitted. "For ourselves we would gladly run the risk, but we must not endanger the welfare of the whole colony. Where will you go, my son?" she asked in despair.

"The prophet Ezekiel thinks my life has been spared so that I may travel through the world hearing the great teachers of our time and trying to discover what is the truth. He says this will be valuable knowledge when we return to our own land."

"I pray that it may happen within the lifetime of your father and me," my mother said. "Perhaps one day we may all be reunited in a new Jerusalem. We must have faith." And faith shone in her eyes.

My father's seamed face broke into a brief smile, then sobered. "It is a worthy mission, son, and I believe with the prophet that you have been spared for a purpose."

"And now I must go," I said.

My mother spoke softly. "Kneel, my son, and receive your father's blessing." Then she stood by his side as my father placed his hands upon my head and repeated: "The Lord bless you and keep you; the Lord make his face to shine upon you, and be gracious unto you: the Lord lift up his countenance upon you, and give you peace."

My parents stood in the doorway of their humble dwelling and waved as I walked away down the deserted street. It seemed cruel that I should part from them as soon as we had found each other. I only vaguely remembered how they looked when they left Jerusalem, but I was shocked to find them now so old. They had suffered. But at least they had each other. Again it pressed upon me that I was alone.

As had become my habit, I used the shelter of darkness to make my departure from the city. The rain which began to pour down on Babylon at the close of that eighth day of January in the year 585, which was the fifth day of the tenth month in the twelfth year of the captivity of Jehoiachin, seemed a fitting symbol of my sadness as I trudged beside the Euphrates. Where should I go next? The river, flowing silently at my feet, seemed to give the reply. I stowed away on an Arabian vessel, and during the night it cast off its moorings and began to move down the Euphrates.

The next morning when I revealed my presence the captain seemed pleased enough to have another member of his crew. The stowaway was soon to learn why, for I was driven unmercifully at work on the ship all the way down the river. When at last we tied up at a port at the head of the great gulf into which the Euphrates emptied, I took the first opportunity to slip away and disappear in the crowded streets of the city. From there, the only way which appeared much traveled and therefore safe was the main caravan route running north and east. I took this route, following up a small river toward a mountain range, passing the ancient city of Susa, and then beginning to climb through mountain valleys.

The character of the landscape soon changed completely. The endless flatness to which I had become accustomed in the valley of the Euphrates was no more. Instead, the land stood all on edge. One jagged ridge succeeded another, and each was higher than the last. Only the channel cut by the river made it possible to penetrate these fastnesses, and a traveler climbed even higher into more desolate and forbidding country. At the top of the pass, there were peaks on every side and it was very cold. Then the route descended to the valley where the city of Hagmatana was situated, and continued on north and east across an arid plateau. In the distance a lofty peak, twice as high as anything I had yet seen, lifted its snowy head. Again the trail climbed into the mountains, then came out on the slopes that descended toward an inland sea. Here, with the white of the high peak behind and the blue of the sea before, I felt an irresistible urge to stay for a time.

It was not hard to find employment in this farming community. Spring was coming on and there were never enough workers to till the fields. The first man to whom I applied welcomed me, and I was shown my new duties at once.

I soon grew accustomed to the pleasant routine of sowing and reaping, training the watchdogs, guarding the cattle, and driving off the marauding wolves that came down from the hills in winter. I was well treated, well fed and housed; my young body was suited to such a life. In the rhythm and sequence of such tasks, days merged into months and months into four years. The parting from my parents became a nostalgic memory; the terrible experiences of my youth were buried in the past and seldom dug up for contemplation; the life of the exiles in Babylon seemed to belong to another existence; and even the sense of a life mission which Ezekiel's injunction had stirred in me had lost all its urgency.

But I was still young and at times I noticed that the women of this land were not lacking in beauty. Beneath their embroidered robes their bodies were strong and shapely. They walked with the erect grace which comes from habitually carrying burdens on the top of the head. Although accepted by these people I continued to feel that I was a stranger in a strange land, that love was not for me in this place. Customs and work habits, food and dress, I was able to make my own. But the religion I was not able to accept. To me it was gross superstition. There was the matter of fire. In every house a fire was kept burning constantly and although the people cherished it carefully, they seemed to regard it with fear and dread. They made offerings to the fire, and every springtime there was a special ceremony that filled me with repulsion.

As the spring equinox approached, the oldest virgin daughter in each family made a doll and clothed it with finery. On the appointed day she presented this doll before the fire, stripped off its garments, burned them one by one, and ended by casting the doll itself into the flames. I had seen this done many times but I did not understand its meaning. My questions were always turned aside, but at times I heard it said that far away in the western mountains from which these people had originally come, there was a fire temple where the priests offered a living virgin to the fire demon at this same time of year. I was inclined to discredit this report as a figment of the imagination and judged the rite more likely to be connected in some way with their practice of placing the body of a deceased person upon a funeral pyre and burning it. At any rate I found these customs unattractive, and was especially displeased by the fascination which the doll-burning ceremony exercised over the women of the community. I knew I could never build a home around such practices. The god of my people made no such demands.

However, I could not help noticing the flashing dark beauty of Samuda. Nor was I alone in considering her the loveliest maiden in the village. Her jet black hair was drawn smoothly back from the whitest of brows. Her eyes—almost as black—were almond shaped and fringed with abundant dark lashes. She had a friendly smile for everyone and I found it impossible not to return it in kind as I watched the graceful swing of her hips when she walked with her water jar securely balanced on her head, without so much as a steadying hand to hold it in place.

One day I came to the well just as she had drawn water from it. She paused, one graceful hand on the vessel. With a brilliant smile she said, "Good morning, Yaush."

"You know my name," I said, pleased and flattered.

"I inquired," she said simply. "I have often seen you hereabouts but I know you are a stranger from a strange land. I wish you would tell me about it."

So it came about that we often met, at the well or in the market place, or sometimes found it possible to sit together on the hillside. Eagerly Samuda listened as I told her the story of my life. And when I paused or seemed uncertain about some episode she drew me on with skillful questions until I had poured out the whole of my starved heart to her.

One day after I had been talking about the close ties of the family life of my people she said softly, "And you have no family."

"And no friend either—until now," I added, trying to control the passionate yearning of my soul.

"I shall always be your friend," replied Samuda softly.

The great emptiness I had known all my life was filled. I felt at home. I forgot that this beautiful girl was the daughter of an alien people, that she practiced the superstitious rites of which I disapproved. I lived in a world of enchantment. I loved and I was loved.

We met daily after that. We shared our thoughts and our hopes. Nothing did we hide from each other. Samuda seemed never to tire of hearing about the land from which I had come.

One day as we sat together on a green hillside above the town I asked her about the custom of the fire worship. She turned earnest black eyes to me, "Oh, that is necessary to placate the Fire Deva," she said solemnly. "His revenge is terrible if he is not appeased. He sends liquid fire that destroys thousands before they can flee. What is the sacrifice of one in comparison with so many?"

"Do you mean that what I have heard is true—the priests still make human sacrifice to this monster-god?"

"Each year at the fire temple far up in the hills," sighed Samuda. And then she added proudly, "And every girl child believes it would be an honor to be the one sacrificed."

I could feel the blood drain out of my face. "Do *you* believe that?" I asked slowly.

Samuda's eyes avoided mine as she played with a blade of grass. "So we are taught," was all she would reply.

One early spring morning I left the village at dawn to go on an errand. I went over the hills to cross the river at an unusual place, and there was Samuda, bathing in the stream. Her garments were laid upon a rock and she was standing in the edge of the swiftly flowing water, dipping it up and pouring it over herself. As she lifted her arms above her head, her firm, pointed breasts made the very outline of beauty, and she seemed the embodiment of all loveliness. I slipped quietly out of sight and went on my way, vaguely troubled.

Later this hidden place at the river became our rendezvous. Often Samuda would lie upon the grass while I recited to her words which

Solomon had written for his Egyptian wife. I had royal precedent for loving a foreign woman!

> How beautiful are thy feet, O prince's daughter!
> Thy rounded thighs are like jewels,
> The work of the hands of a skilful workman.
>
> Thy body is like a round goblet,
> Wherein no mingled wine is wanting.
>
> Thy waist is like a heap of wheat
> Set about with lilies.
>
> Thy two breasts are like two fawns
> That are twins of a roe.
>
> Thy neck is like the tower of ivory;
> Thine eyes as the pools in Heshbon,
> By the gate of Bath-rabbim.
>
> Thy nose is like the tower of Lebanon
> Which looketh toward Damascus.
>
> Thy head upon thee is like Carmel,
> And the hair of thy head like purple;
> The king is held captive in the tresses thereof.
>
> How fair and how pleasant art thou,
> O love, for delights!

When Samuda laughed at the unfamiliar names I would take her in my arms and we would talk of the future. Samuda learned parts of Solomon's poetry and said them back to me.

> My beloved is white and ruddy,
> The chiefest among ten thousand.
>
> His head is as the most fine gold;
> His locks are curling, and black as a raven.
>
> His eyes are like doves beside the water-brooks,
> Washed with milk, and sitting by full streams.
>
> His cheeks are as a bed of spices,

As banks of sweet herbs;
  His lips are as lilies, dropping liquid myrrh.

His hands are as rings of gold set with beryl;
His body is as bright ivory overlaid with sapphires.

His legs are as pillars of marble, set upon sockets of
  fine gold;
His aspect is like Lebanon, excellent as the cedars.

His speech is most sweet;
Yea, he is altogether lovely.

This is my beloved, and this is my friend,
  O daughters of the city!

Then our voices would join as we came to the part of the poem
which we took as a promise of the coming of spring—the time when
we would marry.

My beloved spake, and said unto me,
  Rise up, my love, my fair one, and come away.

For, lo, the winter is past;
The rain is over and gone.

The flowers appear on the earth;
The time of the singing of birds is come,
  And the voice of the turtle-dove is heard in our
  land.

The fig-tree ripeneth her green figs,
And the vines are in blossom;
  They give forth their fragrance.

Arise, my love, my fair one, and come away.
O my dove, that art in the clefts of the rock,
  In the covert of the steep place,

Let me see thy countenance,
Let me hear thy voice;
  For sweet is thy voice, and thy countenance is
  comely.

Even as we talked together in this way and rejoiced when Samuda's father consented to our marriage there were times when the mention of spring seemed to steal Samuda from me for a moment. One day she shuddered as I was repeating to her the lines from our poem:

> Set me as a seal upon thy heart,
> As a seal upon thine arm.
>
> For love is strong as death;
> Jealousy is cruel as Sheol;
>
> The flashes thereof are flashes of fire,
> A most vehement flame of Yah.

"What is the trouble, beloved?" I asked.

"Yaush, what is the meaning of 'flashes of fire' and 'flame of Yah'?" she countered.

"That is only the poet's way of describing the heat of love's flame," I answered, as I held her more closely.

During the winter our happiness was marred by the death of Samuda's father. At his funeral pyre she looked at the flames with intense horror and yet so great was her grief that she had to be restrained from casting herself into them. Afterward she carried on faithfully with all her duties in the home, yet we found much time to be together and to complete our marriage plans. I was happy when Samuda smiled again, and filled with joy when her laugh rang out once more. But each burst of merriment seemed balanced with a period of sudden depression. Was she still grieving so intensely for her father?

There was a custom among Samuda's people that a bridegroom should not look upon his betrothed for one week before the wedding ceremony. Knowing how I would suffer to be so close to my beloved and still not see her, I decided to go on a journey that would fill the days with something of interest. A delay on my homeward way caused me to return a night later than I had planned, so I did not enter the village until the morning of our appointed day.

There was a strange hush over the houses, that the early hour could scarcely entirely account for. The few people whom I met tried to evade me and when I asked a question they gave me brief replies and hurried on. As I came near to the home of my bride I saw people disappear within their houses before my approach. I went straight to Samuda's house and was met by her mother. She stood in the doorway and did not invite me to enter.

"She is not here," said the woman with a set face that masked any expression. Beyond that I could get no information and when I would have grasped her by the wrist the mother shut the door abruptly in my face.

An unknown fear clutched at my heart as I made my way to the edge of the village where lived an uncle of Samuda's, a kindly old man whom I had come to love almost as a father. He saw me coming and met me before I reached the door of his humble home.

"She is gone," volunteered the uncle.

I could scarcely form the words. "But where?"

"She is with the priests," he said. Then after a moment, "Samuda is to be the bride of the Fire Deva."

My whole body turned cold and I stood frozen as the stone statues of Babylon. Suddenly my knees gave way and I reached for the gate for support.

"Come in," said the uncle, "and I will tell you the story."

With a curious mixture of sympathy for a bereaved young bride-groom and pride in a niece who had been signally honored, the old man unfolded the tale.

"The priests came on the very day you left on your journey. They came in their formal robes and pointed hats and said that this year our village had been chosen among all the villages and cities of the land to have the honor of making the annual offering to the Fire Deva. It is the first time within the memory of the oldest inhabitant that we have been thus singled out. The priests sat up on their raised place with the small flame burning before them while all the young women of the village filed past. The flame itself inclined toward Samuda. Then they slew an animal and its entrails spelled out her name. By this double omen she was the chosen one and so it was."

He paused a moment before adding, "You are from a far-off land. You do not understand, but it is an honor."

With this the old man turned and left me. I recognized a conviction of inescapable doom in his words—the same acceptance of the inevitable I had sometimes sensed in Samuda. Belief in the power of that monster-god was in the blood of these people. I left the house, unlatched the gate and walked down the road blindly.

Instinctively I knew there was nothing I could do to prevent Samuda's fate, but also instinctively I had to try. Certainly never again, unless I could free Samuda, would I want to set foot in this village that had offered me supreme happiness only to snatch it from my grasp so cruelly. So I packed my few belongings, took my modest savings, the money I had planned to give Samuda's family as a marriage settlement, and set out.

It was a long and devious journey to the mountain of sacrifice. I had heard that the city of the fire temple was called Shiz, but no one seemed to know precisely where it was to be found. After many days, far back in the western mountains, I penetrated a tortuous defile and saw before me a conical peak with a faint plume of smoke issuing from the top. This was what Samuda had meant by the liquid fire, for here an active volcano smoldered in the depths of the mountain.

I refused to think of the horrible rites as I followed the trail which led upward among weird columns of lava and across fields of sliding volcanic ash. At places the ground was hot, and sometimes the odor of sulphur was strong in the air.

Since I wore the costume and spoke the language of the land I was allowed to enter the city unquestioned. I found its streets nearly deserted but as I neared the fire temple, I saw a great crowd was gathered. My heart rose to my throat. Could this be the day? Unobtrusively I wormed my way among the people.

A lurid light filled the temple and flickered on its walls. It was like finding myself in the very midst of hell. Frantically I asked questions which no one answered. My cries for Samuda were not even heard. Then as the ceremonies began a blessed numbness descended on me. There was a trancelike glassiness in the eyes of the other observers too as they gazed into the cavernous depths of a great pit where boiling lava bubbled up and receded, its red-tinged depths hungry to devour. Almost overhanging the pit on its far side was a grotesque figure made of black lava—the Fire Deva.

In the distance the sound of drums grew louder and the minor strains of a strange chant arose, adding to the incarnate evil unleashed. Out of some inner recesses of the temple emerged a procession. Drummers, singers, dancers, and priests walked by. Last of all came a lavishly adorned platform carried by slaves. Upon it was Samuda borne aloft.

I returned to the agony of consciousness. *"Samuda!"* The hoarse cry was torn from my throat, but immediately other voices took it up and it became a jungle chant.

As she passed directly in front of me I lunged forward, but the guards, judging me a fanatical pilgrim, restrained me firmly.

The procession halted in formation around the fire pit, Samuda in the center facing directly across toward the Fire Deva. As if in obedience to invisible signals, she rose from her reclining position and ascended to the apex of the platform upon which she was carried. She moved with her usual grace, yet there was something almost trancelike in the careful precision with which each action was performed.

The lava surged higher in the subterranean caverns. With it the pitch and tempo of the chanting increased. Timing her motions to the rhythm of the singers and the drums, Samuda began to divest herself of the gorgeous clothing in which she was attired. Unwrapping the veils which bound her bosom, she flung them down into the pit of fire and bared her full breasts to the leaping light. Loosening the robes from her hips, she cast them down and stood forth in naked beauty before the Fire Deva. At last she removed her headdress and tossed it into the flames, letting her hair stream loose in the wind. There was an audible gasp at her beauty, while I looked on, helpless despair and rage and shame warring in my heart.

The chanting began again and the procession moved once more

through all the corridors of the temple. This time when Samuda passed me she looked directly at me, yet there was no sign of recognition in her eyes.

A sense of fear began to be manifest in the crowd. Beneath our feet the earth shuddered from some subterranean convulsions; the lava boiled higher and higher in the pit of fire. Men cried out in terror before a force known to have brought destruction in the past and again threatening a recurrence of disaster. In order to forestall new catastrophe, propitiation must be offered to the demon of the Fire.

The procession halted in its places around the fire pit. Samuda again stood directly across from the black Deva. The red lava gurgled and licked at the sides of the pit. Leaping up, it seemed to will to overpass the limits of its cavern and pour forth again upon mankind in a torrent of destruction. Even the Fire Deva appeared to lean forward with a baleful glare causing a small fissure at its base to widen alarmingly. Panic swept the multitude and a solitary cry of anguish arose so piercing that for a moment it drowned out the crescendo of the chant.

Then sudden and complete silence. The chief priest stepped forward and swept Samuda into his arms. He lifted her naked body high above his head, and all at once it seemed as if she were herself again, struggling to be free. My breath came in great tearing gasps as I threw myself against the guards with all my strength. This time they struck me down, but not soon enough to spare me the sight of Samuda being flung into the boiling caldron. As I sank I heard the sound of her voice as she shrieked one word, "*Yaush!*" No other person in the seething crowd knew its meaning, but it was burned into my mind forever.

3

Zarathushtra

HOW LONG IT WAS BEFORE I RE-
gained consciousness I do not know. But when I struggled weakly
to my feet my first impression was that the scene was exactly as I
left it, with the priests still standing on the platform, empty now of
all trace of my beloved—as empty as my heart would be forever.
My mind worked slowly, and it was not until I began to push my
way out of the crowd that I realized the entire multitude was immo-
bilized as if frozen. Listlessly I lifted my eyes in the direction in
which all the people were staring—to the ledge where the now leaning Fire Deva stood.

I came alive quickly, for there beside the evil monster stood a
strange figure, a tall man with a mighty frame, long flowing hair
and beard and garbed in a brown robe bound at the waist with a
rough rope. He stood with an arm uplifted and his burning glance
compelled attention.

"Who is that?" I asked of the man next to me.

"I know not, nor does anyone else," he replied, never taking his
eyes off the gaunt face of the stranger.

"He is not from our land," said another. "And no one saw him
come—he simply appeared. I fear he is a deva belched forth from
the unhappy earth."

"He is strangely quiet," I said. "Not at all like your priests."

"Listen to what he is saying," said one in a shocked voice.

"He cannot live uttering such words," said another.

79

I listened intently. Why did none of these fire worshipers make a move to kill him?

"Know, all men," the prophet cried, his tones rolling as thunder in the mountains. "Know all men that the sacrifice you have made is an abomination to Ahura. He is Mazda, the All-Knowing One, and he sees what you do. His terrible fires will not be held back but released upon you if you do the deeds of darkness. Renounce now the false and awful ways into which you have been led astray. Return to Ahura and do his bidding.

"As for this false Deva, this black and twisted servant of Darkness," he cried, turning to the lava figure beside which he stood, "his reign is ended." So saying, the prophet braced himself against the wall and pushed with all his might on the grotesque lava form. The fissure, which had earlier opened at the base, widened and with a terrible crash the idol toppled forward into the abyss.

Like a mighty billow the crowd surged a step forward as the cry of "Infidel!" rose up. But the calm voice rose above the shouting, and those nearest the prophet stopped to hear the words, and this pause stayed the movement of the crowd.

Standing motionless, one arm still extended, he continued, "Why do you worship fire as a demon? Know you this day that it is Deity."

A gasp, half anger and half hope, swept over the great crowd.

"Surely you know if you would but heed the truth," he continued more gently, "that the hearth fire which burns in your homes without ceasing"—my mind flew back to Samuda's family where I had so often watched the devotion and fear as they tended their fire "—it is not your enemy but your friend. It warms you up in the winter, and cooks your food, and lights your room. It is Anara, the grandson of the All-Knowing One. You look above and see the great fire which burns in the sky. Its rays descend to the earth and cause your crops to grow. It is Adhar, the son of the All-Knowing One. You see the burning lava which boils in this pit of fire. It is Ruwa, the servant of the Lord of Light.

"When the consummation of this age comes, fiery lava will pour over all the earth. But even that will be a terror only to doers of evil and not to doers of good. The righteous will wade through it and it will be like warm milk unto their skins. These things I have learned from Ahura Mazda, the Lord of Light, the All-Knowing One.

"Know you that fire is the enemy only of the Darkness; that in all the world it is only the Darkness which is to be feared. And you cannot overcome the Darkness by becoming like unto it and doing deeds of darkness. You can overcome it only by fighting for the Light so that the Light may drive the Darkness away. When the sun rises in the sky, worship the Light. When the flames leap upon your hearth, reverence the Lord of Light. When the lava boils red hot out of the earth, think only of the consummation."

With the mention of the boiling lava the spell which the man held over the throng was broken.

"Kill him! Kill the infidel!" went up the cry as the people broke into great confusion. But as silently as he had appeared, the prophet eluded them and vanished from sight.

I stumbled along with the crowd not caring whether I were trampled beneath their feet or not, angry only that my stubborn heart had refused to stop beating when my beloved had been consigned to the flames. Probably those who saw me staggering along through the town thought only that I had partaken too freely of the sacrificial wine.

As soon as I had left the town behind I struck off into the hills where I wandered around all night in a daze of misery. I made no attempt to find any food so greatly did I long for death. The next day was the same, and the next. But I was young and I could not die. It was on the third night that I fell asleep from sheer exhaustion and in a dream I thought I saw Ezekiel gazing heavenward with a rapt expression. "You have been saved for a purpose, my son," he said. "Arise and go upon your journey." In the morning I awoke with greater calm, although my spirits were still heavy with sorrow. I forced myself to eat a few berries and sip some mountain spring water from my cupped hands. Then I started on, not expecting anything, not hoping for anything, not caring for anything.

Leaving the black mountain of the hated fire temple behind, I directed my steps eastward where the peak of white snow soared above the clouds. At the southern foot of the mountain of light was the town of Ragh where I decided to tarry for a while. I secured a room in the inn, hoping that I could withdraw within it and come to some agreement with my own thoughts.

One day an aged and pathetic couple came to the inn and asked for a room. The woman was evidently very ill and not far from the door of death. The inn was full; as there was no place for them I offered my room. I found other lodging but returned frequently to see how the old folks were faring. After several days the husband said to me, "We are Porushasp and Dughdu. Our home is in the city of Urumiah, on the lake of the same name, in the region of Adharbaijan. We have come here because Dughdu wishes to pass from this life in the city in which her eyes first opened to the light of day. We think the time of her passing cannot now be far away, and we know that it is good. But we have one sorrow. Our only son wanders everywhere, and we know not where to find him to call him to his mother's side. He utters teachings which the people of the land do not like to hear, and it may be that he has come to harm. His two wives and his sons and daughters wait in Urumiah and are anxious; and we are lonely."

"My heart aches with yours," I replied.

"You are young for such heaviness of spirit," Porushasp said, "but perhaps it would help to tell it to a pair of older ears. What brings you to this pass?"

"I have lost my only friend, my beloved, to the Fire Deva," I burst out bitterly. "She was both good and beautiful and I rage at her useless destruction. I have lost everything that gave meaning to life."

"No, not everything. Did you not help two strangers?" asked Porushasp, laying a kindly hand upon my shoulders. Almost angrily I tried to shrug it off. Did not the old man realize that that act had been trivial while my sorrow was great as the sea? I did not try to acknowledge his kind words but sat there with my head in my hands.

"Human sacrifice is an evil thing," Porushasp continued. "The people of this land follow many strange practices, my son, but that one is the worst of them all. To those who do not approve it, it is the most devastating of rites. To those who believe, it is the most sacred. I doubt if the two opposing views can ever be reconciled under one roof."

I flashed the old man a sullen glance and had the urge to strike him. Was he suggesting that my beloved and I could never have built a happy home together, differing as we did in our attitude toward the Fire Deva? The insult was too great; but the man was old and I restrained myself.

"In the midst of such pain it is hard to recognize the truth," said Porushasp, "but time will help."

We sat in silence outside the inn for a long time. Within, in a tiny room, life was ebbing from the woman this man loved. Could he once have loved even as I had loved Samuda?

"You have been married long?" I asked finally.

"Forty-five years," replied Porushasp. "Does that seem long to you? It takes a length of time to learn to give and to take, to learn the place of passion and of perseverance, to learn the oneness of spirit. Love, my son, is more deeply experienced at the end than at the beginning of the journey."

I lived again my months with Samuda. Even as I was conscious of my desire for her warm and vibrant body, I was conscious of her unquestioning acceptance of the Fire Deva. I had assumed that our love would eventually blot out her fears; yes, and her beliefs.

"I must go in to Dughdu," said the old man, moving quietly from my side. I looked up at him and knew that here I had found another friend.

"Thank you for your kindness," I said. "I know you are right and there is nothing to do but to go on. I wish I might help you find your son."

After that we talked often, and I told Porushasp of my escape from Jerusalem and of the journey to Babylon. I also told him of Ezekiel's injunction to go through the world seeking truth.

"Truth?" repeated Porushasp. "Who knows the truth? Even my son Zarathushtra, preaches a doctrine that is strange to my ears. But he gives his life for what he calls the truth."

"What does your son teach?" I asked.

"A strange doctrine, that fire is a god and not a demon—"

Excitedly I interrupted. "Have I never told you of the prophet who appeared at the time of the sacrifice of Samuda?" My words spilled out in a jumble. That gaunt prophet was Zarathushtra! But where could he be now?

That night the feeble spark of life went out of the weary body of Dughdu. I assisted Porushasp to prepare her for the last rites. According to the custom, a funeral pyre was built, and the body of Dughdu was carried forth and laid upon it. The corpse would be an offering to the demon of fire, that he might be propitiated and allow the soul to live. The first flames were flickering in the dry grass which was tinder to the wood, when suddenly in our midst appeared Zarathushtra.

Stamping out the incipient fire, he cried to the little group assembled: "I am Zarathushtra. Dughdu was my mother, and Porushasp is my father. By the right of the only son I declare that the body of my mother is not to be consigned to the flames. By the authority of Ahura Mazda, whose message I proclaim, I make known to you that the Fire is sacred and holy. No demon resides in the leaping flame, but the spirit of the Lord of Light, the All-Knowing One. The pure spirit of my mother belongs to the Lord of spirits. Let not her perishable corpse contaminate the fire in which is reflected the glory of Ahura!"

"What then," cried one of the bystanders, "shall we bury her body in the ground as our cousins in the southland do?"

"Not so," replied Zarathushtra, "for the earth, too, is holy."

"Or cast her body to the waters that flow to the sea, as our cousins in the east do?" asked another.

"No," said the prophet, "since water also is sanctified by the Lord of Light."

Without further explanation he took the body of Dughdu upon his back, bore it forth to a high hill and laid it exposed upon a rock. Porushasp made no move to stop his son. This was the old man who had once asked, "Who knows the truth?" He waited with the people for his son's return. When Zarathushtra again joined us he said with assurance, "Her spirit is with the Lord of spirits. His creatures will do their appointed duty when they devour her body." And even as we watched, the vultures swept down in descending spirals and settled upon the corpse.

I had been drawn to this prophet Zarathushtra when I first heard him deliver his rebuke to the worshipers of the Fire Deva and had held the hope that someday I would have the opportunity to talk with him. But when he made such strange disposition of the body of his mother, I was repelled and decided to take my leave at once. Nevertheless, I kept pondering his statement that the spirit of Dughdu belonged to the Lord of Light. His words reminded me of what I had heard from the lips of Jeremiah and Ezekiel—that there was something imperishable within man that united him forever with the Lord Almighty. I sought out my friend Porushasp to say good-by, and even in the midst of his grief the old man expressed a fervent wish that I would find the truth for which I sought.

Not having any particular destination in mind, I set off along the northern edge of the great Salt Desert, a desolate region that well suited my mood. The entire area had once been occupied by a large lake which, as it dried, had left an encrustation of salt upon the soil. For vast distances this profitless surface was all that could be seen, and the glare of the sun on it dazzled the eyes. Some parts of the tract, however, were still swampy, and in them reeds and sedges grew up out of brackish water of varying depth.

At one point I approached a village which stood between marshland on the one hand and hard salt soil on the other. Noting a large gathering of men clustered on the edge of the swamp, I joined them and saw that they held a rope running out into the marsh and that

far out amidst the lush growth, a cow was helplessly bogged down
in the treacherous mud and water. A man was beside the cow, working with great skill and patience to attach the rope to the animal
and to encourage it to turn back to firm soil. When the cow and
her rescuer finally made their way out I realized with astonishment
that the man was none other than the bearded prophet.

Were we destined to cross each other's paths? I wondered if he
had more strange doctrine that I had not yet heard. But after all,
I decided, it was not so strange that we should meet again. He was
wandering across the land in search of converts, and I in search of
something still harder to gain. Maybe it was foreordained that we
should help each other. At any rate, that evening around the campfire I joined the other men to listen to this prophet who both attracted and repelled me.

I admit my surprise that this night he opened up a whole new
area of his teaching.

"Friends, you wonder that I, a stranger, endangered my life to
save a cow that belonged to one of you," Zarathushtra began. "Do
you not know that the care of cattle and the practice of agriculture
are the noblest of the occupations? To water ground that is too dry,
to dry out ground that is too wet, to cultivate corn and grass, to
raise crops and to tend animals, is to serve Ahura Mazda, the Lord
of Light. I make known to you that in heaven the Ox Soul stands
in the presence of Ahura Mazda, the All-Knowing One." There was
a murmur in the crowd but Zarathushtra did not heed it. "Yes, the
Ox Soul watches over all cattle upon earth. When the cattle are
well treated and handled with kindness, the Ox Soul rejoices; when
they are mistreated or neglected, the Ox Soul grieves. In the same
way when crops are well tended and there is food for animals and
men, the Ox Soul is glad; when fields are untilled and cattle and
people hunger, the Ox Soul is unhappy."

One of the men replied, "We know that cattle must be cared for
and fields must be worked, or we die of starvation. But we know of
no such Ox Soul living with our god."

"That is why I come to you," said the prophet, "to make plain many truths hidden from man until now. I tell you that many times the Ox Soul besought Ahura Mazda to appoint a protector upon earth to watch over the welfare of the cattle. Now at last the All-Knowing One has sent me to work for the good of cattle and fields."

The listeners who heard the first part of Zarathushtra's speech with approval, took exception to the effrontery with which he claimed such a high commission. Contention arose.

"He claims to come from a god—is he then one himself?" asked one.

"And this Ahura Mazda—did anyone ever hear of such a god?"

"This man blasphemes," they angrily announced, "and should we leave him in our midst to give false teaching to our youths?"

"Out he should go and join his animals. They and the fields can protect him."

Growing hotter in their jibing they turned to chase the prophet from their village, but already he had noiselessly vanished into the dark.

"And I did not thank him for saving my cow," said a timid voice on the outskirts of the group that was beginning to break up.

As I anticipated, Zarathushtra and I were following the same general route so that I met him again on several occasions, but each time briefly. High in the mountains above the Salt Desert we met for a fourth time. As I entered the village I found its men standing in a knot while one of the villagers recounted a great exploit.

"Did you see it with your own eyes?" I heard one of them ask.

"That I did," replied the storyteller. "I had taken him in for the night, he a plain man with no money and no roll of extra clothing."

"And then what?" asked a newcomer to the circle.

"We were just quieted down for the night when our dog began to bark. I shouted at him to lie down, but he continued to bark even louder. I should have known there was danger, but I was that tired—"

"And then this man runs out of your house, does he?"

"He runs out," the narrator continued, "with me following hard behind and there was the wolf sneaking in among my animals. The next I knew, the wolf was thrown at my feet—dead."

"And he had no weapon?" asked several men.

"Only a club he grabbed as he ran," was the reply. "He did the deed singlehanded, and that quick."

I spoke for the first time. "And who is this hero?"

"We will know that tonight. Today he is wandering in the hills, but he promises to sit with us by our fire come evening."

"I am another stranger," I said. "Can I find food and shelter in your village and stay to listen to this man?"

So it was that I remained with the village men, expecting to see some wild man of the desert exhibit his mighty muscles in exhibition feats and to hear him recount tales of prowess among wild beasts of the forest. To my surprise I heard a deep, familiar voice greet us, and as if from nowhere Zarathushtra stood in our little circle. I think I never saw the prophet seated when he talked. He towered above all others, and often had both arms extended in magnificent gesture.

Without any preliminary remarks he began: "In the beginning Ahura Mazda, the Lord of Light, created the good animals, the ox, the dog, the cock; but Angra Mainyu, the Lord of Darkness and the Great Enemy, made the evil creatures, the serpent, the wolf, the lizard, the fly. Whoever kills the harmful things and protects the good animals, wages warfare for the Light. Give heed to your friend, the dog. Has not Ahura Mazda said: 'I have made the dog self-clothed and self-shod, watchful, wakeful, and sharp-toothed, born to take his food from man and to watch over man's goods. Whosoever shall wake at his voice, neither shall the thief nor the wolf steal anything from his house without being warned; the wolf shall be smitten and torn to pieces. For no house could exist on earth but for these two dogs of mine, the shepherd's dog and the house-dog.' "

"'Tis true," said the men in unison.

"But," added one, "who is this Ahura Mazda?"

"Ahura Mazda, the Lord of Light, the All-Knowing One—"

Immediately the men turned angry. "Infidel!" they shouted. "We know of no such god. Out with you!" Plainly they expected Zarathushtra to rage back against their shouts, but he withdrew and his shadow crossed their fire no more.

After the other men had gone to their homes I sat long by the smoldering ashes of the fire, and I thought about Zarathushtra. Why did not the men hear him through? He preached a different god, it was true, but how could man ever learn truth if he did not listen to every teaching which presented itself? There was something good in respect for the life of lowly animals, but what about the Lord of Light and the Lord of Darkness? Had I not been taught that the Lord God is one? I would make a point of finding Zarathushtra and would ask him personally some of these questions.

Some time later I picked up news of him in a city on the plain.

"He was here with his two wives," the people told me, "and he said to us, 'Let him who is faithful to the Lord of Light erect a house and fill it with wives and children!' But who can support more than one wife?"

"What trouble would we have with more than one wife in a house!" exclaimed a small man with an anxious face.

"So we chased him from our city," said another.

I caught up with Zarathushtra on the far frontier of this land. He was exhausted and in need of rest and I also was glad to stop a few days on my journey—whither? So the prophet and I talked together. Forthright I asked him how he knew he was truly a prophet of a true god.

"For thirty years I lived at home," said Zarathushtra, "married wives, and begot children. Then I went across the river which flowed past our door, and sat down in a quiet place in the forest to meditate. The angel of Good Thought came to me. In a flash I saw how it was at the beginning of time. The Lord of Light and the Lord of Darkness fought with each other. The will of the one was set against the will of the other. Thus it was that the struggle went on for three thousand years.

"Then the Lord of Light created our primeval ancestor, Gayomard, and with him the primeval Ox, his helper. In peace they lived for three thousand years, but then the Evil Spirit rushed in again, with a myriad demons on his side, and the age of confusion began. The Lord of Darkness masqueraded in the garments of light. He appropriated the fires in which the true glory of Ahura Mazda shines and deluded the people into thinking that they are manifestations of his own evil Devas. His minions are the priests who teach the people to be afraid, and call for sacrifices of virgins and first-born children to appease the Devas."

I shuddered, wondering if I would tell Zarathushtra of my love for Samuda. But he was engrossed in his story.

"The age of confusion lasted for three thousand years, but it has now come to an end. The truth has been made known to me, and I am proclaiming it throughout the land. This is now the age of decision. In the age of decision every man must choose whether he will think evil thoughts and do evil deeds, or think good thoughts and do good deeds. One rule only can guide him aright. It is this: That nature alone is good which shall not do unto another whatever is not good unto its own self. He who follows this rule fights on the side of Ahura Mazda."

"But of what use is it to fight for Ahura Mazda if the battle is going to go on forever?" I asked.

"It will not go on forever," cried Zarathushtra. "The age of decision will last for three thousand years, then will come the consummation. The fires of Ahura will be poured forth over the earth. To the doers of evil they will be torment and destruction; to the doers of good they will be as the gentle zephyr and the cool river. The Bridge of the Separator will be set upon the Peak of Light. The doers of evil will find it narrow as the razor's edge and will plunge down to death. The doers of good will walk up it as up a broad street into the paradise of the Lord of Light."

I remembered the high snow peak at sunset. All the range was cold and white. The lofty cone was bathed still in the rays of the setting sun and glowed with a rosy light of unearthly beauty.

"Part of what you teach is indeed beautiful," I said. "I also worship the creator of heaven and earth, ruler and sustainer of my people. My god is Yahweh."

"And where is your land?" asked Zarathushtra.

"Far to the west; far beyond where the two great rivers flow side by side in the valley."

"Someday I shall go to your west and take there the truth of Ahura Mazda," mused Zarathushtra.

"But we have our own prophets," I replied with a touch of pride, "Isaiah, Jeremiah, Ezekiel—"

"I know not of them," he replied.

"And we know not of you," I said. "But tell me, did you receive your truth in a single flash, or did you learn from other teachers and then weave it all into a system of your own?"

"Many revelations I have had, and all from the angel of Good Thought."

"Prophet," I said, "I have seen you spurned many times. Have others accepted your teachings more readily?"

"In ten years only one man has understood me," answered the prophet honestly and sadly. "That is my own cousin, Medyomah, son of Arastai. He works now in the West, setting forth the doctrines. And I go to the East, seeking converts."

Ten years and one follower! I had not the heart to question his teaching further. I would think about it.

I stated simply, "I go to the East, also."

"And what do you seek?" asked Zarathushtra.

"Truth," I answered, and felt puny beside the giant man of such great wisdom vouchsafed him by his god.

"May the search not be in vain."

So saying Zarathushtra passed into the night; and I thought never to meet him again.

4

Flame from Heaven

AT THIS POINT IN MY JOURNEYING
it was time to replenish my dwindling funds. Because of my experience with camels, I could always find employment with a caravan; or because of my strong body I could become a porter; but I decided that I would try for something higher first. After all I read several languages, at least slightly; I spoke many dialects, and I had traveled through every country from Jerusalem to Balkh.

Upon entering the city I was pleased to find, as I had expected, that there were gathered people from other parts of the country. On the northeast side of the city was a large caravansary. Here I spent many hours, ostensibly interested in the camels, but actually picking up bits of information about the travel routes into the East, the nature of the inhabitants, and the hazards of the way. I learned that Balkh was the last great city west of Rajagriha—a journey of many months south and east.

Next I loitered in the market places, picking up a little of the language and customs of the people, studying their dress, and in general trying to feel at home among them. Within a short time I had acquired enough confidence to try my bold plan. Spending my last money to purchase the cloak and other garments of a gentleman, I assumed the air of a scholar and went to the palace. Being brought before the keeper of the archives, I stated that I had been apprised that the palace had need of a translator and tutor for members of the royal family. I hastened to run through my credentials in a way that sounded very impressive.

My plan succeeded far beyond my hopes, for I was escorted into the presence of the king's vizier and after much interrogation, was informed that I would be hired to tutor the vizier himself, and his brother, who hoped before long to travel abroad. I would be required to live in the palace so that I could instruct these dignitaries in formal geography, and also converse with them informally in various languages, from that of the Babylonian to the Egyptian. I humbly informed them that my knowledge of some languages was very slight, but this they took as modesty and were the more eager to have my services. So it was that I found myself living in more opulent surroundings than I could ever have imagined.

The palace was situated in the geometrical center of the city with streets radiating from it in all directions. The exterior was of red granite, recessed and crenelated. The rooms within were finished in white and gray marble, while in the royal chambers and baths the marble was carved into a fretwork of lace. The audience hall of the king was inlaid with stones of many colors, and the entire floor looked like a meadow in bloom in spring. Streams ran through the palace in marble channels so inlaid as to cause the water to shimmer with color. At night the lights were reflected from a thousand shining surfaces and multiplied into dazzling splendor.

My pupils were Frashaoshtra, the vizier, and Jamaspa, his much younger brother and assistant vizier. Jamaspa was about my own age, still in his twenties. Between the two brothers was a close comradeship, which came to include me also as daily we worked together. Depending upon my memory I would draw for them the outlines of some distant region or city and describe it so clearly that they felt they could find their way in the dark. Between our lessons they would tell me things of interest within their realm, so that I learned as much from them as they did from me.

One day they took me to visit the royal gallery. Pausing before the picture of a bearded monarch which occupied the place of honor, Frashaoshtra said, "Manushkihar was the remote ancestor of our kings. He lived long ago and did great deeds. Kai Kabad was his lineal descendant and became the first king of the present dynasty." Leading me to a position in front of another portrait he continued, "He was dwelling by the Mountain of Light when the barbarians from the north invaded our pleasant land."

I remembered the numerous armed bands I had seen as I journeyed and recalled some of the tales of horror I had heard as I sat around the evening fires in remote villages.

"Kai Kabad came forth from his retreat," the brothers went on with the story, "and defeated the barbarian king, Afrasiab. He bound his royal captive with a girdle and would have slain him, but the girdle broke and Afrasiab escaped alive. So the two made peace, and the river remained the boundary between our kingdom of Iran and their land of Turan."

Jamaspa then took up the story. "It is the account of Kai Kaus, Kai Kabad's son, that most intrigues me," he said. "He went often against the advice of his counselors and therefore suffered many misfortunes. Once when he invaded a foreign land, the sun grew dark at midday, and his soldiers were frightened and ran away. He wished to travel into the sky but, after getting so high that the earth looked like an apple beneath him, he fell back again."

"What do you mean by 'travel into the sky'?" I inquired curiously.

"Come, look at the device in the picture," laughed Jamaspa.

Looking more intently at the dim portrait of Kai Kaus, I saw that the king was standing in a small box.

"At each corner a tall spear was affixed upright, and on each spearhead was a chunk of raw meat. To each corner of the box a strong eagle was tethered, its line being of such length that the meat was just out of reach above its head. As the eagles flew upward seeking to get the meat, they carried Kai Kaus into the sky. But at last the eagles grew tired," Jamaspa concluded, "and all fell back to earth."

After this introduction to the early rulers I often walked in the gallery hall to study the portraits. One face attracted me particularly because of its fine features and sensitive mouth. I asked Jamaspa about it.

"That is Siawush, son of Kai Kaus, but he never ascended the throne. He led a troubled life."

"How was that?" I asked.

"He loved a girl of the common people," came the answer, "but he was not free to pursue his choice. Also a woman at court, the wife of a noble, was passionately fond of him. She arranged to have him brought to her bedroom where she lay, veiled only in gossamer, and she besought him to lie with her. He refused to touch her, and fled from the chamber. Thereupon this woman accused him to her husband of having attacked her, and his life was in danger. So he took the girl he loved and fled to Turan. Afrasiab appeared to receive him with honor but in a few years made false charges against him and had him executed."

"Was that then the end of the dynasty?" I asked.

He shook his head. "Siawush had an infant son who was hidden away by his friends and later brought back to Iran. He became the great king, Kai Khusrov, who warred against Afrasiab, took him captive and put him to death. Thus he avenged the murder of his father."

I looked with new respect at the venerable figure in the portrait.

As we moved on to the picture next to that of Kai Khusrov, Frashaoshtra said, "Kai Lorasp is the father of our present king. He held the throne only until his son was old enough to reign, then resigned in his favor, and now he lives elsewhere in peace and quiet and comes back to Balkh only occasionally."

As I became better acquainted with life at court I came to realize that under the beauty and splendor there was little enough of quiet and peace in the royal palace. Kai Vishtaspa sat upon the throne with dignity and seemed sincere in his desire to rule well, but he struggled against many obstacles. On the northern frontier there was a continuing threat of invasion by the barbarians. Within the kingdom, Gaumata, head of the priestly caste, was constantly engaged in insidious machinations aimed immediately at increasing

the power of the priests and undermining that of the king, and ulti-
mately at seizing the throne for himself. And in the king's own
family there was grievous disappointment. Hutaosa, the queen, had
not yet borne the king a son although there had been several daughters. It was obvious that she would soon bring forth another child,
but the record had been so consistently in favor of feminine offspring that the odds in the market place were a hundred to one on
the side of another girl.

The priest, Gaumata, realized that as long as there was no male
heir, the maneuvers in which he himself was engaged would more
surely lead to his usurpation of the throne. To insure a girl child to
the queen, every day he took a priestess with him into the innermost
shrine of the royal temple and lay with her openly in the presence
of the sacred fire. Then by sleight of hand he produced the effigy
of a girl baby and offered it in the flames. "O mighty Deva," he
commanded as much as supplicated, "cause that which leaps within
the womb of Hutaosa to be born a daughter, weak, puny, and of
short life."

Gaumata's most recent plot against the monarch's life had gone
amuck and had nearly cost his own life. He had dispatched an emissary to the barbarians to advise them to watch a certain pass, then
invited the king to ride with him through this pass on a hunting
trip. However, the emissary was intercepted by the secret police and,
under torture, confessed the plot. When Gaumata rode into the pass
with the king it was not the barbarians but the royal guards who
met them. In order not to alienate the entire priesthood the king
spared Gaumata's life, but for a reprimand and warning caused his
ears to be cut off. This accounted for the low-wrapped turban which
Gaumata afterward combined with his tall pointed priest's cap.

One day I asked Frashaoshtra if this story were true, and after
the vizier affirmed it he continued to recount other acts of violence
perpetrated in earlier years. The story that filled me with loathing
for the priest concerned a reader in one of the temples who had
plotted the priest's downfall. Hearing of the plan, Gaumata had
had the man flayed alive, then ordered the reader's chair to be cov-

ered with his skin and forced the man's son to occupy it and continue the father's work.

Established now without a rival in the highest priestly position, Gaumata used methods that were less obvious than those of former years, yet no one could doubt that his ultimate intentions were of the most sinister sort. However, there was little that could be done except to keep a close watch upon him.

One day our lessons were interrupted by the appearance of an attendant who announced that a bearded, brown-robed man who styled himself a prophet had appeared at the main gate of the city and desired audience with the king. Two wives and a daughter, a very attractive young lady, were traveling with the man.

The vizier sent back word that it would be impossible for the king to grant an audience, only to have the messenger return with the short reply, "The prophet says he can wait."

I knew full well who the prophet was, but felt I should verify my surmise with actual sight of the man. Having ascertained that he had established himself outside the gate, I hurried to the top of the city wall where I made my way to a vantage point and looked down. It was exactly as I had expected. Although I had not seen Zarathushtra for two years, I recognized him immediately.

As the days went along, it became evident that Zarathushtra was unswerving in the determination to begin his work in Balkh at no place less high than the court. The rabble which besieged the prophet at the gate, hoping to hear some word from him which would excite their curious minds, received no recognition at all. But when a poor widow besought him piteously to look upon her two small children who were burning with a strange fever, the prophet took pity upon them and ordered his favorite remedy prepared for their treatment. After a single day the fever subsided and the children were restored to health.

A report of this remarkable cure reached the palace where one of the court women recognized similar symptoms in her own sick child. She begged for the services of the prophet, and Jamaspa was dispatched to the gate to extend the invitation to the healer. Zarathushtra was absent at the moment, but Jamaspa found a young lady of remarkable charm seated in front of the prophet's tent. In response to his inquiry she said, "I am Pourucista, daughter of Zarathushtra, and if you care to take your rest here, my father will doubtless return soon."

Zarathushtra was a very long time in coming back, but Jamaspa found the hours passed quickly as he conversed with Pourucista. When the prophet appeared and consented to go at once to the ailing child, Jamaspa took his leave, promising himself he would make up some excuse for returning to the prophet's tent.

When they reached the palace they found the flushed child upon his bed. Zarathushtra studied him carefully, then gave his same prescription. The child was to be bathed every hour with cow's urine, and cloths wrung out of the same liquid were to be applied to the head constantly until the fever abated. The treatment worked with this patient too, although not quite as rapidly as in the preceding instance. It was necessary for Jamaspa to make several trips to the prophet in order to obtain further instructions, and each time he prized the words he had with Pourucista.

Zarathushtra now had free access to the court, and Jamaspa presented him to his elder brother, and Frashaoshtra in turn invited the prophet and his family to his home. The two wives declined, as was their custom, but Zarathushtra and Pourucista came under the personal escort of Jamaspa. Since Pourucista was present, Frashaoshtra had his own lovely daughter Hvovi in the company in order that the two young women might entertain each other. It seemed, however, that Pourucista had much about which to talk with Jamaspa, and Hvovi in turn became deeply engrossed in conversation with the prophet.

Zarathushtra talked at length about his doctrines, and both Frashaoshtra and Hvovi found the new teaching very instructive. At twenty, Hvovi was an intelligent young woman, far more interested in matters of religion and philosophy than most girls of her age. The prophet was gratified to find one of high standing and deep understanding attracted to his teachings. It seemed desirable to Zarathushtra to make frequent opportunities for explaining his more difficult doctrines to Hvovi, and as their sessions together continued he found himself laying fresh emphasis upon one idea he had always advocated but which had slipped of late from its proper attention in his teaching. This was the doctrine of plural marriage and the importance of a man's taking unto himself another wife when the right occasion offered.

Hvovi was also instrumental in bringing Zarathushtra to the attention of the king. She was a favorite of Kai Vishtaspa's queen, Hutaosa, and through the latter it was gently insinuated into the mind of the king that it would be of interest to him to hear the new prophet. So quietly was this accomplished that Gaumata did not even know the first time the prophet stood in the royal presence. Kai Vishtaspa and Hutaosa, great with child, sat upon their beautiful thrones in the audience hall; Hvovi was among the ladies-in-waiting, her eyes intent on the brave prophet. Zarathushtra stood forth with such courage and enunciated his teachings so eloquently that the king desired to hear him again; and that was much to have accomplished at a first hearing.

The second hearing did not go off as smoothly. Gaumata learned that it was to take place and attended it. In the midst of Zarathushtra's address, he broke in. Drawing himself up with all the dignity of the foremost priest of the Deva temples of the realm, he said, "I propose that if this unknown and self-styled prophet has new doctrines to promulgate it should be done in the presence of the learned of the kingdom that they may judge their truth, and that the priesthood of the ancient and honorable Deva temples should have opportunity to speak at the same time."

Kai Vishtaspa approved the proposed disputation although he knew, as did the rest of us, that the "wise of the land" meant the priests and that as chief priest Gaumata would be the spokesman. Then the king added one stipulation that changed the nature of the occasion—the public was to be admitted to the disputation.

Such a gala occasion was not to be missed, so the great audience hall was packed with the curious public, while over against one wall sat the panel of "wise men," the priestly judges.

After extended formalities the first phase of the verbal contest centered around credentials. Gaumata questioned the origin of the prophet, implying that he was nobody come from nowhere. In contrast, he claimed that the priesthood which he represented was an institution that could be traced all the way back to Kai Kabad, founder of the present dynasty. From him through an unbroken succession the priestly authority had been handed down even to the present, to Gaumata himself.

When his time came to answer, Zarathushtra made a simple recital of his ancestry and produced genealogical tables to prove its authenticity. He established his line all the way back to the illustrious Spitaman whose antiquity was as great as that of Gaumata's first predecessor. But the prophet did not stop at that point. With a certain inexorability, he continued to recite a genealogy which went on back to Manushkihar. When the assembled crowd heard the name of the ancient ancestor of all their kings, and realized that Zarathushtra was his lineal descendant and therefore a person of royal blood, they sent up a great roar of approval, and even the panel of judges emitted an audible gasp of amazement.

The hearing adjourned to meet again seven days later. At this meeting the second phase of the disputation was focused on the possession of predictive power. It was proposed that each of the antagonists utter a genuine prophecy which should be verifiable within a limited period of time. One month was the time agreed upon for this testing of prognosticative ability.

Gaumata was given the opportunity to prophesy first, and he used a trick that could not but prove him clever. Since Queen Hutaosa was already overdue for the delivery of her child and since he had been practicing his magic assiduously, looking toward the determination of the sex of the expected infant, he felt safe in making this forthcoming event the subject of his prophecy. Taking a rigid stance before the queen, he fixed his eyes in a glassy stare and addressed her.

"O noblest Hutaosa, queen of queens, and mother of queens, from whose womb an unbroken series of daughters has come forth, each more beautiful than the last, I foresee that within this month yet another daughter will be born, whose hand will be sought by all the kings of the earth, and who will occupy some throne with all the grace and elegance of her illustrious mother." At this eloquent declamation a stir of appreciation went through the crowd, but Kai Vishtaspa looked displeased and the queen held her fan carefully before her face.

Zarathushtra accepted the challenge and made his prophecy deal with the same subject.

"I predict," said Zarathushtra simply but with confidence that impressed his hearers, "that the queen of queens will soon bring forth a son."

At this the king looked pleased, and the queen lowered her fan to look more closely into the face of the prophet.

Zarathushtra proceeded: "I also foresee that this son will grow up to be a very great king. When the empire is endangered by an impostor without ears, this son will put down the rebellion, and will rule from the Nile to the Indus."

Zarathushtra had spoken entirely impersonally and without so much as a glance in the direction of Gaumata, but every eye was now turned toward the latter's turbaned head. Gaumata himself flushed with rage, but by the rules already adopted there was nothing to do but adjourn the proceedings and await the forthcoming natal event in the king's household.

There was not long to wait. The very next day the word was heralded throughout the city that the queen was delivered of a son. Moreover, Zarathushtra's word "soon" was judged to have been more accurate than Gaumata's "within this month." The child was given the name Darius. Gaumata was covered with chagrin which he attempted to hide by retiring to the innermost shrine of the temple.

There seemed no reason why the prophet and priest should not proceed to the third phase of the disputation, but Gaumata insisted on waiting for the expiration of the month which had been allotted for the proof of the prophesying. The ostensible reason was strict adherence to agreed-upon rules; the real reason was that Gaumata had sent to the distant city of Shiz in the western mountains for a priest skilled in magic beyond any Gaumata had yet mastered.

Gaumata announced that the third and climactic phase of the disputation would be a trial by ordeal. When Hvovi heard this she tearfully entreated Zarathushtra not to participate. Frashaoshtra and Jamaspa also advised strongly against it, for they were sure Gaumata would engineer some trickery. However, the prophet did not falter, but professed himself ready for the test.

When the time came the assembled crowd was so large that, in spite of a storm which appeared to be gathering, the proceedings were transferred from the king's audience hall to the large courtyard at one side of the palace. The people were held back by ropes, leaving an open arena in the center.

Gaumata stepped forward arrogantly. He announced that he had been the first to risk himself on the preceding tests and he would not hesitate on this one. He allowed himself to be staked out flat upon the ground and so bound that his mouth was held wide open. The only person in the arena with Gaumata was the high priest from Shiz, who was laboring over a fire where a caldron of lead was being brought to the boiling point. When it reached the proper temperature a portion of the boiling lead was drawn off into a large container, and the priest from Shiz ran to the prostrate Gaumata, opened a trap door on the bottom of the container and allowed liquid to pour into his mouth. Gaumata was then set free and showed himself none the worse for having apparently swallowed a quantity of boiling lead.

I knew there had been some trick to this spectacle, but it all happened so quickly that my eye could not detect where the false move had been made.

As I moved out of the crowd I saw the vizier hurrying in the same direction. When I overtook him he said angrily, "There is foul play! The container held by the priest from Shiz had a separate compartment which held milk. I saw a trickle of it when it was not turned off at exactly the right time. Let me to the king!"

But before we could make our way to the king to call for fair play, Zarathushtra was led forth, fastened immovably to the ground, and rendered speechless by the cruel device which held his mouth helplessly open. His last words were the supplication, "O Ahura Mazda, hear me and help me."

However, the Lord of Light seemed deaf to this plea, for the sky had grown more and more black with towering anvil-shaped clouds, and nature itself seemed to be conspiring to heighten the sense of terror and tragedy. The only illumination came from the fire which the high priest from Shiz was forcing to greater intensity as he brought the lead to the boiling temperature.

In all that great, watching crowd there was no sound. Hvovi had fallen in a swoon and Pourucista clung to Jamaspa in terror. People looked at each other with white, tense faces. I watched in frozen horror this hideous repetition of the fire temple rites.

The moment came. Gaumata watching from the sidelines had an undisguised look of triumph on his face. The high priest from Shiz filled his large container to overflowing with the boiling lead, walked toward the center of the courtyard, swung his container of hot lead in a high arc over Zarathushtra's head. At that moment the black storm released a single bolt of lightning which flashed down, striking the metal container in the high priest's hand so that he fell backward, and the boiling metal descended upon him in a searing torrent. The cry with which he expired was lost in the terrific clap of thunder which followed.

Gaumata fled at once from the city, and the populace tore down the temple in which he had ministered. Kai Vishtaspa and his queen espoused the doctrines of Zarathushtra, and Frashaoshtra and Jamaspa were free to confess openly the faith which they had already come to accept.

At the royal bidding a new temple was erected at the very point where the flame from heaven had struck, and thus this sanctuary stood at the side of the palace in the center of the city. In it Zarathushtra took Hvovi to wife, and Jamaspa was married to Pourucista. From it the king issued the edict which went forth throughout his realm, forbidding human sacrifice and converting the temples of the Devas henceforth into holy places of Ahura Mazda.

I heard the reading of the royal decree with a stab of pain that it had not come in time to save my beloved. But it had come. The prophet had triumphed over superstition. I decided my work in Balkh was done. I took my leave of the court and began once more my lonely way to the East.

Book Three

ENLIGHTENMENT

1

Cult of the Śakti

river valley which led along the usual tortuous route through many mountains. I pushed on rapidly for fresh snow was already beginning to fall on the mountain peaks and I wanted to cross the last pass before it was closed by winter.

On this route I was seldom long alone for there was an almost constant procession of caravans composed of heavy-laden asses, bullocks and double-humped Bactrian camels. It was comforting to have company and safer to hire the use of one of these animals, for the pass itself was a narrow limestone gorge where the trail clung to precipitous cliffs negotiated with more ease by the sure-footed beasts than by humans.

After a precarious descent down the narrow mountain trail, I at last looked out over the valley of the Indus and its five tributaries. Here I became again a solitary traveler. The river valley looked somewhat similar to that of the Tigris and Euphrates, and I wondered if at an early date great cities had existed here also. By now I had trained my eye to try to answer my own questions and I was rewarded when I saw a large mound evidently formed from the ruins of an ancient metropolis. From the contours still discernible it was easy to trace the outlines of the former walls and the course of some of the streets. I was interested to find that the streets were broad and laid out in a careful pattern, intersecting at right angles.

Where rain had washed away the side of the mound I could see remains of brick houses and even recognize installations for bathing and sanitation.

Perhaps my greatest asset had always been an insatiable curiosity and in this far land I smiled as I recalled the worry of my foster mother when I explored the gratings across the waterflow from Hezekiah's tunnel. As I sat on a pile of rocks I relived some of the days of my childhood. I thought on the paradox that I, who at one time had had two sets of parents, had now been for ten years without a home. As I contemplated life and fate, I was absent-mindedly poking the ground with a stick. It hit against something hard and within a few minutes I had unearthed numerous small square pieces of stone, carved with detailed designs hollowed out in the stone. I pushed one of these stones down into the soft mud to see the raised impression. Clearly here were figures of elephants, tigers, rhinoceroses, crocodiles, buffalo, and cattle with great humps on their shoulders.

On one stone there was the figure of a three-headed person sitting in a strange fashion with legs bent double beneath him, feet placed heel to heel, and toes turned down. He was surrounded by what appeared to be wild animals. After studying the figure awhile I tried the same pose but found it would require much practice to accomplish the posture. I laughed to myself at the sight I must make, sitting on top of an abandoned city trying to look like I knew not what!

The next object I picked up was a clay statuette of a nude woman with swelling breasts and pregnant belly. There were several of these small statues, and also a good many cylindrical stones with rounded ends whose significance I could not understand. Both interested and puzzled by these strange objects, I stored a few of them in my roll of possessions and moved on.

Continuing eastward, I crossed plateau and plains country and entered another valley. Here people were living in small village clusters. I found their language had some similarities to that which I had learned in Balkh so I was able to make myself understood, and even more easily I could understand them.

When I came to the first river I asked a chance fellow-traveler its name and he told me it was the Jumna. I contemplated stopping there but I found no large settlement and nothing of great interest, so I continued on until I reached the Ganga River which wound back and forth in serpentine curves, then swung to the north and northeast. There, nestled beside a great crescent sweep of the river, lay the city of Kaśi.

In my wanderings I had of course become accustomed to strange people, strange sights, and strange customs. Nowhere would I ever find a woman as beautiful and graceful as my beloved Samuda, but still Hvovi in the court of Balkh and Zarathushtra's daughter had been good to look upon. I sometimes wondered if from sheer loneliness I would someday take a wife and settle down. Our own sacred books and our prophets encouraged family life and the very order of man's nature made him long to give and to receive love. Such I knew was the better course, but I also knew I could never be satisfied unless I loved with my whole heart. Were the words of old Porushasp true which he had spoken when his wife lay dying? "I doubt if two opposing beliefs can ever be reconciled under one roof." If true, then I was heading the wrong way for happiness, for I was wandering farther and farther from my people. Even in exile, my people lived according to their own customs and worshiped their own God. Always at this point my mind trailed off, and whether I lacked the courage to turn back or whether I was fulfilling a destiny as Ezekiel had suggested I did not know. Irresistibly I seemed pulled east.

What new adventure would Kaśi hold for me? I had come to accept the idea that people find what they are looking for; the merchant is drawn to the markets, the money-changer to the stalls, the adventurer to the dives of evil. My interest seemed to center in the ideas of people. In this mood I approached the new city and certainly my eyes saw a new sight. Even while well outside the city limits I found myself caught in a crowd. However, they were not bound for the city, but apparently were trudging around it. Still more baffling was the nature of the crowd, composed almost entirely of the aged and infirm; the only young people being those who were supporting some individual who could not walk alone. I was also struck by the number of evil-looking characters and instinctively felt for my moneybag. Removing myself from the main body of the crowd, I leaned against a tree to watch. There I was joined by a man who was obviously too tired to continue on his way.

"Is this a procession of some kind?" I inquired.

"You are a stranger," he replied. "Have you never been to our city before?"

I assured him I had not.

"Then you have not come to gain merit?" he asked.

"I have come only because I am on my way farther east. But I might reside in your fair town a short while. It lies in a beautiful valley, and your river is wide."

"The river is most important. But I must join the other pilgrims again."

"You have not yet told me what you are doing," I said anxiously.

"We are making the six-day pilgrimage around the city," he replied. "Many pilgrims come to Kaśi to gain this merit. Some of them will die as they circle the city, but this also is gain, because the pilgrim who dies while making the circuit will be transported directly to paradise. Will you join us?"

"I think I will take my chances on gaining paradise by some other route," I said, perhaps a little too lightly. As I looked over the band of people, almost crawling, I felt that a good many souls were destined for an early arrival in paradise.

I entered the city through one of the many narrow gates that gave the wall the appearance of a circular comb. Oddly, the wall was made of wood, and compared not at all well with the walls of Jerusalem or Babylon. Within the gates there was a labyrinth of narrow, crooked streets, too constricted to permit the passage of any kind of vehicle, crowded with people on foot, and overhung by precariously constructed houses. The dark holes at the ground level were evidently shops, faced on narrow streets which were nothing more than filthy alleys with most evil-smelling gutters running through them.

I stepped into one of the shops whose overhanging balcony excluded the sunlight; an ornate brass lamp cast a fitful gleam through the room. Once accustomed to the semidark my eyes rested on a brocade shimmering with silver and gold threads in a pattern so beautiful as to become a princess. How exquisitely this cloth would have set off the dark beauty of my loved one! Although I became conscious of the presence of some person in a far corner, no one came forward to interrupt my reverie. I walked to the next table upon which there was a profusion of brass objects. I picked up several in turn and studied them; each was intricately carved and delicately lined. What beauty in the midst of such filth! I was tempted to buy one small piece. When I had left the palace at Balkh, my services had been well rewarded so that I had money enough to live for a while and to squander a bit—if such one could call the purchase of beauty. But as always I faced the question of what to do with a treasure after I purchased it, so I left the shop.

Finding the city itself most unattractive I made my way to the river, where I found throngs much larger than the one making the pilgrimage outside the city. No wonder the shops had been deserted —everyone was at the river's edge. In fact, the entire crescent of the Ganga was alive with milling human beings. Although I could not interpret the scene I was witnessing, I knew that I had reached Kaśi during a time of the exercise of their religious rites. I joined the crowd. At frequent intervals along the riverbank flights of steps led to the water. By the hundreds the pilgrims waited at each stairway for a turn to make their way, or be carried down and into the water.

Respectfully I said to a man at my side, "That water is very dirty. Why do not the people bathe in some clear stream or pool?"

He looked at me as if I had profaned the very gods themselves and replied, "This is the Ganga. It is the most sacred act of life to bathe in its waters. If a person can bathe from the five most sacred spots in one day he will ask little more from life." I could only think

that if I bathed five times in that water I would surely want a sixth
bath in some other river.

Along the riverbank all kinds of hawkers vended their wares—
baubles and worthless trinkets, little idols, and small live animals.
Drummers and pipers and fiddlers made music for a recompense.
Trained monkeys gyrated in monotonously repeated antics, and
shaggy bears ambled through their tricks, their trainers accompanying their motions on small drums. A snake charmer squatted cross-
legged before a basket out of which rose the hooded head of a cobra.
Making music on a small flute and then moving his hands in slow,
rhythmic gestures, he caused the snake to sway back and forth. A
magician flung a coil of rope upward where it straightened and
stiffened in the air until a monkey climbed to the top. These and
others marvels were available to any person who had money to
spend, and I must confess that I left the river front poorer than
when I came to it.

I might have loitered among the magicians longer except that my
attention was drawn toward the throngs gathering around raised
platforms along the river. When I drew near I found that the platforms were funeral pyres, some being prepared for use and others
with the flames already licking at the corpses which would be quickly
consumed as the fire broke into terrific heat. A short distance down
the riverbank I saw the flames leap high, watched by the widow of
the deceased who sat immobile as stone, among the relatives. Suddenly she jumped up and flung herself into the heart of the fire. No
restraining hand was moved to save her, and her cry of anguish
went as unheeded as the chattering of the monkeys and the hawking
of the vendors.

Although these pilgrims at Kaśi practiced the rite of corpse-burn-
ing, it was plain that other tenets of their religion differed from any
I had come in contact with in my previous sojourns. Did they have
temples and priests?

I had only to follow the stream of pilgrims that was moving away
from the river to find an answer to my question. We soon came to
an area so crowded with temples that I marveled at their number.

They were of all sizes and kinds, some of wood, some more handsomely constructed of stone. In one temple garden innumerable monkeys chattered in the trees; in another snakes slithered out of the path of approaching footsteps; in yet another, tethered goats awaited slaughter in sacrifice; and everywhere humped cattle wandered freely about the grounds, as they did in the streets of the city.

I entered one shrine where I found women seated on the floor, chanting and swaying to the accompaniment of high-pitched music, while a priest strewed flowers and swung a censer of incense in front of a many-armed idol. Going into an elaborate sanctuary, I passed through corridors lined with statuary until I came at last to a spot where I could peer into the murky innermost recess. There loomed the colossal bust of a three-headed deity. It looked vaguely familiar and then I remembered the small stamp seal that I had picked up in the ruined city to the northwest. I asked a priest the significance of the idol.

"That is Śiva, the great Lord of the Universe," began the priest in a singsong voice, "whom we worship here as Maheśvara. The three faces are like wind, fire, and water; they are also thoughtful, wrathful, and blissful; at the same time they see into the past, the present, and the future. Śiva is the procreator and the destroyer. He rules the destinies of all creatures which are born and die. If one would ever escape the wearisome cycle of birth and death, one must learn the higher doctrines which the great Deva has to teach."

An involuntary shudder ran through me as I heard the god called a Deva. Was I never to be free of that haunting memory of fire demons? But soon I recognized that here the name was employed as a title of the highest reverence.

"I would learn more," I managed to say.

"Then you must go to the temples of the Lingam and of the Śakti," replied the priest.

Following the directions given by the priest, I reached one of the most inaccessible parts of the city. There I saw the temple of the Lingam rising before me. A lofty tower with bulbous top loomed high in the air. Studying its architecture, I saw that it was made up of successive reduplications of itself, so that smaller curved towers were built together to make the greater, all of them recessed and channeled and carved in almost infinite detail. Lesser buildings clustered about the main structure.

Entering one of the smaller temples, I could make out nothing until my eyes became adjusted to the darkness. Sounds of a chisel on marble reached me, and looking into a corner my eyes rested on a sculptor working at an upright block of stone. A male model slipped away out of sight, and suddenly I recognized that the stone was a large, anatomically detailed phallus. This was the symbol of Śiva as the god of reproduction. Then I remembered the small more crudely shaped stones that I had seen at the ancient city on the tributary of the Indus, and for the first time realized their religious significance. From this building I hurried on through a court and passed under the shadow of the major tower, adorned with innumerable sculptured figures. In almost every group the ithyphallic god was central, offering himself to the outstretched hands of some celestial consort.

From here I entered into the central temple building, passing a great stone bull that stood in the antechamber, and then came to the innermost shrine. Other pilgrims, more devout than I, were passing in and out of the temples and I was sure they experienced a deeper religious fervor than did I. Yet, as I watched their faces and movements I wondered if they actually experienced a religious uplift or only a sensuous, emotional excitement? But perhaps that was their religion! I thought there must be something I had not yet sensed, so I would not pass judgment.

I entered the most sacred shrine. The largest phallic stone I had yet seen rested in the middle of a richly ornamented enclosure. Chanting priests circled it; they poured water over it in gushing lustrations; they bedecked it with flowers, and sat in silent meditation concerning the noble Lingam.

I left this temple, puzzled, wondering if all the temples were replicas of the huge one I had seen. On inquiring I was told that the Śakti had great importance, also. Again at this temple I was greeted with the sound of a sculptor at work. The model here was a young

woman of ample physique who stood upon a small platform and
raised her right arm to seize the branch of a tree above her head.
This brought her large, round breasts prominently forward, one
lifted somewhat above and ahead of the other. A single necklace of
jewels fell gracefully across them, resting gently against their raised
tips. Her abdomen curved forward, and around her hips were two
bands of gold which were knotted in front and allowed to fall between her legs. Her left hand rested upon the golden knot. The right
leg was straight, the left lifted and turned outward with the heel of
the foot resting against the other ankle. Around each ankle were five
narrow circlets of gold. This figure the artist was reproducing in
stone, accentuating even more the feminine characteristics.

Again I was reminded of the female statuettes I had unearthed
in the ruined city. Here was certainly a religion of long standing—
centuries old no doubt. As far west as Jerusalem, and later in Babylon and at other points along my wanderings I had heard rumors of
the cult of the mother goddess, but I had ascribed them largely to
a period long past. But now I realized I was in the heart of a very
live and contemporary city whose sole purpose for existence seemed
to be to keep alive the traditions and rites of the cult.

Moving deeper into the recesses of the temple I found a priest
and asked him to explain the significance of the symbols used so
profusely in the decorations. To the priest the story was old and he
chanted his way through it. I found it difficult to follow but seldom
interrupted him.

"Śiva and Śakti symbolize the highest truth—yoga or union.
When in the beginning the purusha or soul of the universe was
united with the prakriti or primordial essence, all things came into
being. All things are now bound in the endless cycle of birth and
death, of creation and destruction, over which the Mahadeva, the
Great Lord, presides. The Great Lord is the destroyer, but by re-
fraining from destroying he creates. Thus all things ebb and flow in
him, and the breath of his body is the pulse of the universe."

The priest paused briefly but I felt this was no time to question him. Besides, I did not yet have any basis for an intelligent question, so I listened as he continued.

"But Śiva is also the great Yogi, and when he sits cross-legged in abstraction his breathing ceases and all things rest. Whoever would be free, therefore, from the weariness of death and rebirth, of dissolution and reconstitution, must be united with him. The perfect union is that of Śiva with his Śakti. In this union there is absolute ecstasy and absolute rest. When all the universe has become the Śakti of Śiva, all things will experience the ecstasy of being one with nothingness. It is for this reason that we ourselves begin the work of emancipation by sitting cross-legged in meditation like the Mahadeva. Then, progressing in knowledge degree by degree, we come to that fourth stage where in the embrace of Śakti we experience a foretaste of the ultimate union toward which all strive."

I was sure I had not understood much of this doctrine, but when the priest suggested that we move on for a further inspection of the temple I followed him, feeling myself so mesmerized by his voice, his words, and the things I had seen that I had little desire to do other than his bidding.

"The Śakti of Śiva is manifest in different characters," he continued. Then he stopped before a large panel sculptured in high relief. "Here she appears with the Great Lord in the form of his wife Parvati, daughter of the snows." With a tiger skin about his loins the figure of Śiva was sitting cross-legged on a mountaintop; beside him, half-reclining and leaning toward him with gentle caresses, was a beautiful young woman, with bare breasts, and limbs wrapped in fine cloth. There was something lovely in the figure of the daughter of the snows and I thought perhaps we were working toward the essential good in this religion. Then we paused before the next statue.

"This is the son of Śiva and Parvati," said the priest. Here was a revolting, fat-bodied, elephant-headed creature. How could this be the son of the shapely daughter of the snows?

"What is his name?" was all I could think to ask.

"Ganesha," the priest replied. "He is the god of wisdom."

I was moved to say that I had never felt wisdom to be so repulsive, but I refrained. We reached the next statue which the priest introduced. "This is Durga, another wife of Śiva." Sculptured in stone and painted yellow was the figure of a woman, beautiful in bust but with ten arms extending grotesquely in all directions.

"Why does she have ten hands?" I inquired.

"You note that each hand holds a different object, a conch shell, a mace, a drum, a spear, and so on. These are the attributes which the great gods conferred upon her when they commissioned her to slay the dragon."

I studied the statue more closely and saw that the woman was standing upon a tiger, a spear plunged into the breast of a demon at which the tiger was snarling.

"During this week we have celebrated the festival of Durga," explained the guide. "Tonight we will carry this statue in ceremonial procession to the Ganga and cast it afloat upon a raft. Tomorrow the sculptor will begin to make a new statue for the next year."

Another figure which he pointed out was a terrible female form, executed in black stone, encircled with snakes and surrounded by skulls. From her protruding tongue the blood of a sacrificial goat was still dripping.

"Kali is the Black One," commented the priest. "Because of her importance we often call her Devi, *the* goddess. She must be propitiated with the blood of slain animals lest her wrath break forth in destruction."

To clear up some confusion in my mind and to show that I was an apt pupil, I said, "Am I right in understanding that these figures all represent wives of Śiva or, as you said, are different forms assumed by his Śakti or female essence?" Even as I put it into words I recoiled at such a concept.

"There are many more besides," approved my priestly teacher. "You see these figures carved upon the pillars around the room?"

I nodded; they were so prominent that one could not miss them.

"These are the Yakshis, goddesses of water and fertility in whom Śiva takes great delight. But lift your eyes higher."

Obeying his command, I raised my eyes to the tops of the pillars and saw that each one had an architrave from which female figures seemed to leap to the beam above.

"Those are the Apsarases, the celestial nymphs, which sing and dance and play for Śiva," the priest explained.

Looking into the dim heights I saw two figures so placed and so carved as to seem almost alive and moving. The priest's voice took on a far-off tone as he assumed an almost trancelike pose.

"And that," came his soft words, "is the union of Śiva with his Śakti."

I offered the priest the customary gratuity, which quickly brought him back to the mundane present. I thanked him for his instruction and left the temple.

Oblivious of the people all around me, I wandered in the streets that night and pondered the Śiva and the religious concepts I had seen expressed in the Lingam and Śakti temples. I found the forms repellent, yet I realized that they were perhaps crude manifestations of a thought that had survived from the beginning of human life—that the nature of man was inextricably interwoven with the nature of the universe. Creation and destruction; male and female; love and wisdom. These people seemed to have all the necessary basic ideas, but were there no prophets in this land to show them that these urges could be brought to a higher level? Surely there was a need for a great teacher.

There were many more temples, hundreds of them I was sure, but I was weary with the sense of uselessness and degradation with which the night's activities had filled me. I would find a place in which to rest. Standing in front of one of the small temples was a man dressed differently from any of the priests I had seen, so unsuspectingly I inquired about an inn.

The man seized me firmly by the hand and pulled me inside the door of the building, saying affably, "Of course. You are a stranger. I can care for you. And you will learn of the mysteries as well."

"It is only rest I want," I said a little gruffly. "I have seen enough mysteries for this night."

"Ah, just so," he continued, half dragging me into another room. "But the Sannyasin ascends through many grades before experiencing the highest." This confusion of words was lost on me for I could see that this was not an ordinary inn such as I wanted.

"It is necessary for you to taste of what is to come in order to know that it is worth your striving," continued the oversweet voice of my guide. "Taste now of that union which is the goal of all creation."

As if by magic the man disappeared and left me standing in a small inner room with little light and foul air. Then from a ragged couch a woman rose, cast aside the robe which was her only garment and came toward me.

"I am your śakti," she said. "Mahadeva has sent you to me." Insinuating herself into my arms she went on: "As the vine clings to the tree, I will cling to you; as the cloth wraps itself around the stone, I will wrap myself about you."

The long hours of this day and the bewildering sights of this night had almost numbed my senses. Could there be truth in the ancient wisdom of this cult? The body pressed against me was neither young nor clean, but soft and yielding. And her arms began to tighten around me. Then suddenly there flashed upon me a vision—I was lying on green grass with rippling water running at my feet. I saw the innocent beauty of Samuda. I flung the śakti from me and rushed from the shrine and from the city, never stopping in my flight until an extra fee had opened the closed gates for me and I stood alone under the waning morning stars.

2

Mahavira, the Last Conqueror

SO EAGER HAD I BEEN TO FLEE
the city of Kaśi that I had not equipped myself for my onward
journey. Fortunately I had money enough to carry me for some time
and a little of it I used in a squalid market outside the city gates.
Here I purchased, at double the ordinary price I was sure, a length
of white cotton cloth which I wound around myself in native fashion, making a garment resembling a combination of skirt and loin
cloth. Another length of cotton I used for a head covering and a
third I purchased for a cloak, a replacement of the articles I wore,
or as a container in which to wrap the few possessions I carried, including the sword that had been given to me the fateful night at
Taloth. How long ago that slaughter seemed! I had nearly doubled
my age since that first adventure with death soon after my sixteenth
birthday.

The air of the Ganga valley was hot, heavy, humid. It lay upon
me like an actual weight and the slightest exertion during the middle
of the day produced a dripping perspiration. Gladly would I have
welcomed the heat of the desert for the desert was hot like the blast
of a furnace but it was dry, and at night sudden coolness restored
one's wilting life. Here in this valley night brought no relief; my
clothes stuck to my body and the very act of living was at times a
burden.

But I had to press on for already I was warned that I was too late for this journey. The rainy season was upon us; for months there would be no respite from the downpours and the heat. Clouds lay over the land most of the time and at frequent but unpredictable intervals torrents of water descended. Along the way the occasional villages were nothing more than clusters of mud huts that housed both man and beast, and I preferred the perils of the journey to stagnation in one of these miserable spots. As I pushed on the engulfing misery of the hours melted into uncounted days and I lost track of time completely.

One day I felt a new quality in the heat; it came from within and seemed to consume me where I stood so that my limbs would not obey my commands. This sensation was followed by chills which set my teeth to chattering. I realized that I was ill, too ill even to stand. I sank down into the grass without giving a thought to the jungle creatures which frequented the region and there I slept.

When I awoke I was in strange surroundings. Slowly I realized that I was lying on a pallet in a dark corner of a small hut. There was no other furniture, but in one corner a fire of dried cow dung burned in a crude stove on which a pot was boiling. Nearby an elderly and emaciated couple sat on their haunches, silent. Once in a while the woman would rise painfully to her feet and hobble over to stir the contents of the pot. It seemed that I lay for hours on the borderline of consciousness before I had enough strength to move my hand. But with this first feeble motion the old woman brought me a bowl of gruel. I could only smile my gratitude, but she smiled back and was satisfied. Some days later I learned from my benefactors that a strange snarl from their dog had taken them outside where they found me lying not many paces from their door. They had carried me into their hovel to protect me from marauding jungle beasts, and then had nursed me through my long illness.

"How long have I been here?" I asked.

"The days are all alike; we do not count them." But from scraps of their talk I estimated it had been about two weeks.

As my strength returned I became fretful of the continued delay.

When one morning I announced that I would leave three days later, the news was received with a strong protest.

"Only a fool would try the jungle now," said the old man. His wife tried a different tactic. "It is a long time since any person has shared our hospitality here on the edge of the jungle. It is very poor, we know, but you would make us happy to stay till the rains are over."

Since the Providence that had kept watch over me in all my ways had brought me through another ordeal, perhaps I should not have tempted that Protector so sorely again, but I had not yet learned that wisdom is better than rashness. I was eager to be on my way and a morning soon came when I felt I could start out once more. The old lady hobbled about the small room, clucking to herself while I tied up my bundle. Suddenly, with more vigor than I would have thought possible, she stood over me, her shoulders held back, adding inches to her bent form. Striking the floor with her gnarled cane she said fiercely, "I wish you were my son. You would not enter that jungle until the rains were over."

I laid my hand on her shoulder and for a moment wished I were her son. "I do belong to you," I said, "because to you I owe my life. But I have a mission and I owe something to it also. I must go on."

It seemed inappropriate to leave them so unceremoniously when suddenly the picture came to my mind of my leave from my own parents. They would be old now—as old as these two. I saw myself that last moment in their exile home in Babylon and I heard my father's voice. Impulsively I said to this man and woman, "Among my people we have a blessing. My father gave it to me when I left home. May I leave it with you, my new foster parents?"

They bowed their heads as I repeated: "The Lord bless you and keep you; the Lord make his face to shine upon you, and be gracious unto you: the Lord lift up his countenance upon you, and give you peace."

As I turned back for one last look I could see the tears streaming down the old woman's cheeks and my only hope was that she would find consolation in the gift of money which I had left for her.

From the anxiety of this man and woman I knew that perils lay ahead for me; had I known how great I might have been tempted to yield to their persuasions to remain with them. Within a short time I was in an impenetrable thicket. Enormous trees covered with thick vines rose about me. Some of them grew into the air, spread out their branches, and sent down roots again, so that going under one tree was like walking in a forest. Rank, lush growth of every kind surrounded me. Bamboo grew in great clusters. Heavy ferns concealed treacherous pitfalls. Exotic blooms lured me aside toward bottomless morasses. Poisonous plants extended their arms to clutch me.

I came to a sluggish river and wondered how I would cross. I stepped on a log to see if it were solid and a crocodile opened enormous ugly jaws and slipped silently into the muddy water as a thrill of horror coursed through my veins. Very gingerly I tried another log. This one was real but it was half rotted with the dampness, and as I turned it over a mass of slimy creatures swarmed out of its sodden depths.

I waited until they had all crawled out, then pushed the log into the water and managed to cross the river by this precarious means. Maneuvering the log under a tree as close to shore as possible, I reached up for a branch with which to swing ashore. The instant my fingers touched the clammy, scaly surface I knew I had seized a live snake, but it twisted out of my hands and glided through the underbrush with only the faintest whisper of leaves.

Shaken, and with more caution than ever, I resumed my journey, proceeding along such semblances of trails as I could find. The jungle was alive with the chatter of birds; the light was eerie and unearthly and I could feel the glare of baleful eyes following my path. The skin on the back of my neck prickled with fear as I caught a glimpse of a tiger in a clearing. It followed me for miles through the undergrowth before it turned aside to some other objective. I saw a boa constrictor crushing a wild pig in its coils. Blood-sucking leeches fell upon me; and everywhere were destroying white ants of great size.

During the heaviest of the sudden downpours there was often no animal in sight and no sound to be heard except the violence of the rain. I would crouch under the shelter of the heaviest growth and wait for a break in the storm. The instant the rain ceased the sun shone as brilliantly as before, the cacophony of jungle voices rose again, and life stirred on every side.

As I emerged from a bamboo thicket and was striding through knee-length grass there reared up before me the hooded head of a king cobra. Lidless eyes glared at me while the ugly head swayed back and forth. I knew that the cobra could be expected to strike with lightning speed, darting forward to lick my skin, before sinking its deadly fangs into it. The snake charmer at Kaśi flashed into my mind. Slowly I began to move my hands and arms back and forth with swaying motions. When the attention of the cobra was fixed, I stepped backward with infinite care until I could reach down with one hand and grasp my sword. As soon as I felt it firmly within my grip I leaped forward and cut the cobra's head from its body.

Rain, the jungle, and wild animals were not to be my only perils. Now the floods came. The height of the rainy season coincided with the maximum amount of melted snow from the high mountains. Swollen rivers overflowed their banks and the entire region was inundated. Low-lying farm lands were submerged and the waters backed up for miles into the jungles. Terrified wild animals whose ordinary habitat was the ground climbed into the branches of trees. High points of land which remained above the water were occupied by elephants and hyenas, tigers and gazelles. For the time being mortal enemies forgot their antipathy and stood side by side as they confronted the common menace.

I reached the edge of one stream as its waters were lapping at the top of its banks. A pile of driftwood so interlaced as to make a compact and apparently impregnable unit rose above the waters. I climbed upon this raft and watched the flood spread all about me. A leopard with a beautiful spotted coat soon joined me, then a wild pig and several snakes. The waters continued to rise, and soon I realized that the pile of driftwood was being loosened from its mooring in the mud. When it broke free the logs continued to hold together and thus our strangely assorted crew were cast adrift.

As we floated downstream I had ample time to think. Once more my fate rested in the hands that had so miraculously preserved me ever since my escape from Jerusalem. This Power had taken me safely through all my wanderings in mountain, desert, and jungle; it had provided me with shelter during my illness and now had rescued me from the flood. I looked at the leopard sitting beside me as peacefully as a house cat; at the wild pig, maintaining a precarious balance among the twigs and other debris of this strange craft; at the snakes, lying motionless. None had any wish to prove supremacy. We were as one. A flash of great insight came to me—unity—that was the idea the people were trying to express at the Śakti temple.

Suddenly I seemed to hear the voice of Ezekiel saying, "Son, you have been spared for some purpose." But I have not worked too diligently for that purpose, I thought honestly. I have been absorbed by my personal happiness and sorrow. If I am spared once more, I vowed, I will prove myself worthy by devoting the rest of my life to seeking throughout the world for the true teaching.

At last we drifted to a junction with a larger river. Here a cluster of mud huts were disintegrating rapidly in the waters which washed around them, and evidently most of the inhabitants had fled, taking with them all the farm animals they could rescue. With the exception of one small party of men paddling about in a crude boat trying to retrieve some belongings, the region appeared to be deserted. I hailed the men, and although they stared in amazement they came to my rescue, and even volunteered to convey me to the nearest city, Vesali, which was situated on high land north of the Ganga. I was glad to accept.

Vesali proved a pleasant place, the capital of a minor kingdom of Licchavi and the home of the benevolent ruler, King Chetaka. I would attempt no more foolhardy travel, so I took up my residence in a suburb called Kundagrama and remained there for several months.

In the vicinity dwelt a small community of ascetics, whose members were frequently on the streets with their begging bowls. They dressed simply, with an under and an upper garment, and received all their food as gifts from the householders of the city. Both men and women were members of the order, but they lived separately as monks and nuns and had no intercourse with each other.

As I wandered through the city I found no great temples nor did I see the people practicing superstitious rites as I had seen in Kaśi; still there were these many religious men and women. One was a young monk about my own age to whom I often gave alms. One day I decided to speak to him.

"Would it be offensive to you if I asked you about your beliefs?" I said this sincerely because I had become a more humble learner than in earlier days.

The monk answered promptly, "It is our teaching that we must not speak any falsehood, and that we must not steal. Also we may not own any property, except—" he added as an afterthought, "these garments, this alms bowl and the huts in which we live."

"Those beliefs are not peculiar to your sect alone," I volunteered. "Do you have other beliefs?"

"We hold it our duty not to destroy any life," continued the ascetic. At this point he paused and carefully lifted from his person a white ant that had climbed upon him and gently deposited it upon the ground before telling me more. "For that reason we carry this little bundle of twigs and sweep the ground before us if there is danger that we might step upon any creature unawares. Also we strain what we drink, lest we swallow any insect that has fallen into the cup."

I thought this was a worthy ideal, within limits, but when I noticed the vermin that crawled upon the monk I wondered if it could not be carried too far. Rather than antagonize the ascetic, however, I would postpone any discourteous questions till a later conversation.

"Who founded the order to which you belong?" I inquired.

"The great sage Parśva was our teacher."

"Is he no longer living?"

"More than two hundred years ago, he dwelt in the city of Kaśi and went forth from there to live the life of an ascetic."

Kaśi! Had the people rejected him and made it necessary for him to look elsewhere for converts? Truth was often more acceptable from a stranger than from a fellow citizen.

I found Kundagrama a friendly city, the people neither suspicious nor fanatical. For the first time in many months I had a sense of well being. One day while walking down the street with an acquaintance we passed a palatial residence, set back in ample grounds.

"That was the home of Vardhamana," said my companion. The name meant nothing to me but the magnificence of the building held my attention.

"One of your princes?" I asked idly.

"Even more important in another way. True, his parents were members of the princely caste and his mother was the older sister of our present king. They became interested in the Parśva order whose members you see begging in our streets. They gave many generous gifts to the ascetics, and while they could be only lay members of the order, they practiced its teachings as far as they could."

"I hope not to the extent some of the monks do," I interposed dryly.

My companion smiled understandingly. "Perhaps not," he said lightly, "but they gave up the pomp and ceremony usually associated with royalty, and lived instead in the utmost simplicity."

"What you say interests me," I remarked. "You know me for a stranger, of course, but you may not know the many hundreds of miles I have traveled since I left my home near a western sea. I have come in contact with many religious practices and there is something in the attitude of Vardhamana's parents that attracts me."

"One of the most beautiful features of their lives was the way they passed from life. Would you care to hear about it?"

"Indeed yes," I answered.

"According to the monks, when Parśva, founder of their order, was one hundred years old he went upon a mountain and abstained from eating and drinking for a full month, and thus he died. Following the example of their leader, when this princely couple, who could have enjoyed the most delicate food and had the services of our best physicians, reached old age and felt the time had come to depart this life, they simply lay down on their beds, letting neither food nor drink pass their lips, until they grew weaker and weaker and expired. Those who knew them say that they were perfectly at peace with themselves and the world."

"I have found peace a very rare commodity," I said. "Do you believe they atttained peace by learning to be satisfied with little in this world?"

"The fewer are one's needs the less strain he lives under," he said simply. "Anxiety comes with great possessions."

"There is something worth considering in that doctrine," I agreed. "But what about this Vardhamana, the son?" I pursued.

"He was thirty at the time of his parents' death. Up to that time he had lived a rather wild life and had somewhat scoffed at the simple existence of his parents. After the funeral he fasted for two and a half days. At the end of that time he arose, called together the poor people of the city and distributed all his wealth among them. Then he put on simple clothes, tore out his hair, and went to live among the ascetics."

"Was it a conversion under emotion at the passing of his parents or was it a sincere acceptance of the Parśva doctrine?" I asked.

"Many people in the city wondered the same thing," commented my narrator, "and they watched closely to see if he would repent his deed. But instead of regretting, he went even a step further. He said the life of these monks was too easy, so he left them and now dwells in the jungle, naked, they say, and alone."

After my recent experiences in the jungle I shuddered to think what it would be like to take up existence there permanently. Later from several other citizens of Kundagrama, I verified the story and found the facts to be accurate. But always when I inquired where Vardhamana might be found I received the same vague directions leading to somewhere in the unsettled region to the east. Again, curiosity and a real desire for knowledge combined to send me into an unknown land, and I started out to locate this man, to see if some of the peace of which I had heard would fill my soul.

As I journeyed I met other travelers who could give me directions for short stretches of the journey. Many of these people added bits of information or legend to my store of knowledge about the strange ascetic. The journey proved to be shorter than I had expected, but the wildness of the country left little to be experienced. Occasionally I came on an open area, however, and it was in one of these that I unexpectedly came upon Vardhamana.

The small vale in the midst of the jungle was pleasant enough to see. Surrounded on all sides by trees and bamboo and ferns was a grassy plot open to the sky. At its edge a spring bubbled up and sent its waters in a little stream across the grass. In the center of the area stood a man. When I had heard Vardhamana called a naked ascetic I had supposed that he wore at least some covering on his head and some cloth about his loins, but the man was completely unprotected from the elements.

He also stood absolutely motionless and gazed straight ahead into some infinite distance. His hands hung at his sides, and no quiver was evident in the muscles of his face. He had stood unmoving for so long that the denizens of the jungle took no fright at him any more but accepted him as belonging fully to their world. At his feet the ants had built their nests, and huge anthills rose beside both legs. Plants of the jungle had also grown up beside him and wrapped their tendrils about his thighs and arms.

A small group of disciples sat on the grass at the side of the glade. When no one made a move to impede my progress I joined them and sat for a long time neither speaking nor moving. After some time I noticed that the disciples spoke briefly to each other, so I ventured to speak to the one sitting nearest to me.

"You have guessed right," he replied in answer to my first curious question. "We are disciples. We maintain constant vigil so that if our master has a word to utter we may be present at the precious moment."

"Does he speak eloquently at times?" I questioned further.

"He is very sparing with his words," was the reply I received. "But there are a few ministrations we are privileged to offer him. We prepare the scant food that he needs to keep his body functioning, and we keep the ground around him clean, using care always not to disturb the ants and growing plants."

"Is there any way of knowing when your master will speak to you?"

"We are waiting momentarily for words from him today." The monk lowered his voice to a bare whisper. "Do you see that little group of monks sitting by themselves?" I nodded. "They are a delegation from the order to which Vardhamana formerly belonged. They have made a pilgrimage here to urge him to return to their group. Yesterday they presented their plea reminding him of his vows—not to kill, not to steal, not to own property; they reminded him that in observing these rules lay salvation."

"And what did he say?"

"He has not yet answered them," said the disciple, "but we think that he will before—"

A strange current seemed to move through the air and we were suddenly aware that Vardhamana was about to speak. Absolute silence reigned. Then he began in a mild tone.

"Truly you have set forth the teachings of the great sage, Parśva, and I adhere to them as you do. But," he came abruptly to the point of dissension, "consider what is meant by the fourth rule, not to own property. Does not one own property who possesses clothing? Do you not have both an under garment and an outer?"

Since the monks were sitting thus clothed, and he was naked before them, it could not be denied that he was applying the rule more rigorously than they.

"Is it not to own property to possess an alms bowl?" Vardhamana pressed the argument. "And do you not carry an alms bowl wherever you go?"

Inasmuch as the monks had brought their alms bowls to receive donations of food on their journey, they could not disclaim possession. It was also well known that on the rare occasions when Vardhamana had traveled he had consistently eaten his food in his bare hands; and when as now he stood in motionless contemplation, his disciples placed the morsels directly between his lips.

"Furthermore," he continued inexorably, "is it not to own property to possess a woman? And have not some among you taken unto themselves a woman either for a night or for a permanent possession?"

The downcast looks of the monks proved that this thrust had not missed its mark.

"Therefore," Vardhamana summed up the logic of his position, "I own no property, and I teach as a fifth rule the rule of chastity."

Since no possibility of reconciliation appeared to exist between the naked one and the visiting delegates, I judged that the interview was at an end. In this, however, I was mistaken. Vardhamana was going to use this opportunity to its fullest. With an enthusiasm I would have thought impossible, he moved from the practical applications with which he had been dealing to an exposition of underlying theoretical doctrines. In these it was evident that he was giving the fruit of the meditations in which he had been engaged for so long.

"The five rules which I have posited are the true essence of the teachings of Parśva. But before Parśva, there lived a long series of other teachers who set forth exactly the same truths. Although I have not yet attained perfect knowledge, already in mystic vision I have seen the long line of these Jinas, these Conquerors. It has been revealed to me that there are twenty-four of them in this age of the world. The first was Rishabha, the perfect ascetic, who lived a very long time ago. After him came the omniscient Ajita; then the holy Sambhava . . ." and Vardhamana continued with a long list of names.

Having little interest in the names, I gave attention to counting them. Others in the group must have been doing the same thing

because when he came to Parśva the twenty-third Conqueror, a stir
went over them as if they wondered if Vardhamana intended to
attribute to himself the position of the twenty-fourth and last of the
great ascetics. I could feel a tension of anger on the part of the
visiting delegates, and of hope on the side of his disciples.

Vardhamana did not name the twenty-fourth, but instead turned
to the time span covered by the lives of the twenty-four Conquerors.
"It has been revealed to me that the first ascetic, the ancient Rishabha, lived ten million times ten million oceans of years ago."

"What is an ocean of years?" asked a disciple.

"An ocean of years," replied the speaker, "is one hundred million
palyas."

The first questioner was abashed, but another took up the inquiry: "And what, O venerable one, is a palya?"

"Consider a receptacle that is nine miles wide and deep," was
the answer. "Think of it as filled with new lamb's hairs, so fine as
are grown within the first seven days of the lamb's life. Then picture
a bird which flies once every hundred years and takes away one hair.
The length of time that it takes to empty the receptacle is a palya."

Again a stir was perceptible among the listeners as they endeav-
ored to comprehend the duration of a palya, of an ocean of years,
and of the span of time from Rishabha to the present. There was a
restless move among the visitors from Vesali.

"Will the twenty-fourth Conqueror come soon?" asked a voice.

"From the Nirvana of Rishabha to the Nirvana of Ajita was five
million times ten million oceans of years, but each interval has
grown shorter, and from the death of Parśva to the death of the
twenty-fourth Conqueror will be only two hundred and fifty years."
This was his reply.

Again the audience was moved, for they knew that Parśva had
died more than two hundred years before. It was unmistakable that
Vardhamana meant someone living even then was destined to be
the twenty-fourth and last Conqueror. The next question turned the
discussion in a slightly different direction.

"If the twenty-fourth Jina will be the last, what will the world then do for a teacher?"

"We are in the descending age of world history," came the answer. "For ten times ten million times ten million oceans of years, the wheel of time turns downward. Once all things were in the best possible state, then came the period that was only good, then the time when there was still more good than bad. Now there is more bad than good, and in the period soon to begin everything will be bad. The truth will disappear and the worst time of all will come."

I recalled what Zarathushtra had said about the wonderful consummation which was yet to come. "Will the world stay forever in the worst possible state?" Someone asked aloud the question that was in my mind.

"The wheel of time turns forever. When the worst has come it will be followed by the bad, then by the bad-good, then by the good-bad, and that is when the great Conquerors will appear again to teach the truth. So the world will climb to the good and to the best."

This was encouraging, but I reflected that if the time wheel kept on turning, it would then start downward again. What is the purpose of these endless, almost infinite cycles, I wondered.

Almost as if my unspoken inquiry had been read, Vardhamana went on: "The purpose of this ceaseless ebb and flow of the universe is to provide an opportunity for the emancipation of all souls. Souls are now imprisoned everywhere. They are in rocks and water and plants, in the bodies of animals and men, in the forms of demons and gods. Through the aeons they are climbing upward. When they reach full knowledge they will attain emancipation; they will dwell in the heaven of perfection; they will come no more back again into the world of flux."

"Who can have full knowledge?" came a skeptical inquiry from among the visiting monks.

"The great Conquerors," was the calm reply.

"He makes the Jinas greater than the gods!" cried one of the visitors.

"He thinks he will be the last Conqueror!" scoffed another.

The members of the visiting delegation got to their feet and prepared to depart, but in the turmoil I heard one of the disciples say, "Vardhamana will conquer; he will be Mahavira, the Great Hero!"

Neither the scoffing nor the admiration touched the naked one. He was again gazing into infinity, oblivious to his surroundings, sunk in reverie.

All that Vardhamana had said was interesting to me, but I found little in it that I would call helpful. The cycles of years, the number of Great Heroes, the extreme asceticism—what was the purpose of it all? When the attendant disciples had resumed their placid waiting on the hillside, glad that the visitors from Vesali had departed, I thought to learn a little more about their beliefs.

"You spoke of Vardhamana as Mahavira. I do not know the name," I began.

"Mahavira shall be the last of the Great Heroes, as our leader mentioned. We think Vardhamana is Mahavira," came the reply.

"Is he then God?" I pushed him for definite knowledge.

"Not God, the creator or sustainer," he replied.

"But do you offer your prayers to him?" again I questioned.

"He does not teach or practice prayer," answered the disciple.

"What does your leader teach to be the purpose of life? Surely he would not have all men follow his example."

The disciple was ready with his explanation. "We follow his example within our limitations. He is greater and sets the example. Our great objective is to learn to control our body, that it may neither suffer ills nor enjoy pleasures. We desire nothing because it is good and hate nothing because it is evil. We must learn to live beyond all emotion, even as has Vardhamana."

"Think deeply, for meditation brings its own reward." These were the parting words of the disciple of Vardhamana.

3

Siddhartha, the Buddha

SURPRISINGLY ENOUGH, I FOUND
a certain release from tension in the weeks that I spent at Kundagrama. I mixed with the people and continued my questioning as
inoffensively as possible, and I found that most of them accepted
the teachings of Parśva rather than the more extreme doctrines of
Vardhamana. Live and let live seemed a simple way of expressing
their philosophy. I wondered what would happen if this entire community were to accept Vardhamana literally; if no one battled
against a marauding beast or exterminated a poisonous insect; if
each person waited to be fed and remained day after day in one
position. I was sure that I had seen a prophet and did not doubt
that he would soon be hailed as Mahavira, the Great Hero. But
what of his teaching of the endless cycles of good-bad-good and the
stress on escape from the world rather than on overcoming evil? I
contrasted this doctrine with that taught by Zarathushtra, who also
taught a great consummation but in the meantime urged men to
practice good agriculture, to maintain good homes, and to love their
children. The life of man was important to Zarathushtra; to Vardhamana the life of the lowest insect was given greater respect than
the life of the noblest man. And wherein was greatness and heroism:
in standing naked in the jungle or in fighting the evil forces in the
world? Or was the ideal a combination of the two?

It was this latter question that puzzled me as I turned my back on the home of Mahavira, crossed the Ganga and journeyed into the realm of Magadha. I fell in with another solitary traveler and was glad to have his company for he was familiar with the territory, having several times visited Kapilavastu, a far northern city at the foot of the great mountains. He described the mighty snow peaks which rose into the sky, and the rich and brave land which flanked them. He gave me details of the fair city of Kapilavastu; and more important, he told me about the priestly caste Sakyas who inhabited it.

My companion talked easily and interestingly, and as is often the case after a man has been alone for a period, he enjoyed the very use of his voice again.

"They are a noble people," he said. "They call themselves the Kinsmen of the Sun, and say that they are descended from Gautama, an ancient Brahman poet."

I noticed the similarity of the name to that of Gaumata, the head of the priestly caste in Balkh, but I soon realized that there was no connection between the two persons. Somewhat facetiously I wondered if this were a land that sprouted religious leaders as prolifically as it did trees in its jungles. I had never dreamed such a variety of priests, temples, rites, and doctrines existed in the entire world as I had come to know since I crossed the Indus River on the western side of this domain.

"Do you know the leader of this Sakya clan?" I inquired hopefully.

"I have seen him, for he holds frequent court sessions which are open to the populace and anyone may attend."

"Is he then a ruler?" I asked.

"The chief of the Gautama clan is the ruler Suddhodana," explained my informant. "He lives with his queen, Maya, in the most sumptuous estate I have ever seen. The grounds extend for miles and there are innumerable mansions and other buildings. In the gardens I saw one pool in which there was nothing but blue lotuses, another with red lotuses, another with white. They built three palaces for their son, one for the winter, one for the summer, and one for the rainy season. They imported gold cloth from Kaśi for all his clothes, and had servants carry a white canopy over him wherever he went. When he was old enough for such interests they gave him many dancing girls. He married and had a son. It nearly broke the hearts of all his family when he went away."

"Went away?" I repeated.

The storyteller nodded. "They say that suddenly he appeared to have a great weight on his mind, but no one thought it more than a passing worry until one morning they awoke to find him gone. During the night he had looked upon his beautiful wife and stood by the bed of his sleeping new-born son; without waking them to say farewell he went out, mounted his horse, and rode off, attended only by his groom. The next day the groom came back with the horse and was not able to report anything except that the master had said he was going away. Also he brought back the son's large gold earrings which he had taken off at the last moment. It is said you will recognize the young man anywhere by the length of his ear lobes which were pulled down by the weight of the heavy gold."

"A curious tale," I said musingly. "When did all this happen?"

"About six years ago. Since that time no one has lived in the son's palaces. They are kept ready for him. His wife and the child are always dressed in their finest to be ready to welcome him. His father and mother sit always where they can watch the gate. But he has never come back."

"Where is he now?" was my next question.

"They say that he goes about somewhere here in the kingdom of Magadha, and that he practices terrible austerities."

"And what is his name?"

"His parents named him Siddhartha. Since he came from the Gautama clan he is called by that name too. And those who think that he is very wise call him Sakyamuni which means 'the sage of the Sakyas.' But I do not think that he is old enough yet to be very wise."

"He would be about our age," I said to my companion, "and I doubt if we have lived long enough to have accumulated enough wisdom to be sages." My friend took this remark in the spirit it was meant and we dropped the conversation for some time.

One day as we were nearing the city of our destination, we met a band of five wandering ascetics. We put alms into their begging bowls but they were more interested in a heated conversation they were carrying on than in our contributions. Since they were talking freely we could not help but notice the gist of their comments.

"Do I gather that you have lost one of your number?" I asked.

"And after six years!" they said almost simultaneously.

Then a self-appointed spokesman continued: "He was with us for six years. Together we tortured our bodies and mortified the flesh. We ate as little food as possible to keep alive, and stayed out in the worst kind of weather. We stood on one foot until our whole legs were numb; we lay on beds of spikes until there were deeply calloused places on our backs. Then, just as we were about to reach the goal, he abandoned the whole undertaking and went away."

"Was the life too hard for your friend?" I asked.

"That is what we think," the ascetics replied. "Look at us! We wear rags, but they say that he has put on fine clothes like those he used to wear when he was a prince. We eat little food, but it is reported that he eats all that he needs and is once again in good flesh. We never wash, but he bathes every day. We lie on spikes, but he sleeps on a pallet. We stand under the hot sun, but he sits in the shade of a tree. He is soft. He has gone back to the world. We are through with him."

The tone of his voice left little doubt but that he was telling the truth.

"Has he returned to his home?" I questioned.

"Not that—yet," they admitted grudgingly. "He is still somewhere in this forest and lives by begging alms. We think he is a traitor to our cause, but he says he is seeking enlightenment." He said the last word with a scoff.

I was sure of the answer to my next question, but I asked it anyway. "What is this man's name?"

"Siddhartha Gautama," they said.

My traveling companion looked as if he had been delayed long
enough, so we took up our way again.

"The same man," he commented. "I am not surprised."

"I think I shall seek him out," I confided. "I have known other
prophets in strange lands and I would know this one also."

As we entered the town we bade each other good-by. After my
companion had gone on his way I began to make inquiries about
this ascetic and found he was known to quite a number of people,
but no one knew exactly where I might find him. Most of the suggestions indicated that he was probably somewhere along the Neranjara River, so I wandered in that direction and one day came
upon him. There was no mistaking the man. He appeared to be
about thirty-five years of age and had exceedingly long ear lobes.
Dressed in a robe of fine orange cloth, his hair neatly curled, he sat
cross-legged in the shade of a large fig tree. His hands rested calmly
in his lap, one open upon the other. He greeted me in a friendly
fashion, thus encouraging me to ask: "Are you Siddhartha, of the
clan of Gautama, the sage of the Sakyas?"

"Yes," was the simple reply, followed by the question, "and who
are you?"

"I am Yaush, and I have wandered many years from the land
far to the west near the sea of blue water."

"How did you know me?" asked Siddhartha without moving.

"As I have traveled in this kingdom, I have been told of you," I
answered. "It was my desire to see you and to learn about the way
which you follow."

"You may ask what you will."

The first question I could think of was a blunt one which I re-
gretted as soon as the words had passed my lips: "Why did you
leave your home?"

Siddhartha took no offense at this abrupt beginning and answered
readily: "I was raised in great luxury and protected in every way
from knowledge of the harsh realities of existence. Then one night
while my dancing girls were performing, I fell asleep, for I was sati-
ated with such amusement. Naturally they could not leave my pres-

ence until I dismissed them but finally they too fell asleep and when I awoke, I found them sprawled out in the most ludicrous positions; the wigs of some had fallen off, some had their mouths open, some were making loud noises as they breathed. It was a most repulsive sight; all their glamour was gone, and I never wanted to see them dance again." He sat several minutes in thought.

"That experience awakened me to the problem of life, and I realized I had to see things as they really are. I slipped out of the palace by myself for the first time in my life, and wearing clothes which attracted no attention, I walked through the back streets of the city. On every hand there was stark poverty, and the misery of the people shocked my senses. I saw an old man tottering along in his decrepitude. It was the first time I had ever seen an aged person, for I had grown up under the illusion that youth was the natural state of all. I saw a sick woman lying on the doorstep of her house, moaning in agony. I had never heard such awful sounds as came from her throat. I saw the corpse of a man who had died on the street. Thieves had rifled his pockets and torn his clothes, and the stench of his putrefaction was already in the air. I asked myself, is this the truth about life! Stripped of the gaudy tinsel which may disguise it for a brief time, this is the underlying reality. Old age, disease, and death—these are the real components of life."

Siddhartha remained silent for some time but I knew this was not the moment for interruption, so I waited for him to continue.

"When I learned that truth—" he began and then paused.

Here again I met that word which was motivating my life— truth. How sincerely each teacher used it, but how different was the content they gave it. I wondered if "truth" was merely the name every person gave to his own beliefs? Or was there some eternal law with which we could align ourselves; or some source of knowledge upon which we could draw—that law or that knowledge being "truth"? My quest was becoming more perplexing and more profound with the years.

Again I picked up the words Siddhartha was saying. "When I learned that truth, it seemed to me more important than anything in the world to learn how to escape from such a horrible existence. I do not mean how to avoid dying, for that is impossible. I mean how to escape from existence itself, how to avoid being born again, going through the cycle continuously."

I wondered how Siddhartha was so certain of the fact of endless repetition of life but I did not break the flow of his thought at this point.

"In a flash it came to me that the only way to escape the suffering of existence is to lose the desire to exist. All suffering comes from desiring something which we do not have. If we desire nothing, not even life itself, then we will be free from the shackles of life."

I sensed a contradiction here but I could not quite clarify it in my mind. Siddhartha had said that suffering comes from desiring something we do not have. But life is a thing we do have; therefore if we have it why should it bring suffering? The argument did not sound consistent to me. By Siddhartha's own definition, attainment should bring satisfaction. But at that moment I could not question because the teacher spoke again.

"My problem, therefore, became how to destroy desire, and that is what I am still working on. At last, however, after many years I feel that I am coming near to the answer."

"Is that why you left your home then, because you desired to stay, and you felt you had to do the opposite of anything you desired?" I persisted, trying to understand this strange doctrine.

"That is right," Siddhartha answered. "When I finally get the answer I will go home again, but only to tell my family the truth I have found. I shall never again live with them, and when they know the truth they will not desire to have me either."

This sounded to me as radical as the teaching of Vardhamana, and I recalled what I had been told of the earlier gruesome austerities likewise practiced by Siddhartha. "Is it true," I asked, "that you used to lie on spikes and torture your body in every way?"

"At first I believed that that was the way to eradicate my desires. Since my stomach desired food I deprived it of food until I lived on a single grain of rice a day. My frame became so emaciated that my bones showed through the flesh; if I folded my hands upon my stomach they rested upon my backbone. Since my body desired comfort I deprived it of comfort. I took up my abode in the awesome depths of the forest; when it was winter and the snow was falling in my north country, I dwelt by night in the open air and by day in the deep thicket. During the broiling months of summer I made my dwelling under the baking sun by day and in the stifling underbrush by night. It was at that time that a verse of poetry flashed upon my mind, which I made the motto of my life:

> Now scorched, now frozen, in forest dread, alone,
> Naked and fireless, set upon his quest,
> The hermit battles purity to win."

"Have you ever heard of an ascetic called Vardhamana?" I asked.

"I have heard of him," Siddhartha replied, "and of others of his kind. They go without clothes, pluck out the hair and beard; they remain standing, and give themselves to practices which torment the body. My own customs were not identical but they were of the same essence. But now I have come to see the falsity and futility of all such practices. They serve only to make one more aware of one's own desires. Therefore they are self-defeating."

I was inclined to agree, but what I most wanted to know I had not yet been told. "What is the nature of the way you now follow?" I asked.

"I now follow the midway practice. Sensuality leads to suffering and dejection; asceticism is painful and unprofitable. My way lies between these two extremes. I discipline my intellect by adhering to a right view of the world; I perceive that it is an illusion and I resolve to renounce it. I exercise my ethical nature by speaking and doing what is right, and by obtaining my livelihood in the right way. I rule my emotions by ridding myself of evil thoughts, and by practicing meditation without ceasing."

I was impressed with these words and was ready to acknowledge that the young man before me was a sage indeed. Vaguely I wondered if he were actually living the dignified philosophy he was expounding.

"Is your way of life entirely satisfactory?" I asked.

"Not yet," confessed Siddhartha. "My goal is enlightenment. When I attain it perfectly I shall be perfectly free. But it may be that I must yet undergo further testing before I am accounted worthy."

This statement raised in my mind the relation between human achievement and divine strength. I asked Siddhartha about his gods.

"I do not contact the gods," was the frank answer, "not in the sense of worshiping them. They are creatures like ourselves, destined for emancipation which they have not yet attained."

"What about your Brahman priests?" For certainly Siddhartha had been raised in the religion of his people.

"My own family is descended from a Brahman. It is from that ancient priest that I have the name of Gautama. In the books of the Brahmans there is much truth, but the practices of priests are often full of lust and superstition. They do not have the way."

I felt that I had asked as many questions as I should, and that they had been answered with candor and wisdom. The speaker seemed entirely sincere, so I thanked him and withdrew.

Siddhartha's place of meditation was close to a small settlement where his needs could readily be supplied, so I decided to seek lodging in that village for the night. In the town I was directed to Mara, the most prosperous householder in the community, whose house and grounds were ample. Here I found a cordial welcome and Mara agreed to supply me with a room and meals for as long as I wished to stay. There was need for the spacious house, for Mara had five daughters of his own and the small daughter of the eldest one living with him. Mara was a talkative individual with definite opinions. As soon as I mentioned my encounter with Siddhartha he expressed himself freely.

"He is a fool and also lazy," said Mara bluntly. "The only reason he can sit there day after day and do nothing but think is that we townspeople work, raise food, earn money, and then give him something for nothing."

He pointed to a poisonous-looking growth hanging from one of the trees in his garden. "That is what we call a parasite. It feeds upon nourishment which the tree provides, and does nothing for itself. The meditator is also a parasite!"

When I commented that it took dedication to an ideal to leave a home of luxury as he had done, it only brought a fresh outburst from Mara.

Soon I discovered that Mara was the self-appointed reformer to do something about it. Daily I joined Siddhartha, sitting a short distance from him for hours at a time. This arrangement allowed us to discuss his views when he was moved to speak, but also allowed for a degree of isolation during his periods of meditation. I made no mention to Mara of this method of spending my time, fearing the knowledge would only call forth other denunciations. One evening Mara's five daughters, all of them young and handsome, came innocently to the water's edge, disrobed and swam in the river. Coming out upon the bank they feigned surprise to see Siddhartha there. Throwing diaphanous robes about themselves, they gathered around Siddhartha and offered to share their delectable food with him. He accepted a small portion but otherwise betrayed not the slightest interest.

The second evening the oldest daughter came, bringing her baby with her. On some slight pretext she asked Siddhartha to hold the child for a moment, and as he accommodated her she talked about the loneliness of a home from which the husband and father was absent.

The third evening the second daughter came alone, threw herself at the feet of Siddhartha and asked him to enlighten her on some problem of Sakyan philosophy. From my retreat I could plainly see that she was more interested in the alluring picture she hoped she presented than in the wisdom of the teacher.

On succeeding nights came the youngest and most beautiful of the daughters who used the wiles of exotic perfumes to stir his senses; then the tallest of the daughters who danced in the moon-light with seductive movements, dropping exhausted on the pallet beside Siddhartha; and then the last of the group who slept at his feet through an entire night. The seventh night the five daughters came again and the purpose of their visit was too obvious. Only once during the entire week of temptation did Siddhartha show any reaction; that once I saw him clench his hand involuntarily, whether from anger, disgust, or desire I could only guess.

During this week no mention of the daughters of Mara passed between Siddhartha and myself, but after they had abandoned their attempts, I asked him one night, "How could you remain so unmoved by the daughters of Mara?"

He answered, "Simply by thinking of them as they will be in their old age, with drooping breasts and withered muscles, toothless, ill smelling, and ugly."

"In other words," I suggested, "you made the desirable present seem undesirable and thus eliminated desire?"

"You are not a dull pupil," answered Siddhartha.

"Then may I take my final lesson from you, for I feel I must leave this place and sit no more with you on the banks of the river Neranjara."

"You have been a good companion," said Siddhartha, "and I think I have noticed you are more relaxed and chafe less at the long hours of sitting."

"I have had so much to think upon that the hours have frequently been too short," I could answer honestly.

"What shall we discuss at this last meeting?" asked Siddhartha.

"If I may, I would like to sum up what I have understood from the many thoughts you have shared with me."

"That would be well," agreed Siddhartha.

I began my analysis. "Your search for enlightenment has led you to expound a philosophy of the middle way; to live without hate, but also without love; to practice no greed but also no liberality; to place no value upon the body, neither to mortify the flesh."

"So far you have learned well," commended Siddhartha.

"Further, you find in meditation the avenue of escape from the anxieties and distractions of the world."

"Meditation is surely the necessary practice," agreed Siddhartha.

"You have talked about an Eightfold Path," I said. "I remember you have referred to this path as consisting of right views, right aspirations, right speech, right conduct, right mode of livelihood, right mindfulness—I do not recall the other two," I broke off.

"They are right effort and right rapture," finished Siddhartha.

"You came from a high caste yourself, according to your own story, but now you do not recognize caste," I made this statement half a question.

"Caste is an artificial and accursed order and does not belong in right relationships."

"I think in this respect you are a true prophet for the people of your great kingdom."

"Do I understand, then, that there are some views with which you do not agree?" Siddhartha asked.

I admitted there were. "I hold a belief in God which your teaching denies."

"Not denies," broke in Siddhartha. "It is only that this teaching is unnecessary."

"We differ there," I said, and Siddhartha took no offense. "Also I do not understand your insistence on the soul's return to life on this earth, when at the same time you seem to deny the identity of the soul."

"Rebirth is demanded by the law of karma," quickly stated Siddhartha. "We have not had time for me to develop that law."

"Karma?" I repeated. "The word has little content for me. I will need more instruction, I see. But I must also add that I am not convinced of the uselessness of life."

Siddhartha remained unmoved at my lack of acceptance of his doctrine so I took courage and finished my statement, "Why should we look at life and see only death, or at youth and see only age, or at beauty and see only ugliness? And why should the ultimate hope of man be to eliminate all desire, the very desiring of which *is* a desire?"

"You would do well to seek enlightenment," responded Siddhartha gently, "even as I am still seeking it. When one attains the great enlightenment all questions are made clear."

"Zarathushtra teaches a Great Consummation," I said, "but it is not like yours."

"Zarathushtra?" repeated Siddhartha. "He is the one who teaches in the far West?"

"The same," I said.

"He is partially enlightened," asserted Siddhartha, "as are all men who seek the truth. I continue the search."

Our conversation was at an end. I expressed the hope that I would meet Siddhartha again and assured him, with all honesty, that I would gladly hear more of his doctrine.

4

Karma

AS I WENT ON MY WAY TOWARD Rajagriha, the renowned capital of Magadha, I continued to ponder the new teachings I had received.

My first view of Rajagriha was from a high point in the mountains, and the view, though imposing, was disappointing—the city looked to be but a mass of ruins. I stopped a traveler who was coming from the direction of the city. "Is that Rajagriha?" I inquired.

"That is the ancient city," answered the young man. "There are two, you know."

"I did not know," I said. "Are you a native of the place?"

"It is my home," and he was proud of the fact. Resting by the wayside with me, he entered into conversation. "The name Rajagriha means 'royal residence,' and we who live in the new city think it is appropriate."

"I'm sure it is," I said politely. "Even the old city lasted well," I added, glancing again at the ruins.

"Those fortifications you see up there"—the young man gestured toward the crest of the hill—"extend for a distance of twenty miles around the top of the hill. They were erected for the old city, and the walls are twenty feet thick."

"Twenty feet thick!" I exclaimed in astonishment.

"And they used no mortar in those days. Go up and look at their construction some time. The new city lies a short distance to the north, and its walls are constructed of chiseled stones laid in mortar, with square towers placed at intervals."

"When was the new city built?" I asked.

"Only twenty-five years ago by our present ruler, Bimbisara, who belongs to the ancient dynasty of Śiśunaga, founded over a hundred years ago. He is a man of both taste and wisdom, although there are those who do not envy him his haughty queen."

I smiled. "Who is she?"

"Her name is Chellana and she is the daughter of King Chetaka of Vesali."

Doubtless it was the surprised expression on my face that made him ask, "Do you know her?"

"I spent some time in Vesali so I know her father by sight," I said. So Queen Chellana was a cousin to Vardhamana, the unclothed ascetic! I smiled to myself as I thought of the contrast between the two—the one doubtless robed in the costliest of silks, the other wearing not a stitch and standing motionless in the jungle. The one haughty in the midst of her court, the other humble as the anthill on which he stood.

I knew that I would have to see this queen. In the city I found lodging, the cleanest I had had on my journeys. The entire city was cleaner than any other I had visited, the streets wider and the buildings whiter. From casual questions I learned that King Bimbisara was considered a genial and open-minded ruler. Inclined to give everyone a fair hearing, he held frequent public audiences and settled most of the cases by compromise and conciliation. It was at these hearings that I saw the queen. Chellana was many years younger than her consort and although she appeared dutifully at court ceremonies and conducted herself with the dignity becoming a queen, it was well known that she would have liked more gaiety and amusement at court than the quiet and conservative tastes of the king allowed. It was also a matter of common knowledge that all her genuine affection was lavished on her only son, born during the first year of her marriage.

Prince Ajataśatru at twenty-five showed the effects of his constant close association with his mother. He was still unmarried, more than a trifle effeminate with a too-graceful walk and unmasculine gestures, which made him a baffling enigma to his manly but gentle father. To the ladies of the court he was a captivating gentleman for he could turn a graceful compliment and his almost feminine appreciation of color and fabric made his advice much sought after. The prince had been taught by his mother to consider his father a doddering idiot whose rule was antiquated. Thus she fanned the flame of ambition in her weak son.

I found life in Rajagriha very agreeable and having established my scholarship, based upon my travels, I was able to live well and meet the upper classes.

About a year after my arrival, I was astonished one day to see Siddhartha, the hermit of the Neranjara, enter the court with some of his disciples. In outward appearance Siddhartha Gautama was still the same. He wore a fine orange robe, his hair was curled tightly upon his head, but there was a new look upon his face—an inner light of peace and conviction—and he moved and spoke with perfect calmness and assurance. From time to time I had heard reports that Siddhartha had attained the illumination he sought, and that those who accepted his teachings now called him Buddha, The Enlightened.

The fifteen men who accompanied him also wore orange robes, adjusted to cover one shoulder, but unlike their leader their heads were shaved. I kept thinking that I had seen some of them before when it flashed upon me that five of these men were the dirty ascetics who had condemned Siddhartha for deserting their company. Now they were wearing coarse but clean garments and were obviously disciples of the Enlightened One.

Two others stood out in the group. One, a youth of sensitive face, fastened his eyes in rapt devotion upon his master and hung on every word the Buddha uttered. The other was a sharp-featured man, distinguished by being the only one to wear a robe that was torn and soiled.

When the king indicated that he was ready to give audience to

the band of monks, Siddhartha approached the monarch respectfully and addressed him.

"O king, it was several years ago that I passed through Rajagriha
on the pilgrimage in which I sought enlightenment. At that time
you invited me to return when I had attained that which I sought."

The king indicated his interest, and Siddhartha went on to tell
of the great peace that had come over him as he sat silently by the
bank of the Neranjara, and of his consciousness of being free from
the shackles of rebirth.

"Would you not also be free, O king?" he asked, and continued
with a brief statement of his doctrines concerning suffering and escape from suffering, such as I had heard from his lips before.

The king was obviously impressed by the words of the Enlightened
One and extended an invitation to the Buddha and his monks to
come into the palace to dine. Siddhartha accepted in his usual courteous way and led his group inside. One disciple, however, the sharp-
featured man with the ragged garb, turned angrily on his heel and
stalked out.

When I left the palace I saw the disgruntled one with his alms
bowl ostentatiously begging a frugal supper.

"Where will your master stay this night?" I inquired of him, for
I hoped for an opportunity to talk with Siddhartha.

"Probably in the palace," replied the sharp-featured one. "He
was born in a palace and he cannot get away from the luxurious
life. Look at me!" he cried. "I too am of royal descent; I am his
very cousin, but do you see me leading that kind of life? Not I," he
added, self-righteously. "It is my belief that we should live in the
forest rather than in the city, that we should dwell under a tree
rather than under a roof, that we should never dine royally but live
only on the alms we beg, that we should never eat fish and meat
such as they will be having there at the king's table, and that we
should wear only the rags that someone else has discarded." This he
said, gesturing toward his own poor garb, then concluded: "And
what I believe, I do!"

"And may I ask, sir, what your name is?" I inquired, ignoring the stream of complaints.

"Devadatta," growled the other, and stalked off.

The next day I came upon Siddhartha and his monks on the outskirts of the city with one of the city's wealthy industrialists, who was pointing out the attractions of a princely estate—its expanse, landscaped grounds, and commanding view.

"If this please you," the rich man said to the Buddha, "I will purchase the garden and build a residence here for you and your monks."

"We should be grateful," replied the leader of the orange-robed band with dignity, while Devadatta muttered to himself. "To whom does the garden belong?" asked the leader.

"It is a part of the large estates of Prince Ajataśatru," was the reply. "I am sure that he will be glad to sell this one area."

We were all startled to hear the contemptuous voice of a man on the other side of the hedge wall say, "Not for as much gold as would pave the whole garden with solid blocks." And Prince Ajataśatru came through the hedge.

"I want no part in locating a band of religious fanatics in this city," he continued insolently.

The industrialist answered quickly, "I take the garden at the price named."

The prince gasped. "There was no bargain meant," he retorted, and turned on his heel as if the matter were settled.

As news spread through the city that the prince was angered by the action of one of its wealthy men as well as at the prospect of having the Buddha settled on one of his estates, the people argued over the merits of the bargain. The king himself was said to have expressed concern over his son's attitude and put the case into the hands of a trusted adviser, a man of scrupulous honor. The verdict was that since the prince had in reality named a price, he was in honor bound to accept the gold. Thus the garden became the property of the industrialist who lost no time in erecting a fine building for the Enlightened One and his monks.

The crafty Devadatta now proposed to the Buddha that he be allowed to undertake the conversion of Prince Ajataśatru.

"You have been very successful in the presentation of the doctrines of our faith to the king," he said to his leader. "To be sure he has not given his full assent to our beliefs, but he has given generous gifts to us and offered us protection anywhere in the kingdom. Would it not be good if I could make known our teachings in similar way to the prince? It may be not long," he added slyly, "until he is on the throne." The Buddha gave his blessing.

The disgruntled monk and the dissatisfied prince established a quick friendship. Each was in a position of second rank, and each believed himself worthy of holding first place. The monk had accumulated a series of imaginary grievances against his superior; the prince was smoldering with wrath against the king.

Strange events suddenly began to take place in the palace. One evening the king was just beginning to eat his dinner when the trembling of his hand caused a spoonful of soup to spill upon the floor. A dog lapped it up greedily, and expired a few minutes later in agony. In spite of much investigation, no light was thrown on the mystery. Another day the king closed his public audience earlier than usual. Hardly had he left the outdoor throne before a loosened cornice of a wall fell upon it. Several days later as His Majesty walked in his courtyard an apparently solid slab of pavement gave way beneath his feet and he was nearly precipitated into a forgotten cistern. In each case Prince Ajataśatru was the first to rush forward with protestations of concern.

This unprecedented series of mishaps was almost duplicated at the monastery. First, a venomous snake was found in the Buddha's bed. A few days later as he took his accustomed afternoon walk in the garden, the heavy branch of a tree crashed to earth at his feet. Not many days later a chariot in which he was riding lost a wheel as it rounded a dangerous curve. Devadatta instituted a series of vigorous investigations which failed to produce any results.

The Buddha's devoted young follower, Ananda, went about with white and stricken face. Like a shadow he followed his leader all

day, looking suspiciously into every corner before he would allow
him to proceed. It was said by some that he took up watch each
night lying on a pallet at the master's feet. Certainly his eyes grew
large and haunted from lack of sleep. Gossip about all these untoward happenings was rife in the city, and there was much specula-
tion as to the possible cause. Then the incidents appeared to die
down and the townspeople occupied themselves with other concerns.

After the monks were established in their monastery the band of
the Buddha's followers increased, and according to reports there
was a difference of opinion among them as to the degree of austerity
befitting to devotees of their doctrine. The Buddha with his middle-
way view was opposed by Devadatta who still held out for asceticism. But when a time came that the Buddha had to be absent on
a trip he left Devadatta as his representative.

I was not surprised to learn that Devadatta's first official act was
to call a meeting of all the monks and extoll the virtues of the true
monastic life as lived in the forest, in rags, and upon alms begged
each day. Nor was I surprised to hear that some of the younger
novitiates had been fired with enthusiasm, and a large number had
voted to go off into the woods with Devadatta. The townspeople
accepted the move with good-humored indifference, but I thought
of Devadatta's crafty, beady little eyes and his ratlike darting
glances and wondered what was afoot.

When the Buddha came back he found the monastery almost
deserted, but he asked only one question, "Did Ananda go too?"

"Not at the same time as the others," was the reply. "He was not
present when Devadatta called the assembly, and when he came
back we told him what had happened."

"What did he do then?" inquired the Enlightened One.

"He made no comment, but he sought solitude and sat all night
in silent contemplation. In the morning he went away without a
word and we have not seen him since."

"Thank you," said the Buddha, and went on about his affairs as
if nothing had happened. A few days later the deserting monks returned with Ananda. He had followed them to their forest retreat

where, after an impassioned and vindictive diatribe delivered by Devadatta, Ananda had quietly reminded them of the beauty, simplicity, and integrity of their Buddha. "He has returned. Are you also returning?" were the closing words of his message. Shamefacedly the group of yet undisciplined followers returned to their leader.

The Buddha received his monks without comment. Devadatta was subdued but by no means defeated. He soon renewed his visits to the prince, ostensibly to instruct him in the doctrines of the Buddha's teachings. The Enlightened One never inquired about what progress was being made, but it was common knowledge around the city that the monk Devadatta and the prince were boon companions.

It was about this time that a naked ascetic appeared at a public audience of the king. His bare sunburned skin contrasted sharply with the costly garments of the people at court, and even with the robes of Buddha's monks. When I first caught sight of him I thought it was the same one I had seen standing in the anthill in the glade, but it proved to be one of his disciples. He had come to apprize the king that Vardhamana had at last attained the highest goal, he was now recognized as Mahavira, the Great Hero. Would the king hear the philosophy of Mahavira? And with his usual graciousness the king invited this unclothed ascetic to enter the palace as his guest.

It was reported that the queen took this act on the part of her consort as a great personal insult, retired to the privacy of her own apartment, and refused to see anyone except her son. Many stories of the queen's former hauteur were revived and doubtless enlarged upon.

The emissary of the Great Hero also paid a visit to the monastery of the Buddha, where he was kindly received. The Master listened to the disciple of Vardhamana with close attention. He even sent cordial greetings to the Mahavira. Devadatta chose to consider this act a personal affront; the Buddha had paid no heed to Devadatta's practice of ascetic austerities!

At this same time Prince Ajataśatru, aided and abetted by the scorn of his mother for a king who welcomed any chance philosopher—clothed or unclothed—decided that some action must be taken. He sealed a secret pact of mutual support with Devadatta. For a drink to the success of both their ambitions the prince produced the headiest wine the palace stores afforded, and emptied glass after glass; but Devadatta shrewdly refused all but the first. No sooner had Devadatta left than Ajataśatru decided to speed up his designs without waiting for the devious plans outlined by his accomplice. He would simply stab his father as he slept. No one would suspect him, a son. As he steadied himself slightly against a chair he wondered why he had never thought of it before, and he reached for his jewel-handled dagger.

Queen Chellana asked no questions as he passed through her bedroom and entered his father's sleeping chamber, but there a surprise awaited him. Due to a pressing problem of state the king had called a night conference in the royal chamber, and his counselors were all seated around a table as the prince burst in. Ajataśatru was too befuddled to think up any excuses, so he was taken into custody without a protest.

However, King Bimbisara was not a man to retaliate. He accepted his son's statement that he had partaken too freely of the wine. For one of the few times in his life, the prince talked to his father, who made it easy for the son to unburden himself. The king learned that the prince felt the kingdom would prosper better under new and younger leadership. Although the king recognized a desire for power on the part of his son, still he was weary from years of rule and he found the idea of passing over the responsibility of the kingdom a welcome relief. So he set a time for his abdication.

The prince manifested great concern for his father. One of his first official acts was to offer his father an entire wing of the palace where he could have complete privacy and the rest he needed. His meals would even be served to him and trays of daintily prepared food were to be seen daily carried through the corridors to the invalid's quarters. No one but the young king and a few well-paid servants knew that the trays never reached their destination.

In the meantime Devadatta was still trying to maneuver circumstances to further his own designs. Each failure enraged him more until he could scarcely sleep at night for plotting. Toward dawn one morning the answer came to him—the mad elephant Nalagiri! Devadatta was so excited that he leaped up from his pallet and went out to pace around the garden until dawn.

Almost daily the Buddha retired to a rocky hill some distance from the city for meditation. This place was known as Gridhrakuta or Vulture's Peak, and was reached through a narrow defile overhung by high cliffs. Sometimes Siddhartha went there alone; more often he was accompanied by Ananda or some other of his disciples, and not infrequently other interested people followed along at a discreet distance.

One day I saw the Buddha and Ananda start off on their usual pilgrimage and decided that I would follow; I was happy to see there were no other townspeople on this morning. As we reached the narrowest part of the trail we heard the thunderous sound of an elephant trumpeting and saw Nalagiri lumbering down the path with that deceptive gait that appears so leisurely but covers the ground so rapidly. His tusks gleamed white in the semidarkness of the narrow pass; there was a menacing look in his small bloodshot eyes; his trunk waved threateningly in the air.

There was no room for the two men ahead of me to step aside; no place for them to flee. I was transfixed with horror, then I saw Ananda step in front of the Buddha and heard him murmur to the Master, "Let this elephant kill me first." But the Buddha pulled him back and faced the charging beast alone.

As the elephant reached the men, Siddhartha looked the mad animal full in the eyes. "Nalagiri," he said in a perfectly calm voice, "has no one ever loved you? Know then that I do."

Nalagiri stopped in his tracks. The Buddha laid his hand gently on the elephant's trunk, led it forward to a place where it could turn around, and took it back to the plantation. To the keeper, whose pockets were heavy with Devadatta's coins, he said, "Nalagiri is a good elephant. If you treat him with kindness, I believe he will be valuable to you."

When Devadatta saw Ananda and the Buddha return unharmed from the morning's expedition, his heart was filled with black rage. At first he thought the elephant keeper had betrayed him. Then he heard the story from the lips of Ananda, and when he saw the added reverence with which the others treated their leader, he was convinced that whatever it was necessary to do to carry out his plot he must do himself.

Nearly a month later the Buddha went all alone to Gridhrakuta. Devadatta, who knew of the plan, left the monastery before daylight, taking a devious route so that none might see him. At a point in the trail where the two sides of the mountains came together like a funnel he climbed to a high point above and stationed himself behind a boulder poised directly over the path the Buddha would have to follow. Here he waited, his heart beating with an almost suffocating intensity. This day his plan would not miscarry.

Soon after daylight the Buddha reached this spot. Devadatta put all his strength behind the boulder. There was a tearing noise as it parted from some surrounding undergrowth, then with a sound like an avalanche it bounded down the mountainside. The Buddha heard it and looked up, his face calm as he raised it to meet the doom rushing toward him. The boulder struck a slightly projecting rock on the canyon wall with such force that the huge rock splintered into a thousand pieces. Devadatta saw one piece strike the Buddha on the foot and saw him fall to the ground. All he could hope was that his superior would bleed to death. Devadatta hurried back to the monastery to be with the other monks when the news was brought.

I was following some distance behind Siddhartha but when I heard the thunderous sound of falling rock I hurried as fast as I could up the mountain path, and so it was that I found the Buddha lying upon the trail, pale and unconscious from the loss of blood. Taking him in my arms, I carried him to the mango grove of Jivaka, the physician, from whom he received the expert attention that saved his life.

At the Buddha's first public assembly after this event he was still

wan and wore a bandage on his foot, but he spoke without any trace
of resentment and without making any reference to what had happened. His theme was karma, and I was glad that at last I would
hear this doctrine explained from the Enlightened One's lips.

"Karma is the sum total of a man's actions," he said. "It is absolutely inevitable and absolutely impartial. A man can escape from
it no more than he can escape from himself. It is the constant sowing and reaping, each reaping a new sowing. Even death does not
free a man from karma, but it is karma that determines the form
of rebirth in the next existence."

The Buddha expressed himself so clearly that no one interrupted
with questions as he went on: "Karma accumulated through many
misdeeds constitutes an intolerable burden; its weight is crushing;
no one knows this better than the person himself who is so laden.
Freedom from karma is the greatest goal."

Even as I listened I told myself that some day when alone with
Siddhartha I would ask him in more detail about the Ultimate.

"Karma cannot be escaped," continued the Enlightened One,
"but it can be worn out. Few may hope to attain freedom from
karma in this life; most will attain it only after passing through
countless existences. But the acceptance of one's present state is the
beginning of emancipation. From that beginning, the middle path
of right views, right aspirations, right speech, right conduct, right
mode of livelihood, right effort, right mindfulness, and right contemplation will lead at last to the goal."

Long I pondered the significance of this lecture. In it I found a
hope that I had not felt when I sat by Siddhartha in meditation the
year before. Not a complete hope, and not a joyous hope, but certainly an ethical content that gave purpose to living according to
the truth which the Buddha taught. Jeremiah, the prophet of Judah,
and Zarathushtra, the prophet in the land of my Samuda—both of
these teachers would find some common ground with the Buddha.
The consummation of which Zarathushtra spoke was less distant
than the ultimate goal of the Buddha's teaching, whose time of ful-
fillment was countless, countless reincarnations away. The Buddha's

realization of hope was more mechanical and inexorable than Jeremiah's. Did the element of God's personal care in Jeremiah's teaching give it the extra warmth and immediacy that were missing in the Buddha's philosophy? Mahavira, I felt sure, would never approve of the Buddha's middle path—that idea would sound like compromise and halfhearted endeavor to the Great Hero.

A last phase of my consideration troubled me the most—the matter of withdrawal from the world. Both the radical asceticism of Mahavira and the more moderate monasticism of Buddha were based upon the futility of life. Although at times when I was deeply depressed I momentarily agreed with them, when at my best I felt a dignity in man and in his attempt to accomplish something in the span of years he spent on this earth. One truth I found ran through the teachings of all the prophets I had known—they agreed that when confronted with the great realities of life man must meet them first within himself. My plans were taking shape at this time to leave Rajagriha but before I left I would have one more talk with Buddha.

During my final days in the city I saw the Buddha's law of karma demonstrated before my own eyes. First it was proved in young King Ajataśatru's life. His father died and the son gave meticulous attention to all the details of a ceremonious funeral. But when he looked for the last time upon the gentle but emaciated face of his father he was struck with terrible remorse and those in attendance said that his face blanched and that he trembled like a leaf. He cried out that he would give his own life if it would restore his father's. When the services were over Ajataśatru went to the Buddha, confessed his crimes and was received into the monastery.

Devadatta's was a different fate. He was not troubled by remorse; he was suddenly attacked by an illness the best doctors were unable to diagnose, and he took to his pallet. He lay there for days and when he felt that he was about to die he was utterly terrified. He sent word to the Buddha asking if he might see him. The Buddha replied that it was not possible in this life, but that after one hundred thousand cycles Devadatta might hope to be reborn in emancipation and then they would meet again. In a frenzy of terror,

Devadatta ordered his pallet taken up and himself borne on it to the Buddha's door. As the bearers crossed the threshold and before he saw the face of the Buddha, Devadatta expired.

When Ananda asked his master why he received Ajataśatru but not Devadatta, the Buddha replied: "Both men must work out the karma which they brought upon themselves; from that there is no escape. But Ajataśatru had never joined the order; he needed to hear my teaching. Devadatta had already learned of the way; for him there was nothing more I could do."

My last interview with Siddhartha, whom I sometimes found difficult to call the Buddha, took place one night at his monastery. The Enlightened One was sitting in meditation and motioned me to join him. We sat long together as we had many nights on the banks of the Neranjara River. I let Siddhartha break the silence.

"We have had many hours together, my friend," he said, and I knew I would always value his recognition of that relationship. "You are leaving? Still restless for a truth you have not found. I, too, spent many years in the quest and had to come upon it myself. May your questing be rewarded as mine has been. What is the matter that is troubling you?"

How typical of him to ease the way for the other person! I tried to thank him for the many hours and the great help he had given me, but when I saw my words were inadequate I came right to the question I wanted him to answer.

"Teacher," I said, "in your philosophy I find so much that is good that it seems childish to dwell on the small amount that I do not understand—or accept. You have broken the chain of caste which has held your people down for centuries. You have given some ethical content to life; you have taught a moral law. Do you find within man himself the power to accomplish all that you teach he must do?"

"I find that a man in each existence does deeds in the body—deeds of good or deeds of evil," answered the Buddha. "He alone can wear out the evil. You understand this law of karma. So if a man's deeds are actually part of the man, how can another person—

a god, if you want the term—assume the responsibility which each man alone must bear?"

I knew that Siddhartha did not expect me to answer the question. Instead the teacher took up the discourse again. "I have noticed that you have looked skeptical whenever you have heard me talk about the highest attainment."

"Skeptical is not the right word, great teacher," I said. "Confused would be better. I cannot comprehend the idea which you offer."

"When one comes to know the joy of undisturbed meditation—and by undisturbed I mean such control of the body and the mind that they do not intrude into one's identity with thought—then one begins to realize the nature of the final state which is desireless, passionless, free from the necessity of rebirth and free from existence itself. This is the highest state."

The Buddha had been patient with me and I would not weary him further with my stupidity. I said farewell to which he replied, "Farewell for this life," and I wondered how many aeons I would have to endure rebirth before I achieved the spiritual stature of the man I was leaving.

Book Four

WISDOM

1

Spirit of the Mountain

IT WAS EARLY MORNING WHEN I
took to the trail again. As always on such an occasion there was a
tinge of sadness at parting with friends and leaving behind a city
which had been good to me. But the exhilaration of being on the
move and the excitement of unknown adventure outweighed the
depression.

Behind me the Ganga followed its serpentine course and the
grasslands shimmered in the sun like lakes. Ahead were green slopes
rising into a sea of clouds. Mighty evergreen trees stood on the hills,
their northern sides heavy with moss. Ferns made such dense thickets
that a tiger could find a lair.

After covering some distance I began to see men and women clad
in woolen robes and wearing large earrings of gold or turquoise—
the women wearing rings, bracelets and other ornaments as well—
making their way toward the mountain stream that cascaded down
the hillside. Here the women filled their copper jars with water, and
both men and women washed in the icy waters. A vigorous race, I
decided, and this thought was confirmed later in the day when I
watched them toiling up and down the hill with prodigious loads,
and singing as they went.

As I climbed farther up the mountain slopes it seemed as if I were
walking into the clouds. Banks of fog swirled about me, now so
dense that I could scarcely see the distance of the next step ahead,

again parting to reveal the depth of the valley below. Persons I met on the trail loomed up suddenly like apparitions and disappeared again in the mist.

At a considerably higher elevation I emerged with relief into the dazzling sunshine above the clouds and into a world of fantastic beauty. The billowing forms of the clouds were of infinite variety, and here and there the fluffy masses formed themselves into white towers and turrets. The dark green ridge I was climbing lifted above this cloud ocean like an island, and clinging to the slopes and crowning the summit were the huts of the mountain village to which the trail led.

For the moment the ridge hid the further view, but when I came to the summit I gasped at what lay beyond. Straight to the north at a distance of about forty miles a rampart of rock and snow and ice rose out of the clouds and soared to a stupendous height in the sky. Three separate peaks marked the ridge of this mighty mountain. The last, which formed the ultimate summit, appeared to be divided by a wall of granite which ran straight to the top, while enormous snow fields descended on either side of it.

Entering the tiny village I asked the first person I met what the great mountain was called.

"We call it the 'Three Sisters,' and over there is the temple of the god of the mountain," my informant explained.

I thanked him, and turned aside to enter a shrine. The first thing that met my eyes was a large gold mask affixed to the farther wall of the inner room. The light from flickering candles illuminated the face, making it both mysterious and malevolent. The lips were drawn back in a grimace, horns projected above the ears, the eyes burned in their sockets with relentless hate. I stood for a long time in front of the mask, watching the shadows play across it, trying to discern the meaning of the grotesque features, marveling at the contrast between the appearance of the mountain and the mountain god.

When I stepped back into the main part of the temple I saw an old man seated in the corner, looking at me intently. I had thought the shrine was empty, but now I realized that this person had been there all the time. The man wore a long robe of dark wool, with a coarse rope knotted about his waist. On his head was a cap like a truncated cone, with flaps which curved out on either side above his ears. Around his neck was a chain of small human skulls cleverly executed in pure gold, and from the end of this necklace hung a replica in gold of the mask of the mountain god. He did not speak, but continued ceaselessly to spin a small metal cylinder attached to a carved stick which he held in his hand. At every revolution the device emitted a clicking sound, and the characters inscribed on the cylinder gleamed in the half light of the temple.

Outside again, I was amazed to find that heavy mists had swept up to envelop the town, and every landmark which I had previously noted was gone; even the great peak was blotted out as completely as if it had never existed. Fortunately the friendly villager who had told me about the mountain and directed me to the shrine was still waiting and guided me to an inn.

During the weeks which followed, clouds rested continuously upon the town. Sometimes glimpses were possible into the great depths of the valleys which dropped away beneath the ridge on which the village was built. Sometimes momentarily the sun broke through a rift, but the more distant ranges never came back into view, and a stranger entering the town could have had no conception of the grandeur hidden from his sight. The fascination of the mighty northern mountain persisted in my mind and I decided to wait for one more view of it; and in the meantime revisited the shrine of the mountain god a number of times. Always the silent, robed man in the corner studied me as intently as I studied the mask.

One morning as I passed down a narrow street, a hand plucked at my sleeve and a voice said, "Go to temple."

For a moment I debated the wisdom of going. Had I angered the god or the priest and was this a ruse to do me harm? But obeying a better impulse, I went. Using my first acquaintance in the village as an interpreter, the priest extended to me an invitation to join the annual evocation of the mountain god. A guide would come for me

—I would know him by a talisman. I welcomed the opportunity to learn what led these people to interpret the spirit of such beauty as I had glimpsed in the mountain in terms of ugliness and hate. It reminded me of the conception of the Fire Deva. Was it a human failing to consider everything vast and unknown as evil—something to inspire terror?

The next day a robed man whose face was totally unfamiliar appeared out of the mist. The stranger pressed a small image into my hand, an exact replica of the mask in the temple, reproduced in pure gold and glaring up at me with all the ferocity of the original. My guide and I left the town at a rapid pace, walked briskly, and at last emerged upon a high and barren hilltop. A group of men, all clothed in identical long robes, caps, and gold chains supporting masks of the god of the mountain, were seated in a hollow square. At their head, obviously as leader, was the priest I had noticed on each of my visits to the shrine.

When we slipped into the places which were reserved for us, the ranks were complete. It was now late in the afternoon, and the sky, still obscured by clouds, was beginning to darken. As if at an unseen signal, all the men began to chant. The song was pitched in a minor key and the rhythm had a barbaric beat, but the words were unintelligible to me except that I recognized the name of the mountain god repeated over and over. Each man also whirled a prayer cylinder ceaselessly in his hand, and the clicking of these machines kept time with the music.

Suddenly the man seated at the right of the leader leaped to his feet and, spinning like a prayer wheel, went all the way around the circle then deposited his prayer wheel in the center of the circle. Each one in turn did the same, except the leader, and when all had finished there was a heap of cylinders. Now the seated men began to sway from side to side as they continued the interminable chant. The eyes of the leader seemed to bore steadily into me and I felt myself succumbing to the hypnotic monotony of music and motion, so that I began to sway in unison with the others and to repeat the name of the mountain god as it recurred in the chant.

Gradually the tempo of the singing was increased and the words were uttered with an increasing intensity of concentration. Then it happened. I saw a cloud form between me and the face of the leader and then within the cloud a grim and ferocious physiognomy took form. This was not the face of the leader for that remained distinct behind it. It was a horrible and repellent visage, with lips parted in a grimace, horns protruding above the ears, eyes glaring with wrath. It was the face of the mask in the temple, the face of the tiny replica I clutched within my hand. Like the mask in the candlelight of the shrine, this face too seemed to recede in the dusk and again to come forward menacingly.

Then the swaying and chanting of the intent ranks changed to a tone of desperate resistance. They were trying to drive the spirit back into the darkness out of which it had come. Only slowly and as if at intense cost did their wills prevail. The phantasm grew less distinct, the features of the awful face were resolved into swirling wisps of fog, and the cloud vanished from sight. The chanting slowed and stopped, the men disappeared one by one into the forest, and I followed my guide through the night to the town.

The next day, in normal surroundings, I could hardly believe that I had taken part in so weird a ceremony. Yet there was the tiny golden mask with the features of the mountain god hanging from a chain about my neck. As I fingered it I knew I had not imagined the journey into the forest. But actually, all I had learned from the experience was that these people believed in the power of black magic. I became possessed of the feeling that I would never shake the spell from me until I had conquered the mountain itself. However, I learned that no one had ever visited the mountain peak and when I inquired about the possibility, no one took me seriously.

This feeling of apprehension hung over me for several days and it was by a sheer act of will power that I made my intelligence triumph over superstition. It was a good experience for me to have had. I realized that I, Yaush, had always been critical of a power whose awful hold I had never known and therefore could not properly evaluate. I was now wiser—and more tolerant.

2

Talisman of Freedom

ON THE NEXT STRETCH OF MY journey I would cross the roof of the world. I was told that there would be pass after pass where the air was rarefied and every step an effort. After much inquiry I learned that there was a way to cut across the ridges and connect with a caravan route which led to the north and east. I decided to try this short-cut, and found that it took me over a series of transverse ridges and valleys. On the ridges the vegetation was sparse, but in the valleys there were dense forests. I was subjected to a constant alternation of climate between mountain cold and tropical valley heat. But the fact that summer was at hand and there would be the greatest freedom from snow upon the passes encouraged me.

The wind was cold and penetrating as I reached the caravan route. Here I found a traveler sitting in the shadow of a rock, resting. The man looked up with a smile and greeted me. "This is a good way to keep out of the wind," he said. "Will you join me?"

I thanked him and sat down. "Which way are you traveling?" I asked.

"Back to the highland," he replied. "I am a trader and I have just finished selling all my wares, so I am on my way back to rejoin my companions at an appointed village. If you are also headed that way I shall be glad of your company."

"And I of yours," I said, "although I'm afraid I shall be more the gainer than you, for you know both the route and the language of the highland and I know neither."

"You will easily acquire all you need to know," he said cheerfully.

With slow and measured steps we started up the pass. Here there were no more wheeled vehicles of any kind. All the goods which moved were carried on horseback, on yaks, or on the bent backs of men and women. The shaggy black-haired yaks were doubtless the best adapted of all animals for the kind of trails which the caravans followed. Ascending this first pass, the way followed the valley of a stream to its source, then climbed the steep walls of a canyon, skirted great precipices, and led up over vast, barren slopes to high places where unmelted snow yet lay in deep drifts.

As we toiled slowly up the mountains we met several caravans coming down. At one very narrow place in the trail we saw the path abruptly broken off at the edge of a sheer cliff. Just before we arrived a yak had lost its footing and plunged over to fall, twisting and turning, thousands of feet to the floor of the chasm below. Now the members of the caravan were trying to lead the other terrified animals across the dangerous spot. We wedged ourselves back into a cleft in the rock so there would be no further disaster.

I had heard blood-curdling stories about the bandit gangs that infested these mountains and I asked my companion about them as we walked along.

"As long as we stay on the main caravan route I doubt that we will have much trouble," he replied easily.

But as we reached the top of the pass an armed band of riders who had been lying in ambush came thundering down upon us with loud cries and weapons flashing in the sun. Obviously we were hopelessly outnumbered so there was nothing to do but submit. The bandits placed us on horseback, flanked on each side by one of their own members, and galloped us off out of sight of the caravan route. There several of them dismounted and rifled our packs, appropriating such things as they could use, including my most valued possession, my sword.

We supposed that we would either be slain on the spot or freed, but as soon as the robbery was completed the band took to the road again with us as prisoners securely held between them. Soon we entered a gorge of red sandstone with the cliffs on either side sculptured into strange forms by the erosion of wind and water. I noticed also that there were some crude carvings, but these were so high above us that I could not make out their nature. After following the steep and winding course of this canyon far back into the mountains, the riders halted and, still keeping us with them, went on foot up a precipitous trail into a side valley. There, high on a cliffside, we were led into the mouth of a cave. Natural passageways had been somewhat widened and extended, and the subterranean corridors constituted a labyrinth in which we soon lost all sense of direction. Our captors brought us into a cavern-room where stalactites and stalagmites depended from the ceiling and rose from the ground. In the midst of these fantastic formations I discerned the outlines of a rudely sculptured idol, so dimly illumined by the single lamp which burned in front of it that I could not make out its features. A watcher at the door kept up a melancholy note upon a horn made of a hollow thigh bone.

A number of raggedly clothed men and women came into the chamber through adjoining corridors. Each carried a lamp which, like the one in front of the image, was a small bowl containing a piece of fat and a wick. The combined light of all these flames now enabled me to make out the nature of my surroundings more distinctly. I was startled to recognize that the idol in the center was a figure of the mountain god. The statue was very roughly carved of red stone, but there was no mistaking that the face was intended to be the same grim visage I had seen in the temple mask. At the base of the idol lay a pile of bones; human bones, as I later learned.

The head man of the cavern dwellers now made a payment to a member of the bandit riders, but instead of leaving, the bandits took their places along the wall as if to await some further ceremony. My companion and I were pushed to the floor in front of the idol. From somewhere in the shadows a woman emerged and began to perform ritual gestures in front of us. I remembered the sorcery practiced on me in the mountain village; also I recalled stories of cannibalism and resuscitations that were associated with these primitive peoples. An uncomfortable prickling rose at the back of my neck and for an instant my hands grew clammy. I glanced at my companion whose face was set and unreadable. Was it possible that the mountain god was to claim my life after all? Then, strangely, my fear vanished and a feeling of detachment sustained me once more.

I still had the small gold mask which the sorcerers had given me, but it was no longer an object of dread; rather I now considered it a symbol of emancipation. Because I wore it on a chain about my neck, concealed beneath my clothes, it had escaped the notice of my captors. I withdrew it now and held it in my hand. A woman noticed the gesture, glanced furtively at the object I was holding and with a muffled gasp fell prostrate on the ground. Others pressed forward to see what had happened and also fell to their knees. Evidently the possession of one of the masks in pure gold signified the highest standing in the cult to which they belonged. In an instant I, and my fellow traveler, became honored guests instead of captives. Food was pressed upon us, our possessions were restored, and we were supplied with fast horses and sent off with obeisances.

As we rode away my companion, hardly recovered from the recent tension, asked, "How did you come by that talisman of freedom?"

I told him the story. When I finished my companion said, "There are many things that cannot be explained in the usual ways, but I have good cause to be glad you were allowed to keep the amulet. Between you and the god of the mountain, I am still alive," he concluded dryly.

"I guess we owe these good mounts to the god of the mountain too," I said, as we came to the end of the red canyon and regained the caravan route.

Before the day was done we reached a small village. Here we found the headman and elders of the village waiting to receive us with a welcome accorded only to distinguished visitors, and the headman took us to his own home for the night.

"How could they know we were coming?" I asked my companion, and found that he was as puzzled as I.

"No one has passed us on the trail, and there is no other road that enters the village by which a messenger could have arrived," he said. "I am somewhat acquainted with this district and I am positive that I am right. But I have also heard that these people have strange powers—"

Our discussion was cut short by the arrival of food, the chief item being their oldest yak butter; we washed it all down—at least I did —with cup after cup of hot tea. My companion asked our host how he knew that we were coming; had a runner arrived ahead of us?

"No one come; we know." I had heard of the power possessed by some people of transmitting thoughts across space, but my companion's vocabulary was too limited to enter into further questioning.

The next day we took leave of our friendly hosts and resumed our journey, with three more passes to cross, all of them at great heights. We were grateful for our horses; the animals were sure-footed and followed the hard-packed trail almost with ease. Our greatest difficulty came when we met an infrequent caravan and had to move over into the deep snow.

At the summit of the last of these passes we turned in our saddles to take a final look at the snowy peaks and barren hills which had surrounded us. Although there were still rugged peaks ahead of us, we had crossed the hump of the world. We spent an occasional night in some small mountain village but otherwise we kept pushing on eastward, past a turquoise lake, across an arid, mountain-rimmed plateau, along a winding river in a deep gorge where we had to swim our horses through the rushing waters.

Often we passed hours without speaking, our solitude being a part of the great silence that lay over the land. Occasionally the quiet was broken by the tinkle of bells from an oncoming caravan, and occasionally we saw dark specks on a distant desert floor to indicate a nomad's settlement with its dark yak-hair tents, its herds and its flocks. When we felt the need for conversation I tried to learn all I could from my companion, for I was aware that the land we were in was peopled by tribes that were of different stock from the inhabitants of the great Indus and Ganga river valleys and mountain rises.

"These people are a different race," my companion agreed. "The straight nose and well-shaped features of the darker people behind us are not found here."

"I have noticed the lower ridge of the nose," I commented. "And the eyes appear to be set in the face at an angle."

"That is not exactly the case," he replied. "The difference is in the way the skin is stretched across the bony framework of the face." With his fingers he tightened the skin across his eyes and temples and became almost a brother to the inhabitants of this land.

"Are their customs and language as different as their physical characteristics?"

"The language is different, but you will pick up enough to get along. I have discovered that you have a rare ability for understanding and making yourself understood."

I thanked him and tried to explain. "I have traveled among strange people since the age of sixteen. One develops a sort of intuition for communication."

"How far have you come?" My companion was eager and curious. "Not as far as Balkh?"

"And as many years of travel beyond as we are removed in this direction," I said. He looked at me with unbelieving eyes.

"But you do not look as different from the people of Balkh as the people we are now among differ from them."

"Our stock has a closer origin," I told him, "but our customs and beliefs are different." This led me into revealing the purpose of my travels.

By now we were entering a more settled region; ahead of us lay a pleasant valley. Although it was at a high elevation, it was well watered and green, and in the center of the plain, perhaps eight miles away, there rose a rocky eminence. On and around it were clustered the houses of a small town.

"I wish I had known of your long travels earlier in our acquaintance," remarked my companion. "I would like to know more, if there were time."

"We part here?" I asked with some dismay, for I had found it pleasant to travel with a congenial companion and guide.

"I am so near the village to which I go that I will push on. But you have a fatiguing distance yet ahead of you and should rest here awhile. I will help you find lodging."

"I have enjoyed your companionship," I said.

"And I yours," he replied. "I wish you well in your quest for the truth," he added with a twinkle in his eyes. "As for me, if you should chance this way again, you will find me plying my trade. Penetrating mysteries is not my business!"

"I do not blame you, friend," I agreed, smiling. "I grant you that it is a peculiar mission and often hazardous, but each of us must fulfill his destiny."

So I was left alone among strangers, but through the good graces of my friend I had been accepted into the home of the chieftain of the town. His house, the largest in the community, was built of sun-dried bricks, whitewashed, although a section in the center was painted bright red. The chieftain and his wife were genial people and we got on together in spite of language difficulties at the start. My first meal was a banquet compared with the fare to which we had become accustomed. The many courses included yak meat and mutton in various forms, turnips, peas, onions, carrots, and large quantities of buttered tea. Later in the kitchen I saw how the tea was made in a large metal caldron kept constantly boiling over a fire, the smoke of which had blackened the walls of the room with a thick and greasy incrustation.

That night I rested well and the following day was ready for whatever it had to offer me. To my surprise it was a sporting contest. That was the last thing I would have imagined in this remote spot. I was evidently in a land of horses for the main sport event centered around these animals. The dog races were of interest but the horse races were definitely the most popular; sometimes the horses raced riderless, but in most of the races the riders were as much a center of interest as the animals they rode.

Toward the end of the day there were contests with slingshot, a common weapon of the area, made of woven yak hair. Remembering my boyhood experience with the slingshots of my own country, I stepped forward and offered to take part in the contest. The people were immensely pleased at this gesture and did not resent my participation, even when I nearly walked off with the honors.

The cordiality of the people was delightful and I soon felt quite at home among them. Still I was greatly taken back when a prominent woman of the village offered me a place in her household as one of her several husbands. Somehow I managed to convey to her that while I appreciated the signal honor, I was committed to a special mission, so that my stay in the town must be short. The chief explained that eking a living out of the land was hard and therefore several husbands were frequently necessary to support one wife and family. The men were an economic necessity.

While in this village I witnessed a funeral that was reminiscent of Zarathushtra's teachings, but with a large ingredient of local magic and sorcery mixed with it. The deceased was an aged man. The priest superintended while the body was rolled up into a ball, the head between the knees. Then to the accompaniment of various incantations, the priest plucked a single hair from the dead man's head. This, I was told, was for the purpose of letting the spirit out. Then bearers from the family of the deceased bore the corpse out to a rocky hill where the priest cut it into strips and cast these to the wild beasts.

I became engrossed in the remarkable powers possessed by the priests and sorcerers. Because I was a friend of the chieftain, I was allowed to watch these men for long stretches at a time. I saw a man seated cross-legged, deep in concentrated meditation until he fell into a trancelike state. Then his body began to vibrate as if powerful charges of energy were pulsating through it, and finally he made a series of prodigious leaps into the air in which, still with his legs crossed, he rose above the heads of people standing near.

Another man, also clearly in a trancelike state, came bounding across the countryside at greater speed than any runner normally could attain, and disappeared up a steep hill without slackening his pace. Yet another, when snow began to fall, took his stand upon a rocky peak and stayed there, wearing no clothing and having no protection whatsoever. "He has the power of increasing his body heat, and is perfectly comfortable," was the explanation given me.

When I questioned these workers of magic about their art, I found I was not so welcome. Their practices were closely guarded secrets. In fact, they said it was impossible to communicate their knowledge, each man had to learn it by experience and if I would remain with them the rest of my life, they would teach me. I did understand that they believed that within man were latent powers that could be developed by the most rigorous discipline, an idea in accord with Mahavira's teachings of subduing the body. But among these people the motivation seemed to be to ward off the evil spirits that dominated the world.

Although I searched closely I did not find any indication of the mountain god, so I decided he belonged to the west slope of the great mountains. Nevertheless I continued to carry the little gold mask that had once won me my freedom. And as it turned out, it was my passport for a visit to the house of evil spirits which was presided over by a priest who had come from the West. Within this temple were ugly idols which represented greed, lust, wrath, and other evil emotions. Men were seated in front of these images, contemplating them intently, hoping thus to perceive the true nature of the vice portrayed, and thus to overcome it in their own lives. After achieving what they considered adequate mastery of their thoughts, they went on into inner chambers where they faced the same temptations in concrete form. They were locked in rooms with golden treasures, with voluptuous women, and with men who reviled and beat them. If they remained unmoved, they were considered far advanced in their training.

It was while staying in this village that I experienced a great longing, like a consuming fever, to return to my homeland. I think it was the little slingshot that did it. Long-buried memories of my childhood, of the home life with my foster parents, of the Jerusalem of my early days, of the women at the pool day after day exchanging little accounts of family happenings—all of these and many others crowded my mind at night and would not let me sleep. I had lost count of the years spent in travel; one or two here, a few more another place; others consumed in tedious travel month upon month. Then my better judgment told me that I must finish my quest; I could not turn back before I had traveled the whole distance east. Having made the decision I was immediately ready to start my trek once more.

The stories I heard of the sages to the east assured me that my trip would not be valueless. Occasional bronze vessels which I saw stimulated my curiosity. This time I thought it wise to join myself to a caravan, thus the perils from bandits and wild beasts would be lessened. So it was that with a long train of animals and men I started again into the north and east.

3

The Old Philosopher, Lao Tzu

THE CARAVAN WOUND ITS WAY over barren plateaus, tawny hills, high, snow-choked passes, waterless deserts, and gorge-riven mountain ranges, to come out at last upon the headwaters of a great river. It followed the river down through the mountains, until it swung away in an extended curve to the north. When the river made a circle of a thousand miles the caravan proceeded five hundred miles eastward and met it again.

Now the river was a mighty stream, yellow with the soil it carried down from above. On its banks were the villages and cities of a race as yellow as the river. Throughout its valley were their farms and fields, every available inch assiduously cultivated. Hills were worked into terraces, and plains were laid out in geometrical patterns. Toiling men, women, and children wrung from the soil the last bit of return. The air reeked from the human excrement which was gathered from the villages after each night and scattered upon the crops as fertilizer.

No smallest corner of land was exempt from cultivation, with one exception, the burial mounds. In some areas the land devoted to graves was greater in extent than the land used to sustain the living. In this country ancestors were the most holy and reverend spirits; their resting places were sacred.

In each of the villages and towns through which we passed I found a mound of beaten earth and I inquired of one of the more intelligent members of the caravan what they signified.

"These people reverence the earth that sustains them," he told me, "and to these mounds they bring offerings to the great earth spirit." There was logic in this conception if the earth, in their minds, were something more than inanimate dirt. Or, I asked myself, could it be they offered their gifts to the spirit of their ancestors, bringing their fruits to the altar? Here indeed was a land it would have been a mistake to have missed.

In a village where the caravan halted, a boy was flying a kite. It caught in a tree, and I helped the lad get it down. The boy's father hurried out, bowed to me and invited me into their home.

"You have been kind to the smallest son of our family, O stranger. Please come into our simple home to rest and refresh yourself, for I see that you have traveled far."

Within, I was served with rice and fragrant tea. But even before food and drink were offered to me, the guest, they were presented before rows of tablets that lined one wall of the room. I watched the ceremony as the father proceeded to take two small bronze bowls from a shelf in front of these tablets; into one he put a few grains of the rice, and into the other poured a small amount of the tea; then he bowed before the tablets several times. The bowls were small, for I could see the family was not rich, but they had the same ornamentation that I had seen on the larger bowls in the village in the highland.

"May I ask my generous host about those beautiful bowls?" I said, speaking as courteously as I could in the language which I had been learning from companions in the caravan during our long journey. "I see that they are carved with many designs, and I seem to see eyes looking at me from their sides."

"Come and look at them more closely," was the friendly invitation. "You know the cloud dragons that are sometimes seen in the sky? These are dragons too. You see their eyes plainly, glaring at you."

Then, pointing to geometrical patterns, "These are their bodies. Like the dragons in the clouds, sometimes you see them and sometimes they elude your gaze. Our artists are very skillful, and they have handed down these designs for many generations."

"Why do they put dragons on the bowls?" I asked.

"In order to guard what is put into them. We place here the best gifts that we can offer to our ancestors. The gifts must be protected and kept safe. and that is done by the spirit dragons for the spirit fathers."

We ate our simple fare with deliberation and sat long over the cups of tea that were renewed with boiling water every few minutes. Since our caravan was unloading part of its wares in this town I knew there was no need to hurry on. And if there were, I think I should have stayed anyway to learn more about these spirits that were given spirit food.

"May I not tire my most gracious host," I began, "but you have shared your food with me, a worthless traveler; and you have taken me into your worthy home although I am but a lowly wanderer. Would it be too bold to inquire from you the meaning of the tablets I see above the shelf holding the spirit bowls?"

"My house is not worthy of your presence," began my host in typical idiom of his country, "but our practice is good to know and I shall tell you gladly."

His wife emptied the tea from our cups and poured more boiling water into the grounds in the bottom of them as my host began his explanation. Of course, I had heard of the ancestor worship of this land but I was truly ignorant of the connection between it and these tablets.

"You have seen the mounds where our honorable ancestors are buried on the countryside, but it is not supposed that their noble spirits are confined to those tombs. It is indeed appropriate to make frequent pilgrimages to these tombs for the spirits reside at times near their moldering bones, but they also reside in our home where a wooden tablet is inscribed with the name of each ancestor."

"This wall, then, is your family shrine?" I asked.

"You use a beautiful word to describe our humble altar," said my host. "This is, as you say, the sacred place for us, where the oldest son pays the honors to the spirits."

In the years of my traveling no teaching which I had heard had approached the belief held by these people. This was only an introduction into their philosophy, and since we were headed for the great capital city of Loyang, it was with renewed interest that I rejoined my caravan and waited impatiently to be on the way again.

On the outskirts of Loyang the caravan was halted by a tremendous concourse of people. Pressing forward, I found that we had reached the Earth Mound of the city. Because this was the capital of the land, this altar mound was the largest in all the country, rising impressively above the plain. A stone enclosure walled it off, and stone steps led to the platform on the summit. The crowd was held back by the wall; within the enclosure were functionaries clothed in gorgeous robes of silk.

"I beg you to tell a stranger what it is that takes place here," I said to a man who was plainly an inhabitant of the city.

The man peered closely to see who it was that could be ignorant of the nature of the most important ceremony of the entire year. Quickly recognizing that he had indeed been accosted by one from afar, he explained: "Today the hours of light and the hours of darkness are equal. This fact our astronomers have told us with the precision of their calculations; you can also observe it, roughly, for yourself. As the summer departs and the winter comes, the great Wang offers sacrifice to the earth in gratitude for the crops with which we have been benefited. He also offers sacrifice to the heaven so that when winter is done, the sun may shine again with increasing warmth."

"Which one is the great Wang?" I asked respectfully.

"Our emperor is he who even now leads the procession up the great steps. He is the most exalted priest in all the land. Heaven will assuredly hear and answer his prayer, for he is the son of heaven."

"And who are they that follow after him?"

"The six who go in single file are his chief officers. You see first the minister of religious rites, next the minister of agriculture, and after that the ministers of the army, of public works, of the monarch's personal affairs, and of punishments. Then come the other high officials of the government."

From the number of high officials that made up the emperor's train, I decided that the affairs of government must have many ramifications. Judging from their costly garments, I decided that a government official was in a lucrative business. I noticed the contrast between these men of state and the poorly clad common people and I wondered if in this country, even as had been true in the Jerusalem of my childhood, the people supported a luxury-loving court by taxes which at times killed both the body and the spirit of the populace. But for the time being my eyes and my mind were fastened upon the ceremony I was witnessing. I turned to my informant. "I see that the officer you pointed out as minister of punishment carries a tremendous sword. Is it in proportion to the punishments to be meted out?"

The weapon was made fast to a belt about the official's waist and hung down in a sweeping curve, the blade both broad and long. In fact it was so long that it would have dragged on the ground except that the minister of punishments had a sturdy page boy who followed him wherever he went and held up the end of the sword. Even now they were ascending the altar in that fashion, the boy tugging hard to lift the tip of the sword over each step.

"There are many punishments in our land," the man agreed. "You see, our system of government is very highly developed, which means that the government regulates everything. In order to do so, it has to pass many laws. The more laws to keep, the more to be broken. The more broken laws, the more lawbreakers, and therefore the more punishments. If it were not for the punishments, the whole system of government would break down." He said this with no flicker of resentment—it was merely a fact.

On the summit of the earth altar the great Wang offered various invocations and prayers, after which all the officials turned toward the base of the mound. There five culprits lay, bound hand and foot, with their heads between vertical slotted posts. The minister of punishments descended solemnly and loosened his sword. The page boy gave his end of the blade to a taller servant, and the latter assisted in lifting the weapon and placing it in the first set of slots. When the blade was allowed to fall it very neatly severed the head of the first culprit from his body. Nevertheless the exertions required in the wielding of the large sword were considerable and by the time all five criminals were dispatched, the minister of punishments was red of face and perspiring profusely.

I sensed, perhaps from the emotions of the people, something in this act which was deeper than the meting out of deserved punishment. Turning quickly to my neighbor I asked, "Why is that punishment performed here? Has it some connection with your annual ceremony?" I could not bring myself to use the words "human sacrifice" of these people who seemed in so many ways to be far advanced in civilization.

"It is true that in ancient times we offered human sacrifice to the spirits," he replied, picking up my thought. "But in these latter days we put evildoers to death at this time because it seems an appropriate occasion. There are many people gathered here, and it makes an impression on them. Besides," he added somewhat lamely but apparently without realizing that he was partially negating what he had just said, "the great spirit above must be pleased to know that we are so ardent for the keeping of the law of heaven."

I thanked the man for his courteous information and left without waiting to see the conclusion of the long ceremonies. I had made a decision and hastened to find the leader of my caravan to tell him I was remaining for a time in Loyang, and to draw the wages I had coming to me.

My new employment was a contrast to the one I had just given up, but in each case my work furthered my quest and I held each task to be good. At Balkh I had found employment in the palace because of my knowledge of language and geography. By this time I had increased in both areas many fold and it might be that they would be an asset in helping me locate work that would reward me by keeping me near some of the scholars of the realm. After a few days I found such employment in the imperial library. The official who hired me said that in this day there were increasing demands for information about the lands to the west, demands from both the government officials and men of commerce.

In my new connection I had an opportunity to talk with learned men and also had access to all the classics. The spoken language presented some difficulties at first, for it was based on the recognition of various delicate shadings of tone. The right word spoken in the wrong tone could entirely change the meaning. The written language was of a new type too, and consisted of drawings of miniature pictures to represent ideas. Great skill was required to execute these pictographs, and many thousands of characters had to be learned before one could read. But the symbolism continued to delight me. Crossed swords to represent the personal pronoun "I" seemed particularly apt, for I, too, had often felt myself at war with myself. "Contention" was symbolized by two women under one roof!

I was also interested in the ingenious construction of the books. Since the writing went in columns from top to bottom, a single narrow strip of bamboo sufficed for a page. As many such strips as were needed were tied together with cords to make a volume. When the book was open it looked like a picket fence; when it was closed it folded together like pleats. Since I was assigned to the department of royal archives, most of the books immediately accessible to me were chronicles from which I studied the history of the country. During many weeks I never met the man called Lao Tzu who was at the head of this department, but he was always referred to with great respect, and warmth as well. Then one day my surprise was unbounded when I received an invitation to tea from no less a person that this keeper of the archives. For the social occasion I shaved freshly, tried to subdue my unruly hair, now streaked with gray, and dressed in the best robe my meager wardrobe afforded.

A servant ushered me into a beautiful garden court where I was met by a benign-looking elderly gentleman who bowed to me and said, "I am Lao Tzu, the keeper of the royal archives."

I was amazed that he introduced himself so humbly. I bowed also and replied, "And I am Yaush, wanderer from the western lands, who now is humbly grateful for employment in your outstanding department."

Tea was served to us and Lao Tzu came more directly to the point than was the custom in this country. We sat, each on a straw mat, while we sipped tea and the master asked penetrating questions about my travels. I gave him the facts as accurately as I could and offered interpretations only when I was asked to do so. Lao Tzu had a keen intellect which made him search for basic information.

On my second invitation to tea I felt free enough to ask an occasional question. "I beg to inquire, sir, if it is not impolite, as to the derivation of your name?"

Lao Tzu laughed. "Ho, so you have heard what the people call me?"

My face reddened but my host took no notice of this. "They call me 'the old philosopher' when they want to be flattering, but 'the old boy' at other times." He enjoyed the little joke for a minute then more seriously explained, " 'Lao' really is my family name, but since it also means 'old' the people sometimes mistake it for a title. It is not so bad, at that, for one of my antiquity!"

Following this hint I asked the question which I had learned was a compliment in this land. "And what, sir, is your honorable age?"

Lao Tzu gave the date of his birth and added with a smile, "But I have looked old ever since I was young." Mentally I converted the date from his calendar into terms of my own land. It was unbelievable! This sage was still in his fifties—not more than ten years my senior. Lao Tzu commented further, "It is a good thing that I have always looked old. Here, you know, one must be old to be respected."

"Have you been long in the government service?" I thought this question would get us onto topics about which I was more conversant.

"All of my life," he replied. "I took the examinations at an early age and have worked in the library ever since. It will not be many more years before I retire."

"You have an interesting system of government in your land," I said, hoping to draw him out a little.

"There is too much government," Lao Tzu affirmed, and added nothing to carry the conversation further in that direction.

For some months the philosopher and I did not again meet informally but when we did, Lao Tzu took up the conversation almost uncannily at the precise point where we had dropped it.

"When I entered the service things were different. The government has now become top-heavy. Every time a new law is passed a new bureau is established to enforce it and new taxes are levied to pay for the new bureau. The multiplication of prohibitions is such that everyone is a lawbreaker. The proliferation of bureaus is such that there are more offices to supervise business than businesses to be supervised. The increase of taxes is such that the people are crushed."

Lao Tzu looked sadly at the volumes by which he was surrounded. "I love my books, and I am bound by my promise. I will stay until I have finished my term, but then I shall withdraw."

"How do you believe the government should be organized?" I ventured to ask.

"It is my belief that the government should encourage and help the people, not burden and strangle them. In order to do that the ruler should lead the people and not drive them. Let him hold a torch in his hand and not a whip. Let him live simply and work hard so that all men will be inspired to frugality and industry. The government should do nothing for a man that he could do for himself. An independent and self-reliant folk will be happier with little than an enslaved and enervated people with much."

"Rightly do they call you a philosopher," I said with admiration. "You should be a teacher, not a librarian."

"I earn my livelihood by working in the royal archives. My mind is not bound by such limitations," replied Lao Tzu.

"Is yours a warlike state?" I felt I could ask this question because my host was in a talkative mood.

"We are not as avaricious as some states," he replied thoughtfully, "but I hold it is preferable to be content with present boundaries rather than to seek to enlarge them. A good ruler will abjure conquest by force of arms. If war comes the ruler will go forth first to battle, and after him the statesmen, for in this way they will confess that they have failed in their duty. The old men will make up the army, the young will be spared for the future. When victory is won, it will be celebrated with rites of mourning."

"That is a new theory. I have never heard it expounded before, and certainly I have never known it to be practiced," I commented.

"Young man," he began with more energy than was his wont, and evidently not realizing how nearly my age approached his, "there are many ideas still waiting for someone to think and then have the courage to proclaim."

"I would like to ask you a question that has been my concern for many years." As the philosopher nodded his assent I framed it simply. "What do you consider to be the good life?"

He had no hesitation in replying, "The simple life is the happy life. It is better to work with one's own hands than with a machine. To make something which is different from what anybody else has made is to be preferred to making a thousand copies from one mold. To think one thought for oneself is nobler than to repeat a thousand phrases which have come from someone else. To love one's home and take pleasure in one's work, to enjoy the taste of food and hearken to the song of birds, to arise eager for the day and to retire weary with toil—this is the good life."

"This all sounds ideal," I remarked, "but do you think such a system would really suffice?"

"It is the manner of nature," rejoined the philosopher. "You cannot make a plant grow by hitting it with a hammer; you can help it grow by exposing it to the sunshine. Think about water. There is nothing so soft and yielding, yet when it attacks things that are hard and resistant it wears them away. This is the manner of nature: it is silent, spontaneous, effortless; it prevails without struggle, and wins without noise."

"I can honestly say that I think this would be a happier world if people practiced your philosophy," but there was a little hopelessness in my voice which gave Lao Tzu the clue to his next statement.

"The sage practices it whether he is in the majority or not. He is kind to the unkind, and thereby they get to be kind. He is truthful even to the liar, and in that way the liar becomes truthful. He remembers that water always seeks the lowest place, but at the same time lifts the heaviest ship; even so he puts himself beneath everybody else in order to lift everybody else."

"Give me time to think this over before I get in any deeper," I said lightly although I meant it respectfully, and Lao Tzu took it in that spirit.

As I turned his words over in my mind I could find no flaw in the argument. The only thing that bothered me was whether it would be feasible to dispense with organization and mechanics to the extent that Lao Tzu seemed to suggest. Would not everyone have to have the high intellect and moral principles that the philosopher possessed to be governed without government? However, it was a very different question that opened our next conversation. It was prompted by the daily evidence I saw all around me of a belief in spirits.

"As far as I can remember, elderly one, in all that you have said you have not mentioned the spirits. Yet I observe that everybody else in this land, from peasant to king, spends much time in making offerings to the spirits of the ancestors and to earth and heaven. Do you believe in the spirits?"

I hoped I had not been too brash and was glad Lao Tzu took no offense.

"I believe that the spirits of men and of ancestors are bound to follow the law of earth, as earth follows the law of heaven. But all of these are things which we can name and hence are not the ultimate. The ultimate must remain nameless because it is beyond our comprehension. It is that which existed before all things and that from which all things sprang."

"But," I made bold to ask, "if you designate that which lies back of everything else as 'the nameless,' are you not with that term itself giving it a name?"

"In a sense that is true," conceded the philosopher, "and as a matter of fact I have spent a good deal of time searching for a name which will express what I mean, for after all if you are going to speak to people about something you must have some designation for it. The best I have been able to do is to name the nameless the Tao."

"Is not *tao* your common word for a path, or something like that?" I hoped I was not displaying too great ignorance.

"You are right. It means 'the way.' "

"Are you suggesting then that the nameless is in reality the way of the universe?" I was deeply concerned with his argument.

"That is as close as I can come to expressing the inexpressible. Look at the haze on yonder hills; watch the sunset touch the sky with flame; consider how tiny is man in the midst of the vast world! There is a mystery about all that is seen which suggests that it is an expression of the unseen. In the expression of the mystery, there is a rhythm and a beauty. That which is manifesting itself everywhere is the Way."

I had no desire to speak as I sat contemplating the scope and profundity of this idea.

Meditatively Lao Tzu concluded, "So if man would also live according to the Way, his own life would become simple and spontaneous. Without striving he would attain, without fighting he would win, without seeking he would find."

For days I pondered this philosophy. I considered it the most mature attitude toward life I had encountered in my wanderings— no magic, no fear, no concentration on evil, no harrowing of the soul or mortification of the body. The way of man in harmony with the Way of the universe, man's insufficient power buoyed up by the all-sufficient power welling up from the heart of things—these were conceptions which appealed strongly to me.

Still there was a weakness and I tried hard to put my finger on it, but for a long time it eluded me. Then one day with no effort on my part it came to me: the doctrine eventuated in quiescence. People could use the teaching as an excuse for indigence. They could conclude that there was no necessity to strive, and would therefore accept conditions as they were. But was that what Lao Tzu actually meant? The wise man could not be so naïve. Perhaps the Way that he taught was a more effective striving. I wavered in my evaluation.

A few days later a handsomely dressed and loquacious man came into the library and before he made known his reason for studying there, he began to talk.

"You have heard of the brilliant plan the government has just instituted?" he asked briskly.

I had to admit that I had not.

"It aims to provide for all the needs of all the people for the rest of their lives," he announced.

"How will it work?"

"Very simple," he replied almost childishly. "The government will take the total income of every person and then from this fund will distribute as much as is needed to each one."

"But how will the fund be administered?"

"A new bureau will be created with branches in every town and hamlet. It will be called the Department of Universal Finance."

"How much will such a development cost?"

"Probably not over half of the total amount that is taken in."

I said mildly, "I have recently talked with an old philosopher who feels that the government is already too highly organized."

The stranger burst out, "Do you mean Lao Tzu? He is a reactionary!"

Thinking to mollify my companion, I asked, "May I inquire in what business you are engaged?"

He answered, "I have just been appointed a clerk in the new Department of Universal Finance."

4

The Oracle and K'ung Tzu

ONE DAY LAO TZU, SPEAKING IN one of his paradoxical aphorisms, had said in my presence, "The farther one travels the less one knows; the sage arrives without going anywhere." I knew he meant nothing personal in the remark, but it sparked me with the desire to continue my journey to the great sea. After all, I had been some years in Loyang. The waves of an endless ocean beat upon a limitless coast, and farther one could not go.

The most direct route led through the state of Lu and this route I followed until it took me into the village of Tsou. Here I was arrested by a sight that made me smile to myself. In the yard of a humble cottage a boy, perhaps twelve years of age, was at play. He had built a mound of earth and constructed the semblance of steps on one side of it. Now he was walking up these steps slowly and seriously. Over his shoulder he wore a piece of cloth evidently to simulate a robe, and held a stick-scepter in his hand. At the top of the mound he halted and began to gesticulate, trying to be very precise with each movement. My mind flashed back to the day of my arrival in Loyang several years earlier when I had watched the emperor mount the ceremonial altar to offer sacrifice to earth and heaven. The lad was playing at the same thing.

Just then a man came to the door of the cottage and shouted, "K'ung." The boy hurried into the house, and I continued on my way.

I found the sea was even more impressive than I had anticipated. Vast, it stretched as far as eye could scan, to the distant horizon. The waves which rolled shoreward breaking upon the rocks with fury, spoke of a restrained but immeasurable power. Water, in this manifestation, was certainly not weak or puny. In the form of a raindrop, water could gently refresh a tender plant; in the form of an ocean, it could overwhelm the world. Was that why Lao Tzu compared the Tao to water?

For no evident reason my mind skipped from the old philosopher to the young boy with the serious face in his purposeful play at Tsou. The man who had called him in looked more like an older brother than his father, yet he spoke roughly. Maybe the boy was an orphan and should have been working instead of letting his imagination run riot. Had the lad ever seen the annual ceremonies? Doubtless he had seen the lesser ceremony performed by the headman of Tsou.

The sea held me fascinated for some time, and I made countless trips to sit for hours on its shores, but there was nothing here to hold me indefinitely. I had reached the extreme limit of my eastward journey. The only direction to go was—back. So I retraced my steps to the little village of Tsou, and as I went a plan formed in my mind. It was not difficult to find the humble cottage where I had watched the boy in his make-believe, and here again, while other boys were wrestling, jumping, and throwing stones into small marked-out squares, I found K'ung in his own yard patiently practicing the ceremonial gestures. Perhaps it was the sight of the other boys that helped me realize why this lad attracted me so greatly. At his age, while the other boys of Jerusalem had played almost identically like these boys of Tsou, I had been intent on my own devices which led at last to my discovery of the entrances and exits to the water tunnel. I saw myself again in K'ung!

It was some time before young K'ung noticed that I was watching him, but even then there was no embarrassment on his part. I greeted him in a friendly way and he returned the greeting.

"As you can see," I began, "I am a stranger in your town. I am heading for Loyang, the magnificent capital of your land, and I would like to find a traveling companion. It is a weary journey to make alone. We would take horses and arrive, as I estimate it, just in time for the autumnal ceremonies of state to be performed by the great Wang."

The boy's eyes glistened when I mentioned the ceremonies at the capital, but he only said, "I am afraid I do not know anyone who could go with you. All the men of our village are busy every day in the fields and cannot go that far away."

"Is there any chance that a young man like yourself would be interested in making the trip?"

"Oh, I would like to!" he burst out; then restraining himself and sobering, he added, "But I am afraid my brother would not let me go."

"May I speak to him about it?" I asked, and, without waiting for an answer, I strode toward the house, K'ung following timidly.

The brother rejected the proposal immediately. "We are poor here. The boy is employed frequently in the silk factory. We need what he earns."

"I am not as young as when I first began to travel," I said mildly. "I need his services badly, and I shall be able to pay for what he does for me. Since I will also pay his expenses on the journey, he can bring home all the wages he has earned." When I mentioned the figure which I could pay it caused the brother to change his mind abruptly.

The brother helped me make the purchase of two horses and the other necessary items for our journey. Preparations were fairly simple and before long young K'ung and I were on our way. As we traveled, the youth never forsook an attitude of modesty and reticence, but from occasional references and in answer to an infrequent question on my part, I pieced together the story of the boy's life. The father of K'ung was Ho. Late in life Ho had married the daughter of Yen. When K'ung was born, the father died, and not long after the mother died also. The one with whom K'ung lived was really only a half-brother, who had a wife and daughter of his

own, and was not kind to K'ung. K'ung had been born with a bulging of the skull, and the other boys often made fun of him. This
turned him increasingly within himself and he devised quiet pursuits
which he could enjoy alone. From his earliest remembrance he had
enjoyed stately deportment and had taken pleasure in the niceties
of etiquette. As he grew older he had become fascinated by the
ceremonies of the court and the rituals of the land. He liked reading
and arithmetic and hoped someday to become a scholar and perhaps a government official.

As we rode along one day I opened a conversation with the mock
serious question, "And so, prince K'ung, what kind of government
would you have for your people?"

K'ung answered in the same vein. "Respected elder, I would have
a serious government wherein the good of every member should be
given equal consideration with every other member."

"Fair enough," I said, "and how would you accomplish this?"

"By what means I do not know, except that I would have every
person follow the ancient customs which I have often heard said
were better than those of today."

"Do you know these customs?" I asked the boy.

"Only part of them, elder one," he said with surprise. "Surely
you know I have had no chance to read many of the classics, nor
have the people whom I know. But I am told the customs of the
good days are all recorded in the classics. These I would have the
people study."

"Would you like to see these books, young K'ung?"

"I have always dreamed of being a scholar but we have no money
in our family to make the dream come true."

"At least I can show you the great books," I assured him. "Have
you any other plans for your kingdom?" For several days we kept
up the pretense between us, and planned a kingdom according to
the desire of K'ung's heart. And I thought it much better than many
I had seen worked out by older heads.

One night when we were both restless, K'ung said to me, "Elder one, I have given thought to our kingdom and I have worked out the most important idea."

"Let's hear it, son," I encouraged him.

"Suppose I were the emperor," he began, "then my first thoughts should be for my subjects. As a husband my first concern should be for my wife. As a father I should care for my children. As an older brother I should look out for my younger brother, and as a friend I should care for my friend's welfare above my own. Now, elder one, what would you think of such a policy?"

I hesitated to say that I thought it was the most profound I had ever heard from any ruler.

We arrived in Loyang in time to see the autumnal ceremonies. K'ung watched every detail of the long proceedings with rapt interest, often making inconspicuous gestures with his own hands corresponding to the movements of the officials. A few times he even anticipated the next move. At one point in the formalities he uttered a startled sound which he quickly suppressed. When I asked him about this later, he said with concern, "That was when the great Wang waved his arms toward heaven. But it is written that at that time he should fall upon his face."

"Are you sure?"

"Yes, it is read that way from the *Book of Etiquette and Ceremony.*"

I made a mental note to check this when we went to the imperial library.

"K'ung, what does it matter whether the emperor lifts his arms or falls on his face?" I asked. "Do you think the spirits pay much attention to these things?"

"It is better to follow the custom," K'ung replied. "It is best to be respectful to the spirits."

Along this line our discussion ran as we made our way to the library. I had hoped we might find Lao Tzu there so I was delighted when I saw the philosopher coming down the corridor, his head sunk on his chest, his mind deep in thought. I interrupted his reverie and Lao Tzu welcomed me with genuine pleasure. He greeted the youth with me and K'ung responded with such respectful formality as to arouse the old man's interest.

"Where is your home, Master K'ung?" he asked, paying the young man a high compliment in the title he gave him.

"I live, sir, in the village of Tsou, in the state of Lu."

"What do you do there?"

"During the day I work in the silk factory, and at night I read in the books with my teacher."

"What do you read?"

"We read the *Book of Etiquette and Ceremony,* and the *Chronicles of Former Times.*"

"What do you wish to be when you grow up?"

"If it is not too much to hope for, sir, I would like to be a student of the ancient books and perhaps even an officer in the government."

At this point I interrupted the conversation to remark, "It is to see one of these books that we have come this afternoon. Young K'ung thinks that the emperor made the wrong gesture at one point in the ceremony."

"And what is it you would like to check?"

K'ung spoke up with decisiveness, "It is this same book that I have just mentioned." He indicated almost the exact spot where the directions could be found. There it was written exactly as he said, that at that point in the autumnal sacrifice the emperor should prostrate himself before high heaven.

The mention of government brought up a topic which was a favorite with Lao Tzu, and a long conversation ensued on that theme between the old philosopher and the boy. I listened with interest and sometimes with amazement. Lao Tzu chose to ask many provocative questions, and K'ung answered with unfailing courtesy but with an independence and consistency of thought that was remarkable. The essence of his idea was that the proper order of things was laid down in the books which came from antiquity, and that the careful following of this pattern would result in the establishment of a good society.

When the discussion ended Lao Tzu again complimented the boy. "Farewell, K'ung Tzu. The world needs scholars and the government needs honest officials. I believe you will become a fine scholar and a good officer in the government."

Hardly were we beyond Lao Tzu's hearing when K'ung remarked with suppressed emotion, "Did you hear what he called me? K'ung Tzu! That means K'ung the Philosopher. I think he does not agree with all that I said, but he was very kind to me. I will always remember him."

When the day came for K'ung to start for his home, I accompanied him through the streets of the city to a temple where we paused to seek an omen for his forthcoming journey, as was the custom. The priest in charge of divination asked each of us for his name, then taking up a round receptacle containing sticks of varying lengths, uttered a long formula and shook out as many sticks as would fall with one inclination of the vessel. He studied the alternation of short and long sticks among those that fell to the ground, then consulted a large book containing many diagrams.

"Two men are going separate ways," he announced. "Each will go to his own home in peace."

I was startled that the oracle included a prediction concerning me, but I paid no attention to it as we rejoiced that the omen was favorable for K'ung's return to his home. When we left the temple we walked directly to a place where a caravan was assembling. There I placed the boy in the keeping of the leader who would be responsible for delivering him to the small house where the earthen mound stood in the yard. As the travelers moved away, I waved a regretful farewell to the serious-faced lad for whom I had come to feel a genuine affection.

The way to the inn where I would stay while I formulated plans for my next move, took me past the temple we had so recently visited. It had no interest for me now, until I was startled from my thinking by hearing a voice say, "Come in, honorable sir, there is more." Looking up, I saw the diviner standing by the temple door.

I hesitated; this kind of superstitious proceeding was not for me, but the priest was insistent and I yielded.

"I hoped you would return this way, honorable stranger in our land. There was more to tell you but your interest was only in the boy. I thought you would return this way and I waited to summon you in."

By this time we were in a small dark room illuminated only by the light of a small charcoal fire. The priest seized a piece of oxbone lying at hand, and wrote upon it a name. I was amazed to read, "K'ung Tzu." That was exactly the way Lao Tzu had referred to my youthful friend. Then the diviner held the inscribed oxbone in tongs over the fire. It glowed in the heat, and finally cracked. Studying the strange outline of this crack, the priest declared, "It is the most auspicious of all indications. He will be a very great man."

I thought this statement enough for an oracle to give at one time, but something in the face of the priest kept me silent in my place. The diviner was staring fixedly at the oxbone which he had again put into the fire. His body trembled with the intensity of his concentration, then suddenly grew limp as he fell back into a trance. He began to speak in a hollow, unnatural voice.

"I see a royal court. The ruling duke is in his council chamber, conferring with his advisers. The post of chancellor is open in the government. Who is to be appointed to guide the destinies of the state of Lu? The first counselor who speaks proposes the name of K'ung Tzu.

"There is confusion now because of many voices which I hear, sometimes all talking at once, but I make out such words as 'incorruptible,' 'good steward,' 'no bribes.' I now see K'ung Tzu holding this important position, second only to the duke.

"I see ahead again a few years. The state is prosperous, the people buy and sell with honesty, weights and measures are checked. Decorum and courtesy prevail.

"The scene shifts to the court of the duke of Ch'i. The duke is jealous of the prosperity of the neighboring state of Lu. The bandits who can no longer work in Lu have come to Ch'i. The good citizens in Ch'i yearn to move to Lu. In their anger the counselors do not think of improving their own province but only of destroying the pre-eminence of Lu. They plot the downfall of K'ung's province.

"I now see one of the counselors to the duke of Ch'i going to the Street of Many Pleasures where he enters the School of Delightful Charms and talks with the matron. Even at his age he is enamored of the beautiful girls with soft voices. I hear the matron say, 'We have eighty beautiful girls about to graduate. They are tall and willowy, trained in ancient and modern dances, practiced in the arts of singing and conversation. They would make fine companions for men of wisdom. They will be ready for presentation at the court of Lu within seven days.'

"Another counselor visits the stables and arranges to have one hundred and twenty magnificent thoroughbreds ready for presentation at the court of Lu within seven days.

"Time has passed. Again I see the capital of Lu. The fields yield little harvest, the peasants are poor and dispirited because of high taxes. In the market places accounts are falsified. A great race track has been built outside the city on the north and the duke and his counselors revel in betting.

"Now I am in a meeting of the duke and his officials. Official documents lie on the table but no one makes a move to touch them. 'Communications from Master K'ung,' says one almost insolently. 'I have had no time to read them. Fragrant Blossom is keeping me busy these days.' His companions wink slyly. 'She does not dance as well as my Marigold,' speaks up another. 'And when my Bright Eyes with her yellow veils—' but this speaker is broken off by the duke's announcement, 'We will consider these matters of state at another time.' And with a yawn he dismisses his court.

"Now I see K'ung Tzu. He is weary and low of spirits. He is putting the records of his office in perfect order—he closes the files—he walks out alone—he wanders in the streets—his pupils gather round —affection in their manner—words such as 'men as brothers,' 'control'—I see a light around the old man as he says, 'Never do to others what you would not want them to do to you'—writing brushes, books, disciples all around him. The scene floats away. I see no more."

The voice of the diviner trailed off into silence. His eyes opened and he sat upright again. Speaking in his natural voice, as if nothing had intervened, he said, "If you wish, you may keep the oracle bone."

I rushed forth from the temple and hastened in the direction taken by the departing caravan. Then my steps slowed and I stopped and stood looking into the distance. Yonder a boy of twelve, his serious face brightened by remembrance of the wonderful ceremonies he had seen, was going home. Perhaps it was better for him to face the future without knowing what it would bring. I glanced at what I held in my hand, an old piece of bone with a strange crack in it. On it was written, "K'ung Tzu."

Book Five

FULFILLMENT

1

Isaiah

IN MY LODGING ROOM AT LOYANG
I sat as in contemplation, an art which I had developed during the
years I had spent in the Far East. But this night I was lost in reverie
rather than meditation. The words of the diviner passed through
my mind: "Two men are going separate ways. Each will go to his
home in peace." K'ung would soon fulfill his part of the prophecy.
What about myself? What had the diviner meant by "home"? I
had none. Could it be Babylon where my parents had been forced
to make a home in exile? It could hardly mean the place of my
birth, for Jerusalem had been laid waste and doubtless the years of
abandonment had added their insults to the ravages of war.

This land, The Flowery Kingdom, had given me more satisfactory
living than any I had known, but it was at the same time the most
foreign. These people faced the east; my people faced the west.
Perhaps I would go to Babylon. Now I could enter that cosmopoli-
tan city as a traveler from the Far East and stand no danger of
recognition or persecution. There I could inquire about my parents,
no doubt long since dead. I could report to Ezekiel—or would he
still be living? The community in exile would know what had happened in Jerusalem in the years I had been gone.

As these thoughts flooded my mind, my lagging spirits picked up
and I found myself in a state of undeniable excitement. My mind
was made up. Now I would make all preparations as speedily as

possible and be on my way again. But what a long way it was! Momentarily I had forgotten the mountains, the rivers, the jungles, the burning deserts. But this time they would lead me home and that made a difference.

Lao Tzu was the one person whom I would bid farewell, so the next morning I went to the imperial library to see the old philosopher. But Lao Tzu was nowhere to be found. After waiting some time I inquired of an assistant.

"He will surely come sometime today," I was assured. "His final pay is waiting for him. You knew that this day begins his retirement?"

I had not known it but I rejoiced that at last he would be free to follow the yearning of his life, to be a thinker, not a keeper of books. The hours passed and Lao Tzu did not appear. I went to the house where I had spent so many happy hours in conversation with the "Old Boy" during the years I had lived in this city. There I was told that Lao Tzu had moved out the day before and had left no word where he could be reached.

As I made preparations for my own departure, I made frequent inquiries after Lao Tzu from merchants and friends who I thought might know something of the philosopher's whereabouts. Most of them had not yet missed him. Regretfully, I left Loyang without seeing my friend. An innkeeper near the city wall told me that a man of ancient look but vigorous movement had passed that way two days previous, in the early morning hours. The gatekeeper on the western wall knew a little more. In reply to my anxious questions he said that a man giving his name as Lao had passed through the gate.

"Are you a friend of his?" asked the gatekeeper.

"A devoted friend," I replied.

"But you are going west. If you were returning to the city I would entrust you with a book," offered the gatekeeper. "I do not want the responsibility—"

"What kind of book?" I broke in.

"The old man gave me instructions to have it taken to the imperial library—"

"Yes, yes," I explained eagerly, "the man was my friend. Let me see the book."

The gatekeeper produced it. I read the opening words:

> It is from the nameless that heaven and earth sprang. When I seek to give a name to the nameless I call it Tao. Great Tao does nothing, yet accomplishes everything . . .

I returned the book to the gatekeeper. "It was Lao Tzu indeed. He is a great philosopher. Make sure that his book is preserved with care."

"Perhaps you will overtake him. He rode off upon a buffalo. He went in that direction," said the gatekeeper, gesturing toward the northwest.

The caravan route which the old philosopher had evidently taken, and which I now set out to follow, led across a desert, a place of utter desolation where were neither birds nor beasts, but rotting bones of dead men and pack animals marked the trail. At times I joined myself to caravans, but when one stopped too long I would move on alone until I came to the next one. During storms I often found refuge in the tents of the nomads and was grateful to the unwritten law of the East that made a family protect the guest within its midst. For months I toiled on, buffeted by strong winds, mired by heavy sands.

Then came the endless wastes of Sinkiang, skirted by the oases of Turfan, Kucha, and Kashgar. More numerous caravans moved in this region, and I was often able to secure a mount and proceed both more rapidly and more easily. Along my way there were elusive traces of Lao Tzu's passing. One had seen him ride by; another had heard an old man talk about the Tao. He had taught briefly in Samarkand and had been seen in Bokhara. Beyond that there were no clues. I crossed the mountains and came down into Sogdiana.

The miracle of the seasons merely changed the nature of the hardships of my trip, as the bitter cold of winter gave way to the heat of summer and desolate autumn followed. I was obsessed with the idea that I was going home; little else mattered. Strangely, as I thought of home it was no longer Babylon, but my own Jerusalem. Here was I, a mature man who for long years had buffeted the world, but now experiencing the emotions of a schoolboy waiting for vacation to begin. In my urge to hurry I bought two mounts and rode them alternately, pressing across the highlands of Iran. Even the old philosopher all but faded from my mind.   .

I was returning by a more direct route than the one I had taken many years earlier. When I had first started the return trip I had imagined myself revisiting some of the places where I had lived in earlier days, but now I was satisfied with what information I could pick up along the way. I learned from the leader of one caravan who frequently visited Balkh that Vishtaspa was still the ruler and still faithful to the teachings of Zarathushtra.

"The king must be along in years by now," I observed.

"But his son Darius is a fine young man," said the leader, "and it is felt he will make an equally wise king."

"That is fortunate," I replied. "What about a high priest called Gaumata? He was stripped of his power and sent into exile before I left the city."

"He is still in exile; some think that he spends his time plotting ways to recover his priestly power, but most of us do not think it could ever happen—at least not during the reign of the present royal house. Of course," he concluded, "Cyrus the Persian is the great power in that part of the world."

"Cyrus?" I repeated. "And who is this Cyrus?"

The man leaned forward from his place by the caravan fire and peered closely into my face.

"How could it be that you have never heard of Cyrus?" he asked incredulously.

"I have been many years traveling in far distant parts," I replied. "I am only now returning and I should like to hear more of this person who wields great power."

"Ha!" said a swarthy young fellow of our group. "Here is a brand new pair of ears to listen to your yarns." The young man flashed a smile.

I could see that in spite of the joking tone the men were interested in the tales of their leader, for they settled themselves comfortably around the night fire and as the flames cast strange shadows on the faces of his companions the older man took up his story.

"It was like this," he began with evident satisfaction. "Astyages the Mede ruled in Hagmatana. One night he had an unusual dream that concerned his daughter Mandane. He saw a stream of water flowing from her. First it flooded his own kingdom and then inundated the whole of Asia. Greatly disturbed, the king sought counsel of the Deva priests, but their interpretation threw him into a state of consternation. He thought to circumvent the prophecy by taking preliminary precautions, so when the time came for Mandane to marry, he selected for her a husband who had a distinguished name and title but no political strength or ambitions that would ever conflict with his own. Just such a person was Cambyses, ruler of the Persians.

"The marriage of Mandane and Cambyses was duly celebrated and for the time being, the fears of Astyages were quieted. Then during the first year of their marriage he had another disturbing dream. This time a vine grew from the womb of his daughter and overshadowed all of Asia. The interpreters told him this dream signified that a child of Mandane would rule over Asia in his place. Mandane was already with child, and Astyages sent for her to come home until she should give birth. It was his intention to destroy the offspring as soon as it was born.

"When the child Cyrus was born, his mother was very ill for many days and under pretext of keeping the child secluded with a nurse, the king instead summoned Harpagus to whom he was accustomed to entrust his personal affairs. 'Harpagus,' he said, 'see to it that you do not neglect the business I am about to entrust to you, lest you bring destruction upon yourself. With all haste take this child to your home and slay him there. Then bury him as you please.' 'I have never failed you in the past, nor will I in the future,' replied Harpagus. 'Be assured that what you command will be done with diligence.'

"When Harpagus returned to his home, bearing the baby in his arms, he was weeping. Upon hearing what had happened, his wife asked what he intended to do. 'I will not perform such a murder as this,' he declared, 'nor would it be safe for me to do so. Astyages is old and has no son. If he should expire and Mandane become queen, my life would be forfeited. Nevertheless the child must be put to death for otherwise my life will not be safe either; but it must be someone of Astyages' own household who does the deed, and not I.'

"Thereupon Harpagus sent a messenger to fetch Mitradates, one of the king's herdsmen who was married to Spaco, a female slave of the king. This herdsman pastured his flocks in the mountains north of Hagmatana, where there were many wild beasts. Harpagus told him, 'You must take this child and lay it in the remotest hills where it will die quickly. This is the command of Astyages, and I myself am appointed to see that it is done. If you allow the boy to escape, you will die the most painful of deaths.'

"Of course, Mitradates had no idea who the child was but he felt this was an unfortunate time to receive such a gruesome assignment, for his own wife was about to be delivered of a child, and how could he perform this grim duty and conceal it from her? Nevertheless, he did not dare to protest, so he took up the princeling and went on his way. When he arrived home he found his wife in her bed, weeping bitterly. Between sobs she told him that despite the assistance of a kindly neighbor, their child had been stillborn. Then she asked her husband what Harpagus had wanted of him. Thinking there was no cause to withhold the nature of his assignment now, he told Spaco he had been commanded to take the child and lay him on the mountain where the elements would soon destroy him or the wild animals would devour him. He also told her that a sly-looking slave had hinted that the mother of the child was none other than the king's daughter, Mandane, and the father Cambyses, ruler of the Persians.

"When Mitradates uncovered the child and his wife saw how

beautiful he was, she burst out weeping afresh. 'If a child must be exposed upon the mountains,' she said, 'take our dead baby and lay it there, and let us bring up this child as our own.'

"Mitradates did as his wife said. They put the royal garments upon the body of their own infant and laid it upon the hills, leaving a helper to guard the body for a time. After three days Mitradates returned to Harpagus and told him that his mission was accomplished. Harpagus in turn sent word to the king, and accompanied the word with the exposed body of the stillborn babe. The king, being satisfied with the evidence, gave orders for the funeral. Thus it came about that the child of the herdsman was buried in royal garb, and Cyrus, the son of Mandane and Cambyses, was raised by the herdsman's wife."

The storyteller ended the tale with a flourish and his audience expressed their satisfaction.

"That was very interesting," I said. "Now I would like to know whether the prophecy of the oracle came true."

"I'm coming to that," said the taleteller, not wanting to be hurried. "When the cowherd's son, as Cyrus was known, was ten years old, he was one day playing with the other boys of the village when in their game they chose him to be king, and he ordered them to build houses, to serve as guards, and to perform various tasks. One lad, the son of Artembares, a Mede of distinction, refused to obey the commands, and Cyrus chastised him with a whip. The nobleman's son was outraged to be treated so, and hurried to the city and complained to his father. Artembares went directly to Astyages and protested. Pointing to the welts from the whiplash upon his son's shoulders, he said, 'This is what your slave, the son of the cowherd, did to him.'

"Summoning the herdsman and the boy, Astyages asked the lad how he dared to behave so rudely to the son of a noble. The lowly boy answered respectfully but firmly: 'Sir, I treated him as he deserved. I was made king by the boys in play, and he was one of those who chose me. All the others obeyed my commands, but he refused to do so and received his just reward. If you think that I should be punished for this, I am here ready to accept what you mete out.'

"Astyages was impressed by the forthrightness and courage of this child. It was exactly the way he would want a son of his to answer. Or a grandson? The thought flashed through his mind. As he talked a few minutes longer with the boy he studied him carefully, urged by a certain resemblance of the nose and brow to the features of his own family. Suspicion overwhelmed him.

"Dismissing Artembares with a promise to settle the affair satisfactorily, Astyages held the herdsman alone. 'Where did you get this boy?' he asked. When the herdsman fumbled in his reply the king knew that the truth was not forthcoming. He had the cowherd dragged to the rack, where the poor man told the whole story. Thereupon Astyages sent at once for Harpagus. The latter, seeing the way the herdsman had been treated, realized it would be useless to try to deny what he had done. He told exactly how he had given the baby to the cowherd with orders to expose it, how he had been convinced that it was dead, and how he had ordered its burial. The king then repeated to Harpagus the story the herdsman had told him and, concealing how he really felt about it, said, 'So Cyrus, my grandson, is alive and that is good. I was very sad over his fate, and my daughter has never recovered her spirits. Fortune has been kind to us. Send your son here to the palace to play with the boy this afternoon and come yourself to a banquet this evening. There we will celebrate what has happened.' At the banquet Harpagus was served with roasted and boiled meat which he said he enjoyed very much. Afterward he was shown a basket in which were the head and hands and feet of his own son, whose flesh he had just consumed. That was how Astyages punished Harpagus."

A shudder passed over the men sitting by the campfire. Even for these hardened camel drivers, the story was too brutal to accept without repulsion. For myself I thought that never in the most benighted regions I had visited had I heard a more gruesome tale.

The storyteller enjoyed the hush he had produced and was encouraged to continue. "But the problem of what to do with Cyrus was still unsolved. Once more the king consulted his diviners. This time the message was encouraging. They informed Astyages that inasmuch as the boy had survived, grown up, and acted as king if only in play, their original prophecy had been fulfilled and there was nothing more to fear. Accordingly Cyrus was sent to his real home, where his parents received him with joy."

At this, another climax, the storyteller paused again.

"Did Mandane forgive her father?" I asked.

"In her joy to receive her son alive—and knowing the power of her father, the king, if she showed any untoward attitude—she accepted the situation."

"And were the prophetic dreams adequately fulfilled by the child's having played at king?" I questioned.

"We will come to that," said the historian. "When Cyrus grew to manhood he united all the Persian tribes under his leadership, then led them in an attack upon the Medes, even against his grandfather, to whom they had long been subservient. Astyages supposed that he could beat off this threat without difficulty, but he made the mistake of appointing Harpagus to command his army. All these years Harpagus had waited for an opportunity to avenge the treatment he had received from Astyages, and now he ordered the army to surrender to Cyrus without a struggle. So you see the prophecy of the oracle did come true. Cyrus became king of the Medes and Persians. Since then he has won many victories. It is rumored that he plans to march on Babylon next," finished the taleteller.

The campfire had burned low and the hour was late. One by one the men rose and walked toward their tents for the night. I followed, my heart heavy with forebodings for Babylon, where the little colony of people from my homeland still lived.

Winter would soon be at hand and Cyrus would not undertake a campaign during that season, so Babylon was safe at least until spring. Perhaps it was part of my mission to end my wanderings by bringing the people advance notice of their impending peril, even as I had first entered Babylon with advance notice of the approach

of the second band of exiles from Jerusalem. At any rate, the idea
made me push faster toward the west.

I reached Babylon on the first day of Tebeth, which fell on the
fifth of January, in the year 539. According to the calendar of my
people this was my birthday. Forty-six years before, a youth just
turned seventeen, I had arrived from Jerusalem with word of the
fall of that city. I relived my appearance before Ezekiel, and heard
again in memory his pronouncement of hope for the future. Where
was that hope now? A people who had been more than forty years
in captivity now faced new disaster in the attack of Cyrus with its
attendant slaughter.

Babylon looked as I remembered it. There was the broad plain,
the great rectangle of the walled city with the Euphrates flowing
through its very midst. Above the city loomed the lofty temple
tower; outside the wall extended the far-spreading suburbs. It was
toward one of the latter areas that I directed my steps, toward the
region of the Chebar Canal, toward the villages where my countrymen were established. Their settlement was now far more extensive
and impressive than on my first visit. Their numbers had been aug-
mented by the arrival of the later exiles and multiplied by the fe-
cundity of the people. The size of their habitations reflected the
prosperity many had achieved through crafts and businesses.

For a short time I wandered about, getting my bearings. I came
to the house where I had last seen my parents and found children
playing in the yard and a young mother sitting near the doorway.
It would be so, of course, for my parents would have been dead
some years by now. I peered into the house as I walked slowly past
and in the dim shadows I pictured my mother as she had turned to
my father and asked him to give me his blessing. "The Lord bless
you and keep you . . ." My heart beat faster as I realized that
once again I would hear the name of the Lord pronounced by my
own people. "And give you peace." When? I must find someone to
talk to.

Near a large structure which I took to be a school of some kind,

I paused and inquired of a friendly-looking person what its purpose was.

"That is our synagogue," he replied, wondering a little at my ignorance. "You—" he broke off and looked more closely at me. "You appear to be of our people, but how does it happen that you know not of our ways?"

"I have been a wanderer upon the earth," I answered. "And what is the purpose of the synagogue?"

"We are a people in exile," he replied without bitterness, "but we teach our boys the sacred books of the religion of their homeland. The synagogue is our school."

"When I was last here," I told the stranger, "there was a prophet named Ezekiel. Can you tell me about him?"

My informant answered politely, "Our prophet now is Isaiah, and he dwells in the Street of the Pomegranate Trees."

"Isaiah?" I cried. "Why, the prophet Isaiah lived long ago. He prophesied in the days when Sennacherib threatened Jerusalem. That was more than one hundred and fifty years ago."

"You know the history of our people well," said the man, "even though you are ignorant of our present situation. This is a second Isaiah. He was born here in the exile and his parents named him after the great prophet of former times. I do not know if the name influenced the course of his life, or if it was an intuition of his future career which led them to bestow the name. At any rate he has grown up to become our leader, and it is his words which have often given us courage in hard times. Come, I will take you to him."

I found myself in the presence of a man whom I judged to be in his thirties. He was slender of build, refined and sensitive of face. The slight stoop of the shoulders suggested the scholar poring over his scrolls, the thin hands and long fingers were those of a poet. But it was his eyes which were remarkable. They were eyes which had seen a thousand sorrows and they were full of tenderness and pity. They had looked into far distances and unto great heights, and there was a sense of wonder in them. There was also an inextinguishable fire, expressive of courage and hope.

When I identified myself to the prophet, Isaiah received me cordially. "Yes, I have often read in the book of Ezekiel where he mentions how one came from Jerusalem and said that the city had fallen," he said. "That was the turning point in the prophet's thinking and teaching. After he heard the worst, a load was lifted from his mind. He could then think about the future. But you must have been a very young man at that time. It was a long journey to make alone."

"I wanted to find my parents," I replied. "And I have come again now to ask about them."

When I gave their names the prophet smiled sadly. "They are both gone," he said gently. "They died at almost the same time. It was as if one could not survive without the other. I myself spoke words at their last rites."

"I am glad that neither had to be long alone," I said. And after a pause I spoke out. "I am afraid once more I am the bearer of ill tidings."

"Speak," said the prophet, his deep eyes undisturbed.

"As once I carried news of destruction from the west, now I have word of impending danger from the east. All the way on my recent journey I heard little but the name of Cyrus. They tell stories of the remarkable circumstances through which he was preserved from death in his infancy. Later reports deal with his successful conquest of the Medes. At present the Persians and Medes constitute a nation the vigor of which has never been seen before. Cyrus has already gone as far west as the Halys River and inflicted defeat on King Croesus. There is no stopping him. But what I have just learned and what I came especially to tell," I went on, "is that Cyrus now plans to attack Babylon. The winter is being devoted to preparations; in the spring he will march here!"

"I knew this would come," the prophet murmured as if speaking to himself, "but I did not know when." Then aloud, "Do you judge this to be bad news?"

"It struck a chill to my heart," I confessed. "I have not forgotten the horrors of the fall of Jerusalem. The older people here went through that experience; I cannot bear to think that the younger generation must face the conquest of Babylon. Our lot was grim enough as a free people in a beleaguered city; it has not been all ease as a captive tribe; what will it be to be a slave people in a city surrounded by foreign armies? Our people will be the last to receive food, the first to be thrust into a breach. If the city is disadvantaged by their life or could be advantaged by their death, they will be forfeited without a second thought. It is ominous news, I fear, which I have brought."

The prophet was speaking again so quietly that he might have been addressing only himself. "It could be that it is good news."

2

The Gate of God

THERE WAS NO WAY IN WHICH I could join the colony of my people, nor would it have been to their advantage to have a stranger try to do so. Still I felt impelled to stay near them. The international nature of my speech and manners made it easy for me to obtain a position as an interpreter at the court of Babylon.

Soon after taking up my duties, my immediate superior, the keeper of the royal seal, hailed me from his chariot, "Come along and I will show you the city." He made room for me beside him, and then drove his span of horses rapidly up the sloping ramp which led from behind the Ishtar Gate to the crest of the outer city wall. The top of the wall was so broad that guardrooms and storerooms were built on either side and there was still space for a street between.

At frequent vantage points we could look out over the plain, where in the far distance shimmered the sands of the desert I knew so well. There were also the extensive cultivated fields of this river valley; and in the foreground lay the suburban areas, in one of which dwelt the exiles from Jerusalem.

The driver pulled up his horses and pointed out to me the defenses of the city. "This moat at the foot of the wall is our first defense." I noted that it was broad and deep. "No boats are permitted on it and the bridges which span it at the chief gates are lifted at night."

"A wise plan," I commented.

The keeper of the seal continued, "The bricks for the wall were made from the earth removed in the digging of this moat. Two ends were achieved with one labor."

"Again wise," I said.

"The bricks were burned in the kiln, then laid in hot bitumen. At every thirtieth course there is a layer of wattled reeds. This wall would stand the greatest earthquake that has ever come."

"It looms high above the plain," I observed.

"High enough that no army could possibly scale it," replied the official confidently. "Nor could they get through the gates. There are one hundred portals in the wall and all are closed with doors of solid brass. Even if men got through the outer wall they would still be stopped by the inner wall there. It is almost as strong as this one."

I had seen many walls in my day and could only admire the engineering work of this one. We drove for miles on the top of the wide wall. The city was laid out in a vast square with the river flowing through it. The outside of the wall, where it met the water, was a sheer drop that terminated in bastions lapped by the flood. Paralleling both banks of the river were lower walls made of burnt brick and closed with gates of brass. At a mid-point a bridge led across the river, new since I was in Babylon many years before. I commented on the fact that the piers were of stone and the span of wood.

"Yes," replied my guide. "Those spans are wooden platforms which are laid across from pier to pier. They are taken up at night so no one can cross from one side to the other. The poorer part of the city lies over there, and thieves and murderers might too easily slip across in the darkness."

"This is a remarkable feat," I said with admiration. "It certainly required expert engineering to construct stone piers in the midst of a deep and powerful river."

"We owe the planning to the genius of a woman," said the keeper of the royal seal. "Our King Nabunaid had a remarkable mother, Nitocris. When she got the idea of building this bridge she went far up the valley and marked out a basin fifty miles around, a basin as large as Babylon itself. Her excavators dug out the dirt and used it for embankments. Then she had the river turned out of its course and diverted into the lake. While it was filling the lake she had the bridge built, the workmen having a dry riverbed. By the time the river had to be turned back into its course, the bridge was finished."

"I would say she was a remarkable woman," I agreed. "But as I understand it, King Nebuchadnezzar was the one who did most of the building at Babylon. These walls were erected by him, were they not?" This I asked without referring to the fact that I had been in Babylon during the reign of Nebuchadnezzar and had seen some of these things for myself.

"That is right," replied the keeper of the royal seal; then as we drove back toward the Ishtar Gate he pointed out, "See how he laid out the whole city. We have two main divisions on this side of the river. In the center of each is a citadel. Far over yonder are the king's palaces and gardens. Across here that great tower stands in the center of the sacred precinct. There the house of rulers; here the house of gods. What a conception! And look at the magnificent sweep of the processional street from the gate to the temple!"

The chariot came to a halt at the top of the Ishtar Gate. "It is said that when Nebuchadnezzar finished all these works he stood at this very place and gazed out over the city. According to tradition he cried aloud, 'Is not this great Babylon, which I have built by my mighty power as a royal residence and for the glory of my majesty?' Come, let me show you his signature."

The keeper of the royal seal led me to the tower wall. Its glazed and bright-colored tiles flashed in the sun. Enameled figures of bulls, dragons, and snarling lions were raised in relief. On each brick was the inscription:

I AM NEBUCHADNEZZAR, KING OF BABYLON

I was not much longer in my new position until I saw King Nabunaid. It was my impression that the glory of Nebuchadnezzar was reflected only faintly in the present king. There was a sort of preoccupation in his manner, as if he were always thinking of something other than the business in hand. His answers were not decisive and he never seemed to make a final disposition of any matter. This vagueness accounted for an undercurrent of mistrust which appeared unmistakable in the court.

Later, as the keeper of the royal seal and I talked in a private chamber, he said, "The King means well and I serve him loyally, but I am afraid he is losing his hold on affairs."

This was an unusually frank statement for a highly placed official to make, but I could see that he was genuinely concerned and had also come to feel complete confidence in me. He continued his explanation.

"It was not so at the beginning; then he rescued us from anarchy. After Nebuchadnezzar died things went rapidly toward ruin. Nebuchadnezzar's son, Amel-Marduk, lasted only two years and was slain by his brother-in-law, Nergal-shar-usur, who held on for four years; and his son, Labashi-Marduk, ruled for only a few months. Then a powerful group of nobles put Nabunaid on the throne and it looked as if the kingdom were stabilized."

"How long has he now reigned?" I asked.

"This spring on the first of Nisan he will celebrate the beginning of his seventeenth regnal year. We hope he will be in the city at that time."

"Why would he be absent from Babylon when the festival of the new year is held? Is that not the most important time of the whole year?"

"He always has his mind on other matters. He goes away for unexplained periods."

"But Nebuchadnezzar went out on many military expeditions too," I consoled.

"That was different. If Nabunaid were out defending the borders or taking new territories no one would criticize him."

"What does he do?" I asked.

The keeper of the royal seal settled himself back in his chair. "Nabunaid is interested in the past," he said. "I think it is all right to study the past if it helps you understand the present and do something about the future. But if it merely offers escape from doing anything about present conditions, it is not good. He goes down to Ur and digs in the foundations of the temple tower there. I admit he has found out a great deal. He dug up inscribed bricks with the names of Ur-Nammu and Dungi, his son. They are the ones who built that tower, fifteen hundred years ago, I presume. All that is good to know, but Nabunaid wants us to go back and do things the way they were done in the time of Ur-Nammu."

"Is that why he seems so abstracted?" I asked.

He nodded agreement, adding, "And he is also thinking about Sin, the moon god. You see, Ur was the old center of the worship of the moon. So the king sent his daughter down there to be the priestess of the moon. And he spends more time there and out at Tema than he does in Babylon."

"Do you mean Tema in the Arabian desert? That must be many hundred miles from here!"

"That is the place. There the moon has been worshiped from the most ancient times. First Nabunaid conquered Tema, then he was conquered by it. From his fourth to his eleventh year he was out there every new year's day and I am afraid he may be going again now."

"I sometimes have a feeling that he is trying to escape from something," I suggested.

"He is afraid of the priests of Marduk here in Babylon," agreed the keeper of the royal seal, "but when he goes off into his retreat it only allows them to take over more and more power. They work against him in every way they can, for they fear that what he really wants is to move the capital to Tema, and if he did that it would be hard on their profits. The way things are going, I am afraid they will be running everything before much longer. When Nabunaid is off in Tema, they tell the people that he is moonstruck, gone mad."

"Who takes his place when he is gone?" I asked as indifferently as possible.

Before the question could be answered there was the clatter of a chariot in the courtyard below. The keeper of the royal seal looked out the window and beckoned to me. I saw a man who might be in his thirties, elegant in attire and languorously insolent in manner, toss the reins to a groom, step from the chariot, and walk into the palace.

"That is Belshazzar, the king's son," said the keeper of the royal seal. "He has the kingship when Nabunaid is absent. We must go quickly to help make a great stir over his arrival." And the keeper of the seal took me with him.

A few minutes later Prince Belshazzar strode into the audience hall, and without giving any recognition to the king's presence, he sat down and swept one of the court women into his lap. Then he seized a beaker of wine, held it briefly to the lips of the woman and finished the contents himself, slamming the beaker down on the table with a resounding noise. "Salutation to the king from the king," he said to his father with an insolent air.

It was not until I visited the sacred precincts around the temple that I located the real power in Babylon. Whereas the court was luxurious and ineffective, the temple area was vibrant with energy. Sharp-eyed priests dominated the scene and there was no doubt about the concentration of wealth here. Animals and produce were brought in a steady stream for sacrifices to the gods and, since only token portions were actually offered and nothing was ever taken away except refuse, the temple storehouses were bulging. Payments of temple taxes and voluntary contributions were made in money, and the accumulation of gold and silver coin was enormous. The deities were also the proprietors of many landed estates, and the management of these by the priests further multiplied the temple income. The control of wealth by the priests was more evident on the surface than was their manipulation of the government, but behind the scenes the lines of influence which extended from the temple to the palace were many.

When Nabunaid was in Babylon the attitude of the priests was one of thinly veiled hostility. At other times they spread a rumor that the king had abandoned loyalty to the proper gods of Babylon and had fallen under the bewitching spell of the moon god. In the desert, so they said, he lived like an animal, exposed to the dew of evening, burned by the sun of day. Beware of this mad mind! Thus they undermined his authority.

In the king's absence, when Belshazzar exercised the kingship, the priests treated him as a comrade, providing him with drink and damsels—and of both they had unlimited supply. Their own distilleries produced the finest liquors in Babylonia; and into the ranks of priestess they admitted only the most beautiful girls. Thus the priests could stimulate the desires of Belshazzar and in satisfying them bring him increasingly under their control. In the end, it was the appetites they had stimulated which led to their own ruin along with his.

The architecture of the sacred precinct was expressive of the power and wealth concentrated there. In addition to the extended complex of storehouses, treasuries, manufactories, record rooms, and residences, there were four main temples and the great temple tower. The first sanctuary was that of Nabu, the god of learning. Nebuchadnezzar, whose name was spelled Nabu-kudurri-usur in the Babylonian language, meaning "Nabu protect the boundary," had been particularly devoted to this deity. The original home of Nabu was at Borsippa, not far from Babylon, and it was due to Nebuchadnezzar that this temple had been erected in the capital. Over the portal was a prayer which was composed by Nebuchadnezzar. Inscribed in ornamental cuneiform it read:

> O eternal prince! Lord of all being!
> I am the king, obedient to you,
> The creature of your hand;
> You have created me, and
> With dominion over all people
> You have entrusted me.
> Cause me to love your supreme dominion,
> And create in my heart
> The worship of your divinity,
> And grant whatever is pleasing to you,
> Because you have fashioned my life.

As was appropriate to the god of knowledge and literature, the temple of Nabu housed a school for scribes and a large library, containing many thousands of clay tablets, covered with close-packed cuneiform script and stored in carefully indexed niches. The composition of original works was constantly in process, and the multiplication of copies of already existent works was carried on as a master scribe read from a document and a row of his assistants copied the text from his dictation.

The next temple was that of Marduk, chief god of Babylon. Expressive of his majesty and power, this building was a massive pile of brick and stone rising in successive step-backs and culminating in a square upper story which had the strength of a fortress. In the center of the building stood a statue of Marduk. It was the figure of a man seated upon a throne with a table in front of him, the entire work executed in solid gold. When the monthly festival of the god was held, a thousand talents of frankincense were burned in front of him, and when the annual new year's celebration took place, he was carried forth in triumphal procession in a circuit of the city and back again, the king himself following humbly like a slave. This was the celebration for which the people wanted their king at hand, for this was the one duty that could not be assigned to any deputy. If the king were not present, Marduk could not be taken from the temple and there could be no new year's procession.

In the temple of Marduk, I sat in a lecture hall and heard a priest expound the greatness of the deity. "Time was," he said, "when the monster Tiamat threatened the gods. From her venomous spittle sprang a brood of gruesome creatures whose veins ran with poison. At their head she marched against the house of heaven. In the council of the gods, fear prevailed. Then Marduk stepped forward, clothed in the glory of the sun. He it was who volunteered to fight with Tiamat. If he should win, the gods offered to give him first place among them all. Marduk made a net of unbreakable strands, seized the lightning as his club, took the hurricane as his weapon, mounted the chariot of the storm and drove forth the steeds De-

structive, Pitiless, Trampler, and Fleet. 'Come,' he challenged Tiamat, 'let us do battle.'

"The monster opened her mouth to engulf him, and he let loose
a fierce wind which distended her belly. He flung the net to entangle
her and loosed the bolt of the lightning against her. Upon her prostrate body he took his stand. With the sword he split her body in
two. The upper half he lifted up to make the firmament; the lower
he left to make the earth. Her brood he destroyed and their blood
he mingled with the good earth to make mankind. The gods he assigned to their places, Anu to the sky, Enlil to the air, Ea to the
waters underneath the earth. Over all he reigned supreme.

"So it is that he is the chief of all deities," concluded the lecturer.
"He is Bel-Marduk, Marduk *the* god."

The third temple was dedicated to Ishtar, queen of heaven and
goddess of love. The shrine proper was relatively small but it was
surrounded by a honeycomb of lesser rooms and all were set in a
spacious, tree-shaded garden. Many women were seated throughout
the grounds, some gazing boldly at passers-by, some veiling their
faces, some richly attired, some in rags.

"Every woman born in the land must come here once during her
life and take her seat in this garden," explained a priest. "The first
stranger who comes by and casts a silver coin into her lap can take
her into one of yonder rooms for his own. The act is a sacrifice to
Ishtar and contributes to making all things fruitful."

The fourth temple was a rambling structure with no uniformity
of architecture; it gave every evidence of having had many additions
built on. This was the sanctuary of the gods from outside Babylon.
Every time a foreign people was conquered and brought to Babylon
in captivity, their gods were brought with them. This tended to keep
the captive people more contented with their lot, and it worked as
well to increase the number of spiritual powers resident at Babylon.
To be sure, there was a difference of opinion on this subject. Some
objected on the grounds that Babylon was the special and proper
home of Marduk, Nabu, and Ishtar; that their supervision of the

city was adequate, and that the introduction of other deities from the outside constituted an affront to the Babylonian gods.

The joint priesthood of the temples of Marduk, Nabu, and Ishtar held to the latter view, which was not surprising. King Nabunaid held the more eclectic view, which was also natural inasmuch as his own first allegiance was to Sin of Ur and Tema. As for young Belshazzar, he did not care one way or the other. Thus it was that the temple of the extramural gods had grown to large proportions, and the idols of Ashur, Susa, Agade, Ashnunnak, Zamban, Meturnu, Deri, and many other places stood there.

I was exceedingly curious to know what the priests would say about the god of my people, so in an offhand way I inquired, "Do you know the captive groups from Jerusalem?"

"They are a baffling tribe," answered one priest. "They would have a god here too except that they say they never make an image of him. It is a backward idea, but their own business," he concluded.

Imposing as these several sanctuaries were, the dominating structure in the sacred precinct was the temple tower which stood in the center of the entire area and soared to a tremendous height. Built of burnt brick, it rose in eight stages, each painted a different color, black, white, yellow, purple, blue, scarlet, silver, and gold. A spiral ascent wound around and around the colossal pile from the base to the summit.

When it became known that I was closely connected with the court I was invited to go to the top. Halfway up was a resting place with seats. At the summit, a railed promenade ran around the outside, and the center was occupied by a temple room. Inside this room were hangings of rich brocade, a table of solid gold, and a golden couch richly ornamented.

"When was this tower built?" I asked.

"More than a thousand years ago by the great King Hammurabi," the priest answered. "Then it was rebuilt, and stories added by the glorious King Nebuchadnezzar. If he could have carried it up a few more stages it might have reached to heaven. But his workmen grew dizzy, their hands faltered, and some came down deranged in mind and incoherent in speech, so he desisted."

Looking down, I saw the multitudes below in the sacred precinct as crawling ants. Gazing up, the firmament seemed almost within reach.

"We call this tower Etemenanki," the guide continued, "which means 'the house of the terrace-platform of heaven and earth.' It is the link between the celestial and the terrestrial. It reaches almost to heaven and the god condescends to come down upon it to meet with men. Every night we send here a different and undefiled priestess, most high in rank, most beautiful in body, to sleep in the divine bridal chamber. Divesting herself of her robes, she reclines upon the golden couch to await the embrace of the god. When the light is extinguished upon the altar table we, watching from below, know that the union has been consummated. Heaven and earth are again joined together, and all is well. Thus it is," he concluded, "that because this tower stands here, our city is called Bab-ilu, 'the gate of god.' "

3

The Feast of Belshazzar

THE JOURNEY TO TEMA WAS NOT
as tedious as I had feared. To travel in a royal entourage was a different experience from tramping alone across the desert. A series of oases provided convenient and pleasant stopping places, and for the marches across the unrelieved wastes of Nefud, camels and men were amply provisioned.

Tema itself rose like a mirage out of the desert sands. Walls, towers, and palm trees made it look like a second Babylon. It pleased Nabunaid to have Tema compared with Babylon. His original conquest of the city had been in reprisal for raids on Babylon by desert tribes, but when he discovered that Tema was an ancient center of worship of the moon god, Sin, he became intensely interested in the place. With a prodigious expenditure of labor, he had ordered stone transported from the mountains, brick burnt by Babylonian methods, and the entire city rebuilt and enlarged. Then as a sort of belated rationalization he argued that Tema might someday become the future capital of the empire, because increasing pressure upon Babylon from hostile forces in the north and east was anticipated, which obviously indicated withdrawal to the south and west.

It was undeniable that Tema was more nearly on a line between India and Egypt than Babylon. Already the trans-Arabian spice routes indicated the course international commerce could be expected to follow in the future. Tema was the strategic place for a forward-looking ruler. The animosity of the priests of Marduk at Babylon and the enthusiasm of the inhabitants of Tema inclined the heart of this timid ruler to the latter city. Nabunaid found peace of mind in the city of his god. As for Babylon, Belshazzar got along well with the priests of Marduk and it was entirely appropriate for an eldest son to exercise the functions of kingship in the absence of the king. So ran Nabunaid's thinking.

On the last day of the old year our royal party arrived in Tema on schedule. In the early evening the king repaired to the temple of Sin to await with bated breath and eager expectation the rising of his god. The spring air was clear and soft, no cloud was in the sky. As darkness came the thin crescent of the new moon gleamed briefly, then sank beneath the horizon. Nabunaid prostrated himself in adoration.

When the king had ordered me to join his entourage for Tema I had supposed that in this crossroad of civilizations there would be much work for me in my capacity of interpreter. But as week after week went by and no demands were made upon my time, I grew restless. My foreboding about the invasion of Babylon, which I had shared with no one but Isaiah, weighed heavily upon my spirits. The prophet had cautioned me to speak only when the proper time arrived. And now I wondered how I would know when that time was approaching since I was far removed from Babylon. With these problems troubling me, I asked the king if I could return to Babylon, and was granted the permission.

When I reached the capital I was sorely tempted to go directly to Isaiah, but I realized that it would cause comment if a court official sought out an individual in the captive group. However, I did have an audience with one important person, no less than the queen herself. She had learned of my return from Tema and wished to inquire about her husband.

It was my first visit to the hanging gardens which I had so often admired from afar. At close hand I could see how the circular colonnades were superimposed to lift tiers of the gardens to a height which I estimated at nearly a hundred feet above the ground. At intervals all the way to the top flowers, shrubs, and trees grew in profusion, watered by hydraulic machines under the operation of slaves.

The eunuch who brought me into the royal presence motioned me to a seat at one side to wait while the queen finished the business at hand. Evidently she was selecting an attendant, for several young women, lightly robed, were awaiting her scrutiny, while one, a black-haired, olive-skinned girl, stood before her, unrobed.

"You will do very well," said the queen. "I like my personal servants to be well-built and strong, and that you are. How old are you?"

"Twenty-five years of age," replied the young woman.

"And were you born in Babylon?"

"Outside the city, by the Canal Chebar."

"Your name?"

"Sarah."

"Good. Tomorrow go to the temple of Ishtar and perform your duty to the goddess; the next day come to me."

At the mention of the sacrifice to Ishtar, Sarah's face blanched. "But sacrifice to Ishtar has never been required of the daughters of our people," she ventured to say.

"No, we have treated your people with consideration although they are captives in our midst. But you were born at Babylon and if you are to take service in the royal court you must comply with the custom of the land."

Sarah turned half aside and was startled to see me and to realize that someone had slipped in during the interview. Her eyes were dark and appealing as they looked directly into mine. I held her gaze for a moment only, then she turned back to the queen and said confidently, "I will go to the temple tomorrow and I will return to your majesty on the next day."

Dismissing the young women, the queen signaled me to approach.

"You have just returned from Tema? I wish to have news of my husband. How does he fare?"

I gave a concise report of the royal journey to the desert city, of the monarch's activities there, and concluded, "I know of no plans beyond an indefinite stay in Tema."

"That will do," said the queen, concluding the interview. There seemed an edge in her voice when she heard that her husband planned to tarry yet awhile, which made me feel that there might be credence in the rumors that she now abetted her son against his father.

The next day I waited many hours at the garden of Ishtar. Late in the day Sarah came and seated herself beneath a flowering tree. Her beauty attracted the attention of many men in the temple area, but I strode forward immediately and tossed a silver coin into her lap. Taking her hand I led her to the temple where a priest motioned us into a small cubicle.

"Fear not, daughter of my people, I will do you no harm," I said as I took a seat upon the pallet beside her.

"I knew you would come," Sarah replied. "I knew it when I saw you yesterday. But I did not know you were one of us."

Sarah related to me how a few days previous the royal emissary had come to the settlement by the Chebar in search of candidates for personal service to the queen, and how she had been brought to the court for inspection. She told the experience with such restraint that I realized I had been correct in estimating her a young woman of understanding and integrity. I, in turn, told her of my position in the court and my concern for our community in exile.

"Do you know one called Isaiah?" I asked Sarah.

"Indeed, yes," she replied with quickened interest. "I do not know how we could endure our lot without the encouragement he gives us. He constantly urges us to look forward with hope."

"Has he spoken of anyone who is coming to Babylon?" I phrased the question cautiously because I did not know if Isaiah had shared the information about Cyrus which I had brought to him.

Sarah looked at me searchingly before she answered. "Do you mean Cyrus the Persian? The prophet has charged us strictly to tell no one outside of our own community, he holds that Cyrus will besiege and conquer Babylon. Those older folks among us who remember the horrors of the siege of Jerusalem are filled with fear, but Isaiah tells us that what Cyrus does will work for our good."

"What do you think, my daughter?"

"I pray that Isaiah is right and I believe that he is. Once when he was speaking about Cyrus, everything grew dark before my eyes and then in a circle of light I saw a king marching across the world, holding a scepter of justice rather than a sword of slaughter. Another time I saw the same king standing before a multitude of peoples saying, 'Go to your homelands, all of you, and dwell in peace.' I ardently desire that it may be so, for I love a young man of our people and we fain would make our home in the shadow of the walls of Jerusalem."

"Those walls are rubble," I said gently, "and the land is desolate. If ever our people go home again, their life will not be easy. But what is the young man's name?"

"Danel," Sarah replied softly.

I dared tarry no longer with Sarah in the temple cubicle. But before parting we arranged that on the infrequent visits the queen might allow Sarah to make to her home, she would gather what information she could and relay it to me in some way. As we left the temple grounds, a priest leered at us and I flung him a coin which he pocketed greedily.

The summer passed slowly. I kept my eyes and ears open for any movement or news in the court that would indicate rumor of an approaching enemy, but nothing disturbed the complacency of the palace. In the community by the Chebar, the young prophet never once veered from his attitude of hopefulness.

In the early fall, at one of our infrequent meetings, Sarah brought me a disturbing report. "Our people are beginning to doubt. They complain to Isaiah that the months and years of their captivity have gone on ceaselessly without change. They are skeptical about the deliverer he promises. There is much feeling of unrest in the community."

"What groups do the most complaining?" I asked Sarah.

"Among them are the businessmen," she said. "Some of them think it would be best to forget about ever returning to Jerusalem, and plan to make the most of their lives in Babylon. They taunt the prophet with his words about Providence, and say perhaps it is the will of this Providence that they prosper right where they are."

"And what does Isaiah reply to all this?" I asked.

"He speaks out more plainly than ever," said Sarah. "When I last heard him he gave a very definite pronouncement." As Sarah began to repeat the words of the prophet, I sensed the same feeling of awareness emanate from her that I had felt in the presence of Ezekiel and young Isaiah. "He said in effect: 'There comes one from the east whom the Most High has anointed to do his bidding. He is the shepherd of the Lord and will perform all his pleasure. Though he bows down to idols, his deeds shall be ruled and over-ruled by the one God of all the universe. By his doings Bel and Nabu shall be caused to tremble and their city shall be humbled to the dust. But those who are oppressed he will lift up and those who are captive he will set free. Cyrus is his name and Messiah is his title.' "

"You have great faith in the words of the prophet, Sarah?"

"You see—" she hesitated, then lowered her voice as she went on, "I hear voices at times and I have had visions. I mentioned my visions to you the first time we met, did I not?"

I nodded assent and she continued without further explanation. "One voice was unmistakably that of my father who died some years ago. He urged me to be of good courage as I await deliverance and to do my work faithfully in the queen's household. He intimated that I was being prepared for some important task and that in some way I would be the channel for a message to the royal court. Sometimes I feel that it is almost too great a responsibility to carry alone."

"You know that I am here to help?"

"Yes, Yaush, I count on that, for I think perhaps you are a chosen vessel even above me," said Sarah calmly.

"Are there any other manifestations among our people?" I asked her.

"There is Danel, my fiancé," and she colored ever so slightly at the happy thought of this upstanding young man.

"What about Danel?" I encouraged her.

"He has unusual dreams which he says portend some major event about to take place. He says we must live resolutely and patiently and be prepared when the time comes."

In the royal court of Babylon in the fall of the year 539, excitement was mounting in anticipation of the great fall festival. The astrologers, after careful study, had decreed that it should fall on the day which began at sunset on the sixteenth day of the month of Tishri, or the thirteenth day of October. On that evening a specially chosen priestess from the temple of Marduk would ascend the terrace-platform of heaven and earth to sleep with the god. On that evening also, Belshazzar would preside at a palace feast for a thousand of his lords, and banqueting and revelry would prevail throughout the city.

I had never before been part of a court when such extensive preparations were being made for a festival, and I found the expenditure of money almost beyond belief. Among all the people, even to the poorest, the same spirit of profligacy prevailed. They would have this one fling and then settle again to the hardships of life.

In the midst of these high-wrought spirits, the blow fell without warning. Just two days before the festival a messenger galloped into Babylon at high speed. The horse he rode, although the last of a series of relays, had been pushed so hard that it dropped dead in its tracks as it was pulled to a halt. Breathlessly the messenger rushed up to young Belshazzar.

"Your Majesty," he gasped, "I come to warn you that the Persian army is marching toward Babylon in overwhelming force. Sippar fell this very day. Even now the first column of Persians approaches this city."

Even though Sippar was only fifty miles up the river, Belshazzar heard the message without apparent dismay. Not only did he have implicit faith in the fortifications of Babylon, but he had partaken of such generous samplings of the wine to be served at the feast that his mind was in no condition to come to sharp focus upon affairs of state. However, he realized that something was required of him, so with a show of kingly power he summoned one of his officers.

"Send a detachment of troops to the plain to the north of the city tomorrow," he ordered, composing his face into an imperious frown. "That should take care of those Persians."

The military engagement thus casually arranged turned into a rout for his troops. The numbers, strategy, and discipline of the detachment of Babylonians were totally inadequate. As soon as this fact became evident, the soldiers abandoned the struggle and made a precipitate and disorderly withdrawal into the city, consoling themselves with the thought that they would be back in Babylon for the great festival!

Belshazzar received the announcement of the unsuccessful skirmish as if it were a matter of minor importance. Let the Persians sit out there on the plain for a while. Let them contemplate the mighty walls of Babylon. Let them visualize themselves as corpses floating in the moat or as flies being brushed off the smooth stones of the towering ramparts. These thoughts would melt their insolence in presuming to attack Babylon! And if the Persians got a little hot for battle they could do no more than attack the outlying suburbs that were peopled with exiles. On with the festivities!

The sun sank beyond the horizon. The chosen priestess climbed the spiral steps to the golden couch to satisfy the desire of the god. Merriment began in all the houses of Babylon. The acting king, Belshazzar, took his place with a thousand lords and their ladies in the great hall. This was the proper worship of Marduk—and if the young ruler was a little weak in his theology he was strong in his knowledge that there was good entertainment to satisfy the soul this night.

I was among those who made their way to the royal feast of Belshazzar. The gigantic basalt lions at the gateway of the royal palace were bedecked with flowers; the yellow bricks of the palace walls were illumined by flaring torches. Fine lords and ladies in elegant attire strolled through the palace rooms. The men wore linen tunics reaching to their sandals, and long white mantles; their hair was long and carefully curled; their bodies redolent of perfume. Each carried a staff carved with his own distinctive insignia, an apple, a rose, a lily, or an eagle. The women, clad in graceful gowns of iridescent hues, tightly belted at the waist and open at the breast, wore circlets of gold on their brows, bands of gold on their arms, and golden rings set with precious stones on their fingers. I walked across the polished floors of white and mottled sandstone, past the wall reliefs of bright blue glaze, and found my place at a table near the front of the enormous banquet hall.

Above me on a raised platform were the places of Belshazzar and his mother the queen, his favorite wives and concubines. Also above the floor level of the hall was the stage for the performers who would entertain us. At one side of Belshazzar's platform, within call of the queen yet in a subordinate position, was Sarah. I saw her there, her face strikingly framed against the wall behind her.

Slaves came and went on noiseless feet, laden with huge trays of food. The rich produce of the Euphrates Valley and the exotic delicacies from the corners of the empire were available in limitless quantities. Only more abundant were the wines and the liquors, which every guest would attest came up to the demands of the king.

The feast progressed and Belshazzar's spirits rose with the hilarity of his guests. Of a sudden the beauty of Sarah caught his eye and he asked his mother the queen about this girl.

"Her name is Sarah. She is a child of the captives from Jerusalem who reside at the Canal Chebar. She serves me well." The last statement was made by the queen not only because it was true, but also with the hope that it might tend to dissuade her son from adding Sarah to the number of his concubines and thus taking a valuable servant out of her own ranks.

"The captives from Jerusalem?" cried Belshazzar. "The stubborn ones who still think their defeated god is better than the gods of Babylon! The obstinate ones who will not let their women sit in the garden of Ishtar! And yet they work well and their craftsmen are skillful. Do you remember the incomparable gold and silver vessels which Nebuchadnezzar brought from their temple?"

Then, as the climactic idea came to him: "Let us drink our wine from them! We will drink to our gods from the vessels of the god we destroyed."

Shortly they arrived and, gleaming and glittering in the light, the magnificent vessels from the Jerusalem temple were laid upon the banquet table. Beakers and flagons, tumblers and bowls, they were put in the hands of the king and his lords and ladies. The wine of the priests of Babylon was poured into them.

One of the lords rose to his feet, lifted a gold tumbler and offered his toast.

"I praise the lord Marduk, slayer of Tiamat from whose body he made the firmament and the earth. Marduk who ordered the stations of the other gods. Marduk, chief of all gods, the god of Babylon!"

These words were the signal for the appearance of the dancers who enacted the myth of Marduk. The army of Tiamat was a repulsive horde. Some of the dancers were dwarfs, some giants, some horribly deformed, and all wore gruesome animal beards. Tiamat, the personification of chaos, wore billowing garments that alternately swathed and revealed her body which was painted in bizarre patterns of black and red, while her hair streamed wildly and her eyes glared fiercely. Marduk was preceded by sword dancers whose blades cut patterns of light in the air, and the god himself was armored in gleaming silver. As the dance ended he stood triumphant over all the demons and received the homage of all the other gods.

A wave of applause swept through the banquet hall. When it subsided another lord rose to his feet, lifted his vessel of ancient gold and declared, "I praise Nabu, god of wisdom; god of the arts and sciences; god of the mystery of numbers and the lore of the stars; god of all learning, past, present, and future!"

With these words the pageant of the scribes was enacted on the platform. Rows of scribes writing beautiful cuneiform script were superseded by astrologers who swung orbits over their heads as if measuring the heavenly bodies. After this, prognosticators gazed into the mists of the future which dissolved to reveal Belshazzar ruling the entire earth. A storm of applause ended this scene. If any man asked himself if honor should not have been paid to the real king, Nabunaid, none had the temerity to voice the question.

A third speaker rose to his feet.

"I praise Ishtar, goddess of love, source of fertility, queen of heaven. Her womb is pregnant with creative power. Her breasts nourish all things. Her beauty is beyond compare."

A line of tall and stately young women, garbed in shimmering brocade, wearing high jeweled headdresses, moved across the platform. A row of priestesses came forward, each with a golden serpent wrapped around her leg and smaller snakes of gold encircling her breasts. These serpents were so cleverly contrived that they seemed to writhe as the priestesses walked. Next the loveliest girls from the corners of the empire performed the love dances of their own lands, some stormy with passion, some intoxicating in their abandon, some subtle in their allurement. Finally the immediate attendants of the goddess appeared. These girls, whose bodies were powdered with dust of gold and dust of silver, drew the carriage of their mistress with ropes of pearls. Then Ishtar herself, personified by the most beautiful girl who had passed the temple portal during the year, came into view and the entire audience gasped at the perfection of her form.

Small wonder that Belshazzar, intoxicated with the beauty before him and his mind benumbed from drink, gave little heed to the words of an aged fisherman who had forced his way even to the royal table.

"My lord," the fisherman gasped, "I have come from the quays —the river is almost dry."

"Go back and tell this to the guard. Why bother me?"

"But, my lord, there is no guard upon the walls. The soldiers have come down to the feast."

An angry scowl settled over the face of Belshazzar, but before he could speak a shriek of such poignant and piercing quality came from behind the queen as froze everyone in his chair. Looking in the direction from which the cry came, I saw that Sarah's place was vacant. Then I could see her fallen back upon a couch in an apparent trance. Guests near her began to move about and the queen started to rise. But she immediately sank down again, horrified, for a strange vapor seemed to emanate from Sarah's body, rising into the air and hovering against the lofty wall, plainly visible to everyone in the banquet hall. Then the vapor contracted into the form of a human wrist and hand which, moving of its own volition, wrote three words upon the wall in large, clear characters. The language was evidently Aramaic for the words consisted only of consonants for which the proper vowels would have to be supplied. Clearly before us stood the words MN, TKL, PRS.

I could see Belshazzar trembling violently. He tried to pull his befogged mind into some degree of clarity. "The priests of Nabu!" he commanded. Had he not just seen their powers extolled on the stage before his very eyes? But the priests could make nothing of this strange handwriting on the wall.

The queen moved to her son's side. "My lord, this girl comes from the captives on the Chebar. She loves a man named Danel who is known to be an interpreter of dreams. Let us have him brought."

While a chariot thundered through the streets of Babylon, out to the canal, and returned with Danel, the people in the banquet hall remained in their places. Sarah lay motionless in her trancelike condition, the mysterious ectopod remained suspended in the air, and the characters of the writing stood out plainly on the wall.

When Danel came he stood in the center of the great hall and read the words, MENE, "numbered," TEKEL, "weighed," PERES, "divided."

With neither arrogance nor servility in his voice he turned to Belshazzar, now visibly slumping in his place.

"The signification of the writing, O king," Danel said, "is this: 'God has numbered the days of your kingdom and brought it to an end. You have been weighed in the balances and found wanting. Your kingdom is divided and given to the Medes and Persians.' "

Then Danel went to the side of Sarah. Overhead the hand was resolved again into vapor and the vapor seemed to withdraw into the body of the prostrate girl. The letters of the writing slowly faded from the wall. Danel spoke the name of Sarah and she sat up, a look of wonder in her eyes.

4

The Ransomed of the Lord Return

DAWN WAS LIGHTENING THE SKY
when Belshazzar and his guests came forth from the banquet hall.
Their minds were none too clear and all were shaken by the mystery
of what had taken place within. Some were beginning to wonder if
they had really seen the phenomenon which they were now dis-
cussing.

There was no mistaking, however, what confronted them outside
the palace. Armed warriors were drawn up on all sides. The first
ranks were swordsmen with short weapons and small round shields.
The next were spearmen with large shields and long lances. Behind
them were archers with powerful bows in their hands and large
conical quivers over their shoulders. All wore low helmets and gleaming breastplates. Their hair and beards were cropped and curled.
It was the army of the Persians and Medes.

In the light of day it was easy to read the story of what had taken
place during the night of Babylon's revelry. Up the river above the
city the invader had emulated the earlier deed of Nitocris, but for a
different purpose. Like the famous woman of earlier years, Cyrus
had cut the embankments of the Euphrates and turned the river into
the vast low-lying side basin. When the water in the main channel
had fallen to the depth of a man's thigh, he had sent his army into
the stream where they had marched directly into the heart of Babylon. Alert forces on the city walls could have trapped and massacred

them there, but no one had seen any sign of what was happening except the old fisherman who had gone in vain with his message to Belshazzar. The brass gates in the low walls paralleling the river-banks were not even closed, and the soldiers had walked directly into the streets of the city and occupied the entire capital without a struggle.

When Belshazzar emerged from the feast and found himself face to face with the captain of the Persian guard, in a brief burst of kingly spirit he whipped out his sword and made a frantic attack, but his opponent swiftly and unerringly ran him through. Babylon now belonged to Cyrus.

It was on the sixteenth day of Tishri, which was the thirteenth day of October in the year 539, when Babylon fell, but it was not until the third day of Heshvan, or the twenty-ninth day of October, that Cyrus himself made his personal entry into the city. The entourage of the Persian was impressive, for this conqueror brought even his own food and cattle with him from home. He also brought his own drinking water direct from the Choaspes River near Susa, his winter capital. This water, boiled, was contained in silver flagons transported on four-wheeled mule carts. Despite the elaborateness of such equipment and the overwhelming strength of his accompanying forces, the demeanor of the new conqueror was modest and simple. He entered the city on foot and walked up the processional street to the temple of Marduk. There, to the surprise of the people of Babylon, he addressed them in the name of their own god.

"While in my own land I worship my god," he said, "but it was your lord Marduk who bade me come hither. He summoned me to proceed to his city, Babylon, and he marched with me as a friend on the way. I stand upon the steps of his temple with gratitude for his help and with thankfulness that he has permitted me to enter his city without battle and without conflict. He spared suffering in his city, Babylon, and gave it intact into my hand. For this I am glad.

"The lord Marduk is angered when many foreign gods, the gods of Sumer and Ashur, of Ashnunnak and Meturnu, and of many other places are given a home in his own sacred city. I therefore decree that all foreign gods shall be returned to their own lands together with their people who were carried into captivity here. In their homelands the temples of these gods shall be peacefully rebuilt and hymns of praise shall arise in their honor. There may all these gods, whom I thus bring again into their cities, pray daily to Nabu and Ishtar for me, and may they speak a gracious word for me and say to Marduk, 'May Cyrus, the king who worships you, be granted a long life and a peaceful reign.' "

A murmur of approval arose throughout the great concourse of listening people. The citizens of Babylon were delighted with this recognition of their god, and the representatives of people who were in exile could scarcely believe the good news they had just heard. They were to be allowed to go back to their homelands! The priests of Marduk, who feared for their power when Belshazzar was slain, were also somewhat mollified and less hostile to their new master.

I made my way to the community of my countrymen and arrived in time to hear Isaiah address them, assembled in great numbers by the Chebar.

" 'Comfort my people,' saith the Lord. 'Tell them that at last the sins of Jerusalem have been punished twice over and the hour of their deliverance from exile and captivity has come. The sufferings of a generation have paid the price of the accumulated misdeeds of the past and the time of liberation is at hand. Lift up your heads and look. Behold, a way opens across the wilderness, a highway in the desert. It shall be so smooth that even the halt and the lame may walk upon it. Cyrus, my shepherd, has cast down the barriers and now bids you go forth in freedom. Walk upon the way which leads again home. Rebuild the fallen walls and replant the barren fields in the land of your ancestors. Make a place of hope and opportunity for your children's children.' "

The proffered return to the homeland was received with mingled feelings by the exiles. Many of the older people wept for joy, and many of the younger were fired with a desire for adventure. But many of the middle-aged murmured at the abandonment of their prosperous businesses and comfortable homes. In the end, many matters had to be taken into consideration in making up the companies that would leave Babylon to return to the homeland. There were some aged and infirm persons who could not undertake the trip, much as they wanted to. Other persons, prosperous and at the height of their careers, abandoned everything for the sake of making a new start in Jerusalem. The liquidation of Babylonian holdings and preparations for the long journey took time. In some cases, groups cast lots among themselves to determine who should go first and who come later.

It was the outcome of such a lot which caused Sarah and Danel to remain behind when the first contingent finally set off on the long march. Their eyes were shining as they watched the fortunate ones move away, for they themselves would come later. I waved them farewell with affection in my heart and good wishes on my lips.

I was to be among the first band to return to Jerusalem. It was with mixed feeling that I started on this last lap of my wanderings. Nostalgically I remembered the high resolve of my youth to return to the city of my birth; poignantly I recalled the blessing of my father that final night in Babylon; reassuringly I recollected the words of the oracle in the land of young master K'ung.

As we trekked along, our pioneer band of returners from exile sang the songs of their homeland, related experiences of joy and sorrow which they had experienced, shared their hopes and ambitions. But there was also much time for quiet and thought. My mind often strayed to the peaks, the jungles, the deserts, the streams, the prophets, and the seers that had dominated my years of wandering. And my heart lingered with Samuda.

Everywhere I had found men seeking—seeking within the world and seeking within themselves. I came to the conclusion, which I had tentatively reached many times, that those seekers who found something in the depths of their own souls related to something in the heart of the universe were the ones who found a peace which the others did not have. They were the ones who could endure adversity in the confidence that a purpose ran through life and would be worked out in the ultimate consummation. They were the ones who looked forward with hope. I realized that this was a very inadequate statement of a profound truth which I felt within me.

I glanced at my own people marching beside me. Who could have believed that the time would ever come when they would actually return to their homeland? Yet here they were, on their way. Jeremiah had said it would come to pass; so too had Ezekiel and Isaiah. The impossible was being accomplished. To be sure, for years ahead Jerusalem would be little better than a desolation and life would be hard, but the miracle of return would be followed by a miracle of rebuilding.

Surely, in the long view, there was some reason why this people had been preserved through an exile in which they might have perished utterly. There was still something great to be accomplished through them. I dared to wonder if there might yet arise in the midst of these people one who would bring together all the truths of the world? How diverse they were, rugged Zarathushtra, punctilious K'ung, middle-of-the-way Buddha, extreme Mahavira, and all the others. Yet in some sense they were all engaged in the same quest, each had torn a fragment from the great page of truth.

I realized this was no time now to tell my fellow countrymen about Mahavira, Lao Tzu, Siddhartha Buddha and the others. These returning exiles had their eyes fixed upon an immediate goal; they had far to go and much to do. Yet I knew that the teachings to which I had listened were not meant for me alone. I must preserve them against the time when all people would need them and could profit by them.

So I sit in a lean-to shelter which has become my home beside the ruined walls of Jerusalem, now rebuilding. As soon as I have finished these last lines I shall seal this manuscript in one of the earthen vessels that the exiles brought back from Babylon. I shall retrace the path of my youth down the rocky defile to the Jordan depression. There, where crumbled bricks and broken shards mark the former site of Taloth, I shall climb the steep hill and enter the cave which once gave me refuge. There I shall place the jar, safe until such time as I need it for reference. Then I shall bend my head in salute to the past, and raise it with hope for the future. A wanderer upon the earth no longer, I shall enter Jerusalem.

A Note on Chronology

THE EXACT DATES CONTAINED IN
the manuscript center around the destruction of Jerusalem in 586
B.C. and the fall of Babylon in 539 B.C. Between these points ap-
proximate dates may be inferred from the sequence of events. The
manuscript implies a time around 580 for the happenings connected
with Zarathushtra, popularly called Zoroaster, 570 for Mahavira,
560 for Gautama Buddha, 550 for Lao Tzu, and 540 for K'ung
Tzu, better known as Confucius. I have compared these dates with
chronological data derived from other sources and find a rough
agreement as follows: Al-Biruni puts the appearance of Zoroaster
258 years before the attack of Alexander on Persia in 331 B.C.,
hence the prophet began his public work in 589; the conversion of
Vishtaspa ensued twelve years later in 577. Jaina sources date the
birth of Mahavira about 600 B.C. and state that he left home at the
age of thirty, hence in 570. The Mahabodhi Society places the birth
of Gautama Buddha in 624 B.C., the Mahavamsa suggests 566.
Taking as reasonable a mid-point between the two traditions, we
may put the birth at about 595; enlightenment came at the age of
thirty-five, therefore in 560. According to Vincent Smith the change
of rule between Bimbisara and Ajataśatru was in 554. Taoist tradition points to 604 B.C. for the birth of Lao Tzu; in this case he was
fifty-four years of age in 550. Ancient Chinese histories put the
birth of Confucius in 552 B.C.; he was therefore twelve years of
age in 540.

Date Due

APR 12 1972			

Demco 293-5

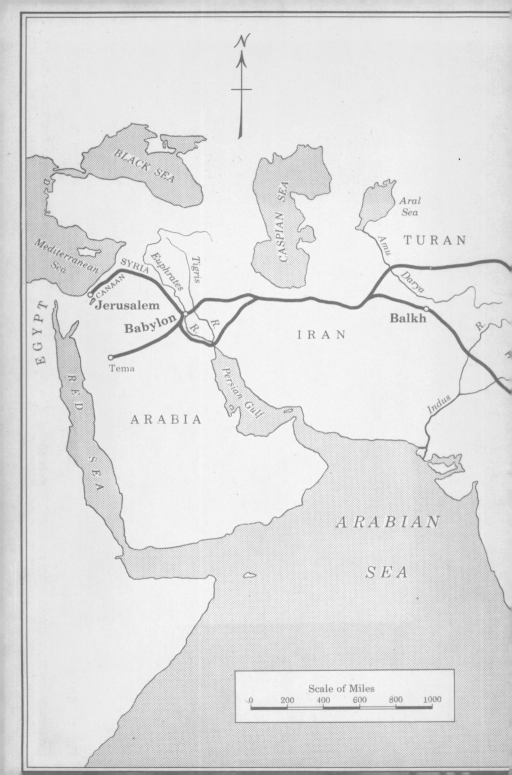

N

BLACK SEA

CASPIAN SEA

Aral
Sea

TURAN

Mediterranean
Sea

SYRIA

Euphrates

Tigris

Amu

Darya

CANAAN

Jerusalem

Babylon

R.

R.

IRAN

Balkh

R.

EGYPT

Tema

Persian Gulf

ARABIA

Indus

RED SEA

ARABIAN

SEA

Scale of Miles

0   200   400   600   800   1000